Richard Smitten lives in California and is currently involved in film projects relating to his books. He is the author of *The Godmother*, the story of Griselda Blanco and her crime empire, and co-author with Robin Moore of *The Man Who Made It Snow*, about the Colombian drug trade, and also the novel *Legal Tender* (Headline 1992). *Capital Crimes* is his third novel.

Also by Richard Smitten

Legal Tender

Capital
Crimes

Richard Smitten

First published in Great Britain in 1992
by HEADLINE BOOK PUBLISHING PLC

First published in paperback in 1993
by HEADLINE BOOK PUBLISHING PLC

A HEADLINE FEATURE paperback
10 9 8 7 6 5 4 3 2

ISBN 0 7472 3959 2

Typeset by Keyboard Services, Luton

Printed and bound in Great Britain by
HarperCollins Manufacturing, Glasgow

HEADLINE BOOK PUBLISHING PLC
Headline House
79 Great Titchfield Street
London W1P 7FN

This book is dedicated
to my mother and father,
for their unyielding support,
prayers, and encouragement.

AUTHOR'S NOTE

The story you are about to read is based on the truth;
the names have been changed, some locations altered
and characters invented.

The original money to fund the Colombian cartel
came from Wall Street – stolen by an American. It
was the biggest heist in the history of Wall Street.

As a result of the theft, he became the most wanted
man in the world – hunted by the CIA, stalked by
Interpol. He became a man without a country. This
did not stop his criminal mind from flourishing, nor
did it stop him from establishing the 'Bank of Death',
where all borrowers were welcome. If the interest or
principal was not paid, the penalty was death.

This story is the prequel to the plague that was to
envelop the world.

This is how the horror began.

RICHARD SMITTEN

'It is the law of nature that causes all things to be balanced. A law that says: nothing comes free, all things must be paid for, all wrongs must be righted.'

Sioux Medicine Man

1
The Rip-off – Wall Street

She couldn't get out of the cab fast enough. The stale smell of an unsmoked cigar hung in the fetid air like death. The cab pulled to an abrupt halt in front of the WOS building on Canal Street. The cabbie stared at her legs as she stood on the curb and handed the money to him through the open window. She didn't wait for her change.

The lobby was packed with people running helter-skelter, like their lives depended on it. As she waited for the elevator to take her up seventy-seven floors to WOS headquarters on the penthouse floor, she noticed that the clock said 3:40 – twenty minutes until the bell rang and the stock market closed.

Wall Street was her beat; the market-closing aftermath on the trading floor, where she once worked, always reminded her of the day after a party – part elation and part letdown.

The elevator finally arrived and disgorged its

1

passengers, like sardines packed in a can suddenly coming to life.

She had never met Leonard Immke and wondered what he would be like. His rise in the financial world had been astronomical; like a fiery comet through a dark sky, he was highly visible but there was little known about him.

Only a few weeks ago Immke had bought the troubled World Overseas Securities mutual funds from the high-living Manny Rothman, who had basically invented the concept of mutual funds and sold it to the world: spread your investment by purchasing a group of securities, and thereby limit your downside risk – safety in numbers, don't put all your eggs in one basket. Manny Rothman, a tough kid from Brooklyn, a great salesman, surprised even himself with his success, and when the money came showering in, he couldn't resist the excesses that the money allowed. Rumor was that Manny had personally tapped into the funds themselves to support his insatiable pleasure habits. That was when Leonard Immke, an even greater salesman, stepped in.

She stepped off the elevator into carpet that was so deep it seemed to brush against her ankles, even in high heels. The receptionist sat behind a green Italian marble desk that was just low enough to show her well-developed breasts. The desk was rectangular – like a dollar bill, Sarah thought.

The receptionist directed Sarah to Leonard Immke's office. Immke had three secretaries in the anteroom to his office. They all had one thing in common: they were beauties. They took their time in assessing Sarah Baxter, who was as beautiful as any of them. The secretary closest to Immke's office rose.

'You must be Sarah Baxter from the *Journal*; we've been expecting you.'

'Yes,' Sarah answered.

'I recognize you from your byline picture. Mr Immke reads your column every day.' The secretary opened the door. 'Go right in, Ms Baxter; Mr Immke will be with you in a second.'

Sarah counted her steps from the door to the soft low-slung seat in front of Leonard Immke's desk; twenty-four paces – at least fifty feet. The desk was huge, marble, the same color as the reception area. The high-backed chair looked almost double size. She wondered how big Immke was.

Sarah got her notepad out and started making notes. This interview might turn out to be fun after all.

Leonard Immke watched her through the one-way glass between his office and the 'Boiler Room'. Great ass, he thought, great legs. Class, real class; maybe Brynmore, Smith, Vassar, Hunter College . . . Where the hell did they get those stupid

names for girls' schools? he thought. He slipped his
jacket on and straightened his tie, paying no
attention to the rough-looking Hispanic man at his
side. He turned from the one-way window and
walked over to his Chief Floor Trader, Sydney
Rosenburg. The Hispanic male followed.

'Sydney, you got what I asked you for?' Immke
asked.

'Yeah.' Sydney handed an attaché case containing one million dollars to Immke who opened it,
took a fast look and snapped it shut.

'Here,' he said, as he handed the case to the
Colombian. 'Take it and go. If Sydney says the
count's good, you can take it to the bank.' Immke
paused. ''Course in my case, I am the bank.'

Immke smiled and slapped the man on the
shoulder. The man seemed to recoil slightly from
the slap, to tense up, but Immke paid no attention.
The two men walked through the Boiler Room to
reach the fire exit door.

The room was frantic with activity. Sydney
Rosenburg followed the two men, stopping for a
second here and there to speak to the traders he
controlled. The Boiler Room consisted of twenty-
two people, all normally buying and selling stock
for the WOS funds.

There was a difference today: today the traders
were all selling.

The Boiler Room was the heart of WOS. There

were two thousand salesman around the world, working night and day to sell shares in the WOS various funds, but only twenty-two men and women spent that money by buying and selling securities.

When they reached the fire exit door, Immke spoke to the Colombian. 'Take this down two floors, then take the freight elevator to the first parking level; a car will be waiting.' The man nodded and pushed through the exit door without a word or a gesture.

'All right, Syd, how the hell are we doing?' Immke asked as he strode quickly toward his office.

'We're doin' good. The real estate fund has been cashed out and transferred and the commodities fund is in cash as well,' Syd said, walking fast to keep up with Immke.

'That's swell, Syd, but what about the main fucking fund? How we doin' there?' Immke stopped at the door with the one-way glass, waiting for an answer.

'Well, a lot of the specialists know we're selling and they're dropping the bid on us.'

'Fuck the specialists, Syd. Who do I have to fuck around here to get myself understood? When I tell you SELL at the fucking market,' Immke turned and yelled for all in the Boiler Room to hear, 'I MEAN SELL AT THE FUCKING MARKET!'

All the trading heads rose from their computers

as one, stared at Leonard Immke, then looked back at their screens.

'It ain't our money, you know, Syd?' Immke whispered, 'So . . .'

'Sell at the fucking market – I got it, Leonard, I got it,' Sydney whispered back, filling in Immke's sentence.

'Good. So do it!' Immke said and pushed through the door into his office. 'I gotta take an interview.'

'An interview? After today, what will be left to talk about?' Sydney muttered out of earshot of Immke.

Sarah Baxter was surprised; Leonard Immke was on the small size, average at best. She was shocked at his clothes. They looked like they were purchased off the J. C. Penney sale rack, although she knew better. It was the way he wore them and the color combinations. They didn't work – plaid jacket, black pants, white socks and deep dark sideburns.

Immke waited until he was safely behind his massive desk to shake hands with Sarah. She had to rise out of the low-slung chair to join his outstretched hand with hers. As she leaned over to rise, he checked out her breasts. They were firm, slightly uplifted by her bra. Not a bad set, he thought, leaning forward for one last look as she retook her seat and prepared her notepad.

Immke plopped into his seat. 'So, what can I do ya for?'

'The *Journal* wants to do a feature story on you. Is it true that three weeks ago with only three million dollars you bought control over two hundred million in assets?'

'About two hundred and twenty-five, to be accurate. And we are fully invested at the moment,' Immke added.

'Did you know that the Wall Street gnomes, the men who run the street, are nervous? They think you're trading on margin and that you're over-leveraged.'

'Well, they don't make our business decisions around here, do they?' Immke smiled. 'When they prove they're always right, we'll hand our portfolios over to them to trade,' he quipped, squirming slightly in his chair, starting to tap the tip of a sharpened pencil on a yellow legal pad, making tiny dots in the shape of a dollar sign.

'Two questions: how many WOS funds exist to date, and what are your plans?'

'There are five funds: blue chip, growth companies, foreign investments, a venture capital fund, and a real estate trust.' The phone on Immke's desk rang; he snapped the receiver out of the cradle. Cupping the mouthpiece, he said to Sarah, 'Sorry, it's a call I gotta take.' He smiled and spun his chair round so that he could look over the city and, more importantly, make himself inaudible to the reporter who was left looking at the back of his chair. Immke spoke in a whisper, 'Did the Brinks truck come?'

'Yes, and Wells Fargo as well. We've executed almost all the sell orders and transferred almost one hundred and sixty million offshore.'

'Look, Sydney,' Immke spoke softly but his voice was fierce, 'I want it all sold. Let it go at the fucking market. I want the fucking cash, you understand? You got twenty-five per cent to go and you should have five per cent.' Immke checked his watch. 'And you got ten minutes till the closing bell.' He paused to think for a second. 'Sydney, you tell your traders that there is a hundred thousand in fresh for them at five after four if they empty their portfolios.'

'Leonard, that's two point two million dollars.'

'Three. Three point two million dollars. There's a milllon in there for you, Syd, in addition to what we already agreed. I got your attention now?'

'Yes.'

'Good, I'll call back in ten minutes for the good news.' Immke hung up and smiled as he spun his chair round; he could only imagine the furore in the Boiler Room. 'So where were we?'

'What are your plans for the funds?'

'Basically, we're not changing a damn thing.' He could go for this broad if he wasn't leaving tonight for Nassau. 'What else you wanna know?' he asked,

8

smiling at her. She looked back at her notes, shivering slightly under his feral grin.

In the trading room after the bonus announcement, it was pandemonium. All sense of decorum had been thrown to the winds. Orders for the best stocks, the blue chips, were being executed at the market. WOS was dumping on the American Exchange as well as the Big Board and their over-the-counter stocks were being sold at any bid, with some of the smaller stocks dropping twenty to twenty-five per cent under the onslaught of the selling. The traders couldn't care less. In ten minutes they could make more than a year's wages. And they all knew Leonard Immke was brilliant; after all, he had taken control of over two hundred million in hard assets with only three million dollars, so if he wanted to be in cash, they would help him and they would help themselves.

Below, in the bowels of the WOS office tower, in the secure receiving station that had been specially constructed by Immke, the Brinks and Wells Fargo armored trucks were lined up. Armed men were carrying cash from the trucks to the security room, where the cash was inventoried then fed into a compactor, compressed, and stuffed into duffel bags and suitcases. The armored trucks would stand by until the money was repacked, then carry it back into their trucks. Loaded a second time, they would head for La Guardia airport and a waiting 707.

As Sarah Baxter talked, Immke glanced at his gold desk clock on the green granite base. He wondered if he should take it with him. He decided not to, since the inscription was dedicated to Manny Rothman, his predecessor. He felt good, strong, buoyant – not like a kid who was stealing candy, more like a kid who was stealing the candy store while the owner watched. He was in full form as he began to explain the concept of a mutual fund to this beautiful girl, sitting with her legs crossed in front of him, frantically taking notes, as if his words really mattered.

'So, to sum up. We aim to protect our investors from risk by spreading the WOS eggs over many baskets. You know, to honor the original concept of the mutual fund, Manny Rothman's concept, the concept that got the ball rolling. Safety first!' Immke smiled and looked at his desk clock again: ninety seconds to go until the final bell. He was still torn about taking the clock with him for its sentimental value. 'The three rules of the mutual funds are: diversify, diversify, diversify. We represent a lot of widows, retired folks and folks who would like to be retired who are counting on us. Our slogan around here is: preserve capital at all cost. If you don't have a stake you can't play the game.'

Immke walked round his desk to announce the interview was over. Less than thirty seconds now until the bell.

Sarah understood she was being ushered out. She didn't like it. She spoke as she rose. 'Is that how you look at the Street, Mr Immke? As a game?'

'What street?' Immke stopped on their way to the door. He was from the street; the street he understood. He smiled, 'Oh, you mean Wall Street. Sure, I look on it as a game. It's only a game when all you have to lose is money.'

'Can I quote you on that? This article will be out about this time next week.'

He shepherded her through the door, 'Sure, you can quote me on that, and anything else I've said. If I said it, I gotta believe it, right?'

'Lots of people say things they don't believe, Mr Immke.'

'Yeah?' Immke paused, 'Well, I ain't lots of people, am I? I gotta go now. It's been a pleasure.' He shook her hand and closed the door in her face.

He walked fast through his office to the secret closet door that led to the Boiler Room and the waiting Sydney Rosenburg. He disappeared into the closet, slamming the door and locking it behind him.

He quickly walked the length of the trading room, stopping occasionally to check the sell slips on the traders' desks, thousands of shares of IBM, General Motors, AT&T, Ford, BP Oil, Exxon, Nabisco . . .

Sydney watched as Immke made his way toward

him. As he approached, Immke blurted, 'Yea or nay, Syd?'

'Yea, we blew off the last shares just as the bell rang.'

'And the wire transfers?'

'Twenty more minutes and they'll be completed.' Smiling, Sydney handed Immke the transfer slips. Immke studied them for a second: millions of dollars already safely waiting for him in accounts in Switzerland, the Bahamas, Grand Cayman, Lichtenstein, Panama and the Channel Islands. He stuffed the slips into his pockets.

'You got the cash for the traders?'

Sydney handed Immke a corrugated box with twenty-two envelopes, each containing a hundred thousand dollars. Immke rifled though the box then handed it back.

'Syd, anybody on the Street figure out what we're doin'?'

'No, just a lot of curious traders and bankers who refuse to believe their own eyes. They think it's some brilliant new strategy you have that requires you to get into cash first.' Sydney sat down at his desk and took out his small notebook that held a record of all the current transactions. He extended his hand toward Immke who just stood there for a minute.

'Oh, yeah,' Immke smiled, 'you want these offshore transfers, right, Syd?' Immke dug into his pocket and handed Sydney back the slips. 'Hand these cash bonuses out to the traders when the transfers are finished. There's a clean-up crew in the halls waiting for your signal. When the traders leave, let the crew in. They will shred every single document and crate off the paper. I don't want one bit of paper left in this office – no paper trail.'

'What about the big office?' Sydney asked.

'Who gives a shit about the big office? That's incoming; this is outgoing.' Immke laughed as he made his way back through the secret closet door and into his office.

Once inside, he sat down behind his desk and took a long deep breath to calm down. He spun his chair so that he could overlook all of Manhattan. He had acquired WOS three weeks ago for five million dollars: two million delivered in cash on closing and a cashier's check for three million delivered by his lawyers three weeks later. Manny Rothman would be depositing that cashier's check in his bank. By Monday, Tuesday at the latest, he would realize the check was a phony as it came bouncing back through the banking system.

So, Immke thought to himself, it cost me two million in cash to get two hundred and twenty million in cash. One per cent – that's not bad! That's what there will be in my various accounts after today – two hundred and twenty million, FRESH. It was all he could do to keep from screaming with joy.

He spun his chair round and reached for the green granite clock that had been presented to Manny Rothman. He held it up to the twilight streaming through the window. It was cool to the touch. The inscription read, 'To Manny Rothman for Outstanding Achievement in the Mutual Fund Industry. The Financial Advisor, Annual Bernard Baruch Awards.'

Yes, he would take the clock and that would be all he would take.

Six hours later, after the clean-up crew had done their job, Leonard Immke and Sydney Rosenburg were seated in a stretch limo speeding out onto the tarmac at La Guardia airport and a waiting 707 jet. The back seat contained duffel bags and suitcases filled with cash that had come in at the last minute. The car came to an abrupt halt halfway between the open cargo door and the gangway steps that led to the forward passenger compartment of the airplane. Immke and Sydney watched as the driver and his assistant tossed the cash onto the plane. They stayed until the cargo door that extended from the belly of the plane had been sucked up into the fuselage. Immke handed each driver an envelope with five thousand dollars in cash.

He and Sydney trotted toward the stairs. Immke had to force himself not to break into a run. He wanted out of New York, out of the United States, out of the control of anyone who might stop him.

14

Immke's new pilot, Captain Butler, stood on the top of the stairs. 'All set, Mr Immke?'

'You bet.' Immke hurried by the pilot and took his seat. 'Butler, this is Sydney Rosenburg, the best floor trader in New York. He's gettin' off at Nassau.'

Butler reached forward to shake Sydney's hand.

'Later for the handshaking, Butler. You could say time is of the essence so let's make like the birds and "flock off", right now!'

'Yes, sir.' Butler withdrew his hand and headed for the cockpit. He turned at the cockpit door hatch. 'Buckle up; no stews this trip.'

Immke waved Butler into the cockpit. The plane had been redesigned with a bedroom and a living room which contained four facing seats with a coffee table separating them, and a refrigerator on the side. Immke and Sydney sat facing each other.

The engines fired, warming up for only a brief moment before the plane started to roll toward the runway. Sydney buckled up. Immke reached into the small refrigerator and pulled out a bottle of Taylor New York Champagne and two plastic cups. He put the champagne on the table between them and buckled his seat belt.

'What now, Leonard? You'll be the most wanted man in the world after this, the biggest heist in the history of Wall Street,' Sydney paused to take his plastic cup in hand, 'or any other street for that matter.'

Immke poured the champagne, almost spilling it as the plane came to an abrupt halt, taking its place in line, waiting for permission to take off.

Sydney sipped the foamy bubbles off his champagne. 'The Wall Street establishment will never forgive you for today.' He took another sip as the plane started to roll down the runway, gaining speed. 'What are you going to do?'

The plane was almost up to takeoff speed. Immke watched the airport lights fly by his porthole. He saluted Sydney with his plastic glass. 'To you, Sydney, and your good work! Your efforts will contribute to what I'm goin' to do next.'

They were airborne. Immke picked up the intercom and buzzed Butler.

'Yes, sir?'

'Butler, take us on one long, slow arc over Manhattan before we head out to sea, okay?'

'Yes, sir.'

'Sydney, you remember that Colombian in the Boiler Room?'

'Yes. Rough-looking customer.'

'Well, he's a part of my plan. I'm going to Colombia to become the National Bank of Cocaine. I been plannin' it for a while. That Colombian is a farmer – cocaine growers are only farmers, you know, Sydney. And you know what farmers always need?'

'A banker.'

'You are fucking right, Sydney, a farmer needs a banker the way a man needs a woman.'

'Maybe you should use another example, Leonard.'

'Funny, Sydney! You know, that's the first time I seen humor from you.' Immke paused as the Manhattan skyline appeared. 'They're goin' to need a banker who understands them.'

Immke went quiet as the plane passed over Battery Park, Wall Street and headed up the canyons of Manhattan toward Central Park and the Upper East Side. 'Syd, you know what my greatest strength is?'

'Your sense of humor?'

'I give you one little compliment, Syd, don't be thinking you're a comedian.'

'Sorry, Leonard.' Sydney poured them both another hit of champagne. 'Okay, what is your biggest strength?'

'I always know where the action is going to be, just before it happens. Always, always, fucking always. And I'm ballsy enough to grab it.' Immke held his plastic cup high in the air as the plane veered over Long Island, toward Sandy Hook and the open ocean. 'Sydney, those Wall Street assholes will remember today for a long time to come.'

'That's not the half of it, Leonard,' Sydney affirmed as they clicked their plastic cups together in a salute. 'Not the half of it.'

Both men looked down at the gray-black glaze of the moonless Atlantic Ocean, dark and foreboding in its calm majesty.

2
One Year Later, The Snatch –
Colombia

The lights were still ten minutes away. Tonight
was the night. A year of planning and hard work, no
guarantees.

Dark, moonless nights always gave Butler the
creeps. He was long past the open ocean now,
skimming low over the jungle. Green looks black
when there is no moon. No signs of life, but he knew
there was life teeming below: eating, sleeping,
killing, surviving, striving to see another sunrise.

Flying under a thousand feet you had to watch for
the thermal currents. They could drop you so
swiftly you couldn't move the controls fast enough.
Made it easy to become part of the rainforest. In a
month the jungle would swallow up your remains
for ever.

Butler climbed to five thousand feet, his hand
shaking so bad he couldn't get the RDF signal on
line. Finally, he picked up the frequency, loud and

clear, right on course. He'd done it a hundred times before, but tonight was like those nights in Asia. The talk was over. You were head down and charging, running full speed after the gossamer enemy who was nowhere and everywhere. And you loved it, like a primeval animal set loose to run wild after years of holding back.

No time for thoughts like that now.

Sometimes on moonless nights the clouds took on shapes like big, sleepy gray animals. They could also hide the only landing strip in hundreds of miles of jungle.

But there it was, dead ahead, two glowing strips in the blackness, the strobes blinking like little white Christmas tree lights. The runway was only three hundred feet longer than the minimum for a 707. You hit it right or not at all. Big, black lumbering cow of a plane. The controls had been fighting Butler all night, like they had a mind of their own.

The front wheel squealed as it hit, bringing the nose down tight to the tarmac. He hit the reverse throttles, hard as he could. He could have used a co-pilot, but he would only have been in the way tonight. He broke all the rules all the time, so why not this one.

He made sure to get the aircraft turned nose into the wind, gripping the wheel, taking deep breaths

to get the adrenaline down. The worst was still
ahead of him.

He yelled out the window in Spanish at the
fumbling ground crew that he wouldn't need the
wheel chocks tonight.

A few minutes later he saw the single headlight
of the jeep bouncing up and down as it tumbled
across the flat terrain toward him, its dust rising to
join the clouds. It came into full view, carrying two
men like always, each armed with a night-scoped
infrared M-16.

They hardly slowed down for him to jump in the
back seat. He sat on his duffel to avoid the springs
sticking up through the worn covering. The snow-
capped Andes were visible from here, about four
miles to the north. The villa lay in a perfect basin at
the base of the mountains.

The ride to the villa took six minutes, never more.
The two Colombian Indians sat up front. Butler
liked to watch them fight over the one pack of
Marlboros he tossed to them. They drove like kids,
pedal pressed to the floor, but kids don't carry M-
16s.

The villa sat proud and serene on five acres. A
high stone wall went all the way round, broken
glass and wire strung along the top. Radar beams,
sonar pickup, and laser heat sensors crisscrossed
the property at critical spots, installed by the most

sophisticated security people in the world.

They passed through the steel gates with only a nod and a wave from the guards. The jeep curled a U-turn and stopped at the front door of the main house. One of the two huge oak doors creaked open slowly, just enough to let him in.

Butler took a final glance over his shoulder at the carefully manicured landscaping, royal palms sighing in the breeze, bubbling fountains with bad sculpture in their centers, indirect lighting on the two Olympic-size swimming pools. If one is good, two is better, he thought to himself and went in.

The security people inside were the best money could buy – FBI, CIA, Special Forces, even SAS, hired actives or retired. They all knew Butler. He'd been Leonard Immke's personal pilot for over a year. They didn't bother with a body search anymore. Their mistake. Even the best get careless.

Inside was always a shock. Beverly Hills in Colombia. The world's most wanted man, exiled for the rest of his life, no passport to call his own, Leonard Immke had tried to bring the USA to him. It had been one year ago that he had stolen over two hundred and twenty million in cash from the WOS funds. He was now the World Bank of Cocaine.

Butler was escorted past six smiling showgirls sitting in the immense living room. He had flown them in a week ago from Las Vegas. Roxie, the long-legged willowy blonde with the defiant eyes, smiled as he walked by. 'Hi, baby, how about me in the co-pilot's chair back to Vegas?' Roxie and Butler had flown together before.

'Anytime, kid. It's a long, lonely ride.'

He passed down the black marble hallway into the library. A guard opened the door for him. All the Cowboys were there, gathered around the huge, inch-thick glass coffee table.

Jesus Christ. Immke was supposed to be alone.

He was standing, presenting a platinum coke spoon on a platinum chain to Chico Gonzales, the Cuban from Miami. Butler hadn't expected any of the Cowboys, but there was no going back now. Too many wheels had been set in motion, and he was too far from inertia.

Immke looked over, smiled, and yelled, 'Butler, did ya bring the Opium?'

The library was barnlike, with a big fieldstone fireplace. One lonely six-foot propane-powered log was burning in the center. A large-screen TV was on with no sound, images flashing of uniformed gladiators wrestling each other for a football. Butler pushed aside three kilos of coke and laid the sealed box of Opium on the glass table.

'Butler, you have no idea what this stuff does for my love life. One bottle and it's all over.' Immke carefully unpacked each bottle of the perfume, twelve in all, one hundred and fifty dollars an ounce. He smiled and gently handed a bottle to Sweet and Low, the only Cowgirl. Then he yelled: 'Have a seat, Butler; you know everyone. Help yourself to a beer.' He waved his Budweiser at Butler like a red, white, and blue pennant.

Butler looked around for a seat.

Lynx was sprawled on the white loveseat, his full-length lynx coat pulled tight over his shoulders, with Ike and Tina, his two white Lhasa Apso puppies, each cradled in an arm. Lynx lived in Harlem and took care of the black market.

Butler heard a squeaky voice call his name. It was Billy Siegal motioning him to sit between him and El Hombre, the Colombian, on the main couch. Immediately, the Colombian got up and moved to an empty chair, underlining the fact that he was no mere Cowboy but Immke's main supplier.

The Bear, his bodyguard, was leaning against the fireplace. He moved about a foot or so also, to keep El Hombre in perfect view. The Bear stood silently in the corner, chewing coca leaf, occasionally reaching into his *chuspa* for a fresh leaf. He was six four and weighed over three hundred pounds, the only armed man in the room, with a sawn-off, short-handled pump shotgun. No one was stupid enough to ask for his weapon. The Colombian was never without him. Butler wondered if the

Bear stood in the corner of the room when the Colombian made love, if he ever made love.

After a few waves and grunts from the others, Butler sat down.

El Hombre always sent chills down Butler's back. He had seen how he operated in the mountains. He would have to keep El Hombre away from the plane. Those pale blue eyes in that dark face were staring at Butler without blinking, almost like he knew what Butler was up to. Butler stared back.

Immke finished his ceremony, slipping the coke spoon and chain over Chico Gonzales's head and adjusting the chain. It meant he was now a Cowboy, part of the brotherhood, with certain automatic rights, including a ten-million-dollar line with Leonard Immke's B of C, as he liked to call the Bank of Cocaine: ten million anytime, on call by telephone, delivered in cash or kind anywhere in the world. The Cuban was sweating profusely even though there was a chill in the air. Butler got up to get another beer. Immke never let the help in when the Cowboys were meeting, but Butler was like family.

There was no beer left in the big Igloo cooler. Immke looked up and caught his eye.

'Butler, ya mind grabbing some more beer and a few bottles of champagne from the kitchen? By the way, ya fix the plane like I told ya?'

'Yes, had it done in Miami. It's heating up now.'

'Great. I want to try it out when we're done here. I'll bring a few of the broads, right?'

'Sure, Leonard. Whenever you're ready.'

Butler walked down the hall to the kitchen. It was set up like a restaurant, equipped with only the latest US-made appliances. Even the cordon bleu chef was American. He was resentfully preparing trays of Whoppers, Kentucky Fried Chicken, Pizza Hut pizza, Big Macs, and Dairy Queen sundaes. Butler recognized them; he flew them in frozen from New York once a month, along with the latest Betamax tapes of *All in the Family*, *Love Boat*, *Happy Days*, and all the major sporting events.

He was grateful for this moment away from the others, a chance to compose his thoughts. He would have to move even faster now.

He carried two Bud six-packs and two bottles of Taylor New York champagne back to the library.

The meeting was over. Chico Gonzales was proudly wearing his prize: the top of the spoon was a sculptured cowboy hat. All the Cowboys had their spoons on full display. You had to do over fifty million a year wholesale to get one.

Butler sneezed so hard he almost dropped the champagne. Sweet and Low was dabbing some Opium perfume behind her knees. She took care of the politicos in Washington. She got her name from handing out gram bags of coke sealed in Sweet'N Low packets.

26

Immke laughed. 'He's allergic to that Opium, sweety. Am I right, Butler?'

Butler nodded his way, trying to stifle a second sneeze.

The champagne was served in hollow, plastic-stemmed glasses as the food trays were marched in by the staff.

Immke collared the chef, who was standing in the doorway.

'Did ya send the trays to the plane like I asked?'

'Not yet, sir. We're doing it now.'

'Good. Butler, grab a Big Mac for me. Let's go try out my new toy. See youse on the plane in five minutes,' he yelled to the group.

The invitation was open. Butler avoided looking at the Colombian. He was watching them like a blue-eyed hawk. So was the Bear. They were the last two Butler wanted anywhere near the plane. He was sweating as bad as the Cuban now.

Leonard marched down the hallway, his white socks reflecting off the marble floor. He yelled at the six girls in the living room to shut off the fucking TV and follow him.

'How about it, girls, Butler has put in a hot tub on my fucking plane, can you believe it? The only flying spa in the world!'

'Flying whorehouse, you mean,' Roxie muttered to Butler under her breath.

'Did you bring the Super Bowl tape?'

27

'Yes, Leonard, it's loaded in the VCR on the plane.'

The girls were tittering and laughing as they climbed into the Cadillac stretch limo waiting to drive them all to the plane. Immke sat between two of them, with a third on his lap. He bounced her up and down with the rhythm of the car. The other two were busy rubbing the insides of his thighs.

The ride in the limo was a lot smoother than it was in the jeep. They pulled up to the boarding stairs, which were flimsy, made out of pipe welding. That suited Butler fine. The plane would easily brush the ramp aside.

The two escort vehicles also stopped, one in front and one bringing up the rear. Their headlights reflected off the shiny black fuselage. Six body-guards got out. Two wore strapped-on Uzi machine-pistols in plain view. The one in charge ran up the stairs, while the other stood motionless at the bottom. They were all bored, used to the midnight cavorting of their employer.

Butler helped all the girls up the stairs. Roxie smiled, squeezed his hand, and winked as she disappeared into the black belly of the plane.

The custom-built 707, which used to belong to a skin-book publisher, had lingered on the market unsold for a long time. Immke took one look at it and bought it on the spot.

Butler nodded at the top stair guard and passed through the hatch. He was the last one to enter the main cabin. The salon was solid red, from the thick, ankle-deep plush carpet to the heavy, red damask-flocked wallpaper that crept up to cover the ceiling. The chairs were all covered in shiny black vinyl that looked like patent leather. The tables were built in, made of a plastic wood veneer. They reminded Butler of a runaway Holiday Inn. Right in the center sat the new four-foot-square California redwood hot tub.

Two-thirds of the way down the fuselage a door opened into Immke's private bedroom, also blood-red. An enormous bed spread from one side of the aircraft to the other; on the ceiling was a huge mirror. Butler often wondered what would happen if he dropped into an air pocket at exactly the wrong moment.

He took the hatch off the hot tub and hit the switch. It started to bubble and boil. Steam rose like puffs of cigarette smoke. One of the girls stuck her toe in the water and let out a little squeal. He turned the thermostat down and flipped on the VCR. Terry Bradshaw was dropping back, trying to find Lynn Swann in the end zone. No one in the salon had the slightest interest in the game.

Immke started to undress first, telling the girls to do the same. He threw his clothes on the floor, getting tangled in them, almost tearing the buttons off his silk shirt and kicking his shoes into the nearest corner.

'See what happened to the stuff I ordered, will ya?' he said to Butler. 'It should have been here by now. What's keeping them?' Butler wondered the same thing.

He finally heard the van stop at the foot of the gangway. The chef was struggling with two silver trays, the security men helping him up the stairs. Butler got them all out quick, took the aluminum foil off the trays, and stared down at twenty Double Whoppers with all the trimmings. He popped three bottles of Taylor and took the tray round.

They were all naked in the hot tub. Butler looked back after he set the tray down; all seven were chomping away at the Whoppers, laughing and splashing. A redhead had straddled Immke, both of them face to face eating the same Whopper with no hands – they were busy in each other's lap.

'Come on, Butler, jump in, the water's great.' Immke let go of the Whopper just long enough to speak; then he lunged back into the girl and the burger.

Butler looked out the door and saw the trail of dust rising in the distance. Three carloads of Cowboys were screaming across the plain from the villa. This was it. There was no time left.

He walked forward to the galley to put the trays away. Still only one guard posted on the top step of the gangway; the others were bunched around the cars below, talking, waiting for the rest of the Cowboys.

He moved slowly over to the door and smiled at the guard, an ex-spook Butler knew from Vietnam. The spook nodded and smiled back as he cupped his match to hide the light from his cigarette, like he was afraid of a sniper. Butler slipped his foot in front of the spook and gave him a heave. He tumbled head first down the grated iron steps, his Uzi pistol bouncing rhythm, finally hitting him full in the face as he fell into a limp heap at the bottom.

Butler slammed the heavy black door shut behind him and snapped the lock. He reached down into his boot and pulled out his Saturday-night special, a pearl-handled, snub-nosed .32, and whirled round yelling at the people in the hot tub: 'Party's over! Get out of that fucking tub, real slow. Ladies first, Lenny.' Immke hated to be called Lenny.

One of the girls panicked and started to scream. Immke slapped her as hard as he could; the noise silenced everyone.

'Butler, what the fuck ya doing? All I've done for you, what the hell is going on?' He was standing in the middle of the hot tub, still holding his plastic glass of champagne, half-eaten Double Whoppers floating and bubbling around him.

Butler reached into the crew locker to pull out a silenced Ingram machine-gun. 'We're going on a little trip, Lenny, back to the good old USA. You too, ladies. Get dressed. You all get a free trip to Washington.'

'You motherfucker. Butler, whatever they're paying ya I'll double – triple.'

Butler had never seen fear in Immke before. He looked exposed, vulnerable, standing there naked, drops of water running down his chest, steam rising from his unit. The girls were all in one corner scrambling to get their clothes on, like they had been caught in a raid.

'Get dressed, Lenny. You look ridiculous.'

Immke climbed out, went over to the corner, and dejectedly started to untangle his clothes. Butler ushered the girls into the bedroom, single file, then locked the door from the outside.

He glanced out the window. The Cowboys were piling out of their cars. The plane was surrounded now with people scrambling around like ants. One of the security people was fumbling, trying to load a bullhorn with batteries. Butler clipped a pair of handcuffs on Immke and shoved him into the co-pilot's seat.

'Please, Butler, it can't be money. I'll give ya—'

Butler slapped a six-inch strip of duct tape across his mouth before he could finish. He couldn't stand any distractions now.

He hit the toggle switch and sparks of red started to spit and sputter out of the right Rolls-Royce engine. Butler heard them trying to slide the chocks under the wheels. No problem; he could goose the engines right over them. The left engine fired into life. Immke looked pathetic sitting there, the tape across his mouth, eyes as big as silver dollars with brown centers.

Both things happened at almost the same moment.

Butler saw the feet first – they must have been size sixteen. Then a huge pair of legs slid down in front of both windows, almost filling the panes. They settled on the nose cone just as a massive chest took their place. Two arms like most men's legs were holding a sawn-off pump shotgun, aimed at Butler's head. He was eyeball-to-eyeball with the Bear, who didn't even seem to notice the Ingram pointed at him.

The explosion was like thunder, even over the roar of the jet engines. The plane rocked violently from side to side. The Bear sat solid on the nose cone, like he was riding a donkey.

Butler knew immediately what had happened. He had wasted too much time. They had framed the door with soft plastic explosive, packed in PVC pipe. The door had imploded, flying in one piece across the cabin and smashing up against the far wall. A standard SAS stunt to disarm plane hijacks.

Butler heard voices fill the cabin behind him. They had him front and back. It was only Immke that was keeping him alive.

'Open up, *cabron*.' The butt of the rifle against the door echoed through the cockpit. Butler kept the Ingram silencer pressed against the glass with one hand; the other he used to yank Immke out of his seat. He slammed Immke's back against the cockpit door. His head bobbed forward with the next two thuds against the door.

'You fuckheads start any shooting and Immke is history. Now stand away from the door.' Butler slid the bolt sideways on the cabin door and kicked it open, pulling Immke with him, so there was no line of fire for the Bear. They came through the door together. Butler slammed it shut behind them. The Colombian took two steps backward to let them into the salon. He had an Uzi in one hand and a gold-plated forty-five in the other. Lynx stood looking over his shoulder, a long-barreled .44 Magnum at his side. He waited, looking for an opening. He was fast with his weapon; Butler knew he had to watch the angle between them.

The girls were screaming in the background and banging on the door. Chico Gonzales let them out.

Immke's eyes were bugging out of his head. Butler ripped the duct tape off his mouth with one pull. It sounded like sandpaper on glass. Immke screamed, his eyes watering, but he was too scared to cry.

He yelled, 'Don't shoot! This bastard is crazy. Let's talk.'

'Talk, shit,' the Colombian said and grabbed the redhead as she passed. He had her by the hair, still holding the forty-five. 'Let him go or she dies.' He dragged her over to the gangway door. 'Now let him go!'

The Colombian swung her round by the hair and pushed. She stumbled on the top step in the start of a swan dive. As she arched out he put two shots right between her shoulder blades. Butler heard the thud as she landed.

'I know this guy. It don't matter what ya do. He won't budge an inch,' Immke pleaded.

'So what we do?' the Colombian muttered, those ice-blue eyes never blinking. He grabbed Roxie by the neck.

'We trade, for Chrissake. We trade.'

'He ain't got nothing to trade,' Lynx said.

Butler heard the Bear slide down off the fuselage. He landed square on the gangway, filling the jagged hole that used to be the door. He had the shotgun pointed right at Butler.

'Get the fuck out of here with that scattergun –

you'll kill us all,' Immke bawled. Somebody tossed the Bear an M-16.

Butler decided it was time to get serious.

He slid his free elbow under Immke's chin and rammed his knee into the small of Immke's back, raising both his Gucci loafers off the ground. Immke started to turn red, kicking the air, just able to sputter a few words. 'Fa Chrissake, we got to figure this out. Safe passage. We give him safe passage.'

Butler slowly lowered Immke by setting his knee straight. The Colombian let Roxie free. She stood there, wide-eyed, mumbling, 'You would have let them kill me.'

The Colombian held the pistol in both hands now, left cupped under the right, aimed at Butler.

'Easy. Take it easy. No sharpshootin'. Believe me, he'll take plenty of youse with him.' Immke was thinking so hard Butler could almost feel it. He had hope now, his confidence was coming back.

Butler was slipping. He knew the feeling. He was starting to lose all fear of death or injury, beginning to float, lightheaded, almost like he was outside himself looking in. He knew where this could lead. He had to go slow now, move with the flow.

He must try to feel what the others felt. If they moved, he would move. This fluid feeling had saved his life many times. He pressed the silencer hard against Immke's temple. Immke knew there was

36

little time left. Butler could get the Colombian first, then either Lynx, the Bear, or the Cuban, but not all of them.

'I got it! I got it!' Immke was screaming now. 'We give you the Bear. You let him jump out just before you leave the ground. You're on your way; we get him back.'

'No,' the Colombian snarled.

The Bear had been with him since he was old enough to walk, had been his father's bodyguard until his father was shot to death on one of the coca steppes.

'Ya have to! He won't believe it any other way. There's a million for each of you. Ya need me for the harvest. Believe me, Butler ain't gonna do nothin' to him.'

He talked about Butler like he wasn't there. Butler could see why Immke was one of the world's great salesmen, how he could have talked an experienced player like Manny Rothman out of control of a huge mutual fund with a bad check.

'How we do it?' the Colombian growled.

Immke answered, 'Easy. The Bear stays in the doorway. He jumps the same time the wheels leave the ground. We clear off now.'

The Colombian translated for the Bear. There was no need. The Bear understood English even though he never spoke a word. The Colombian wanted time to think. They nodded to each other.

'We do it.' He looked at Butler for a few seconds. 'If anything happens to him, there is nowhere you can hide.'

Butler believed him.

In seconds the plane was clear except for the Bear, Butler, and Immke. Butler positioned the Bear in the doorway and did a fast body search for weapons. He was clean.

Butler took Immke up forward with him and checked the controls. The engines were still running. If he sat in the co-pilot's seat he could keep the Ingram pointed at the Bear and one hand on the controls.

Butler walked Immke to the door, pushing the Bear off to the side.

Below him the girls were scrambling to get into the food van. Two men were carrying the redhead's body off. Immke turned to him.

'I'll never forget ya for this, Butler. Why? Why—'

Butler pushed him down the stairs. Immke swore all the way to the bottom and got up running. He lost a loafer but never missed a step.

Butler positioned the Bear back in the doorway as cover, in case any of the sharpshooters got itchy.

'Arms up here.' Butler pointed to each corner of the doorway. 'You make one move, motherfucker, and you're gone.' He did as he was told, staring at Butler, chewing his ever-present coca leaf.

'You get any thoughts of jumping early and you'll

have twenty holes in you before you hit the ground.'
He understood. Butler went forward.

He inhaled slowly, then jammed the throttles.
The thrust almost jarred the Bear out of the
doorway, but he held on. Butler had the aircraft
rolling now; it was only seconds before the wheels
would lift off. The ground-speed reading was eighty
when the wheels started to spin free.

The Bear turned in the doorway. With his yellow,
slanted eyes and black, coca-stained teeth, he
grinned the smile of the devil. Butler had met this
devil before, and he knew they would meet again.

The Bear leaped, his huge bulk slipping under
the wing. Butler saw him rolling off behind him like
a tumbleweed.

Butler tossed the Ingram and rammed the
throttles full forward, then raised the flaps to the
sound of small-arms fire and bullets ricocheting
around the cabin. He prayed they had no SAMs.

He veered hard left over the jungle, disappearing
into the murky night, the snow-capped Andes
fading behind him.

At ten thousand feet he put on the automatic pilot
and went back to check the plane. Lots of bullet
holes, but the most serious damage was the blown
door; there was no way to cover it.

He returned to the cockpit and the controls. The
oxygen mask was hanging down in front of him. He
slipped it on. He put his Special Forces jacket on

over his jumpsuit. It wasn't too bad now, but it would be freezing over the ocean.

Both hands started to shake at the same time. He was coming down.

He yanked off his oxygen mask and washed his face with his hands. Would he really have done it, like Roxie said – let her die? The roar of the engines was deafening, reverberating off the walls. He put the oxygen mask back on.

Twenty minutes later he saw whitecaps below and dropped down to five thousand feet. He would hug the coast now almost all the way to the Yucatan. Then it would be a straight shot across the Gulf, to the Keys and Miami.

His hands were almost under control. He couldn't get the redhead out of his mind. He tried, but he couldn't feel anything for her, or Roxie . . . or that fucking, grinning Bear. He probably should have drilled him right out the door.

Butler had to concentrate all his thoughts on flying the aircraft. The US government had spent a fortune checking him out on anything that flew. He was going to need all of it tonight. He was a lone plane flying in from the general direction of Cuba. He knew he was on the Key West scope already, and 'Fat Albert', the blimp on a rope three thousand feet in the air over Big Pine Key, had his eye on him.

Two hours later, both hands numb with cold,

teeth chattering, Butler saw the two F-4 fighters. He gave them the designated signal. They had been alerted by Harry Ormsby to escort Butler to Miami. Butler and his escort circled north of Key West and followed the Keys up to Homestead Air Force Base.

He shuddered when he thought Immke might have blown out the tires; there was no choice but to assume that they were okay. He braced himself as the wheels hit, bounced, and screeched along the runway. He waited for the pull; there wasn't any. The aircraft stayed flat and true. The only thing that deflated was him. He could feel the air come out of him in a big whoosh. He was alive.

They hustled him to a waiting Intertel Lear jet, and he was flown direct to Peacehaven in Georgia to meet with Harry.

Mission accomplished. The only thing missing was Immke.

3
De-briefing – Peacehaven, Georgia

Butler was slumped in a corner of the six-door armored Mercedes limo, the Georgia pines flashing by, almost mesmerizing him into sleep. But there would be no sleep until after he had seen Harry. Harry hated failure. There was no sense in trying to predict his reaction.

Harry owned Intertel, the largest international security agency in the world. It had over a hundred offices worldwide; headquarters was five floors of a large glass office tower in the heart of Washington. He also owned Peacehaven, where Butler was now headed, a fifty-acre farm in the beautiful rolling hills of Georgia.

Peacehaven was a state-of-the-art school for anti-terrorist training and mercenary skills, including hand-to-hand combat, small-arms, explosives, telephone bugging, listening devices, automatic weapons, and the use of advanced drugs for interrogation. A Disneyland for dealers in death.

The irony of Peacehaven was that by teaching how to disarm Plastique bombs, Harry also taught how to make them. The students learned to dip bullets in Teflon so they could pierce bulletproof vests. Harry's graduates were lethal. They could either fight or initiate terrorism, using the same basic tactics.

Among Harry's Intertel customers were the Who's Who of big business. It was this group that wanted Immke. Washington wanted him too, and they were Harry's largest client. Harry was careful with all his customers. Like J. Edgar Hoover, he kept a 'death's-head' file on anyone who counted.

The driver turned left onto Rural Route 12 for nine miles, then turned right onto a dirt side road. There was no great gate to Harry's preserve, no sentries, no guard tower. Only an innocuous green mailbox that said Peacehaven Farm. It was as though Harry was issuing a challenge for someone to try trespassing on his domain.

Butler knew this country well; he had spent a month training here before the Immke assignment. The road ended on a high, treeless knoll. He entered Harry's electronic fortress. It looked like any prosperous Georgia farmhouse from the outside.

Everyone at Peacehaven wore uniforms. Most were veterans of the US military and wore the uniform of the force they had served under. The others wore the Peacehaven Special Forces uniforms: red berets and marine camouflage. Two Red Berets directed Butler down the main hall, past the computer complex, into Harry's office. Butler heard Harry on the phone before he saw him.

'So why can't you be there? I sent the plane an hour ago. Just grab a cab, put it on the company.'

Harry was big but not fat. He loved uniforms and wore one of whatever service he felt like. Tonight he had on Marine dress blues.

Behind the king-size desk was a giant Plexiglas map of the world. Harry had seen the original in the DEW-line war room under Lake Nippising in Canada. It had impressed him so much he had to have one. Green lights twinkled on every Intertel office around the world. The red lights were war zones like Cambodia, Belfast, and Beirut. There were over twenty red blinking dots. Business was good for Harry.

He turned finally and noticed Butler.

'Fuck, fuck, fuck!' He slammed the phone into the cradle and hurled his braided, peaked officer's hat across the room. It fell with a final spin on the floor. He tore off his jacket and threw that next. It landed in a heap on his hat. He was standing now in his dress-blue pants, red suspenders, and white T-shirt that said Airborne Rangers where the pocket should have been.

45

'Harry, look, I'm sorry—'

'It's not you, Butler. It's a broad. Stood me up. Tits like McIntosh apples and the cutest ass in Washington, and legs – my God.' He pointed Butler over to the couch. 'I heard you came real close.'

'Not close enough.'

Harry shrugged. 'Drink? Anejo, right? How many rocks?'

'Four.'

He walked round the Plexi world map and yanked out Australia. It slid out easily on a cantilever. The bar followed. Harry loved doing this. Each time he did it he looked over to see if it impressed his visitor. The first time Butler had seen it was almost two years ago, when he was in serious trouble with the CIA.

Harry poured each of them a stiff one.

'To your safe return, Butler. Goddammit, I thought we had the slimy little son of a bitch this time.'

'The Cowboys were there, all of them, and the Colombian.'

'I know. Our mistake. Sorry.'

'Thanks, Harry, but it puts me on a worldwide shit list. I won't make a year.'

Immke would have already set his wheels in motion, wheels with many long spokes that reached almost every corner of the earth.

'What is it with these young broads, Butler?

Stood up again, I can't believe it.'

'It happens, Harry.'

'Easy for you to say, the way you look. I hope it's as easy for you in a couple of months. I have a plan for you.' He took a long belt of his drink. 'God, I hate it when they don't show. It took me a fucking hour with this uniform tonight.'

Harry was long in coming to the point, but he was never without a point to come to. He had been in the first landing at the Bay of Pigs, first up the river into Cambodia, the organizer of the aborted attempt to take over Abaco in the Bahamas. His company had been successfully hired to assassinate at least three major leaders in Africa. Butler settled back in the heavy leather sofa. Harry would tell him when he was ready.

'She was coming down from DC. I even sent the Lear to pick her up. And to top it off, she fucking works for Intertel. Used to work for Intertel,' he added spitefully. 'Where were we? Oh yeah . . . the plan . . .'

He poured another drink for both of them, plopped down on the couch, and swung his feet up onto the coffee table, sending a miniature wheeled cannon flying in Butler's direction, who caught it before it hit the ground.

'Ya know, Butler, when they called me from Langley about you two years ago, I wasn't sure. You had been real naughty, you know. You were in big

47

trouble. What saved you was your old man and all
the dough the CIA had spent on you.' Harry had
picked up Butler on the rebound, and planted him
undercover with Immke, based on a tip he was
going to rape WOS. But Immke had moved too
quickly for them to stop him.

Harry stood up, one foot behind the other, trying
to get his shoes off without untying them. He did
fine with the first; the second hurt his big toe, so he
leaned over and untied the laces. The shine was so
good it gave a perfect reflection of his face, including
the waxed circles on the ends of his handlebar
mustache. The shoes became missiles that joined
his hat and jacket. He sat back down.

'Might as well be comfortable. You made me
nervous at first. Overtrained, itchy trigger finger,
and that shrink report scared the shit out of me. But
I liked you. Wanna know something? I thought you
might be a match for Immke. So I was wrong.'

'Nice vote of confidence, Harry.'

'As far as I'm concerned you did okay. Came close.
Believe me, I'll find out how we missed that Cowboy
clambake. If Immke had been alone we would have
nailed him. So anyway, I owe you one, and I got a
good retainer for this job. But I hate to tell you how
much I lost tonight. Dead or alive, it would have
been a huge hit. The Wall Street WASPs, ya know,
he fucked them real bad, and they're deadly. They
never forgive a major screwing.'

Butler could feel the second drink sneaking up on him. It was hard, concentrating on what Harry was saying. He had been up for over twenty-four hours now. He was losing it. He knew Harry was lonely and wanted to talk, but he hoped he would get to the point soon. Harry must have picked up on it.

'Okay, Butler, here's what's happening. First, the good part: I deposited three hundred thousand in your Swiss account an hour ago, when I was sure you were going to make it back. I know it's not the million we agreed on, but you didn't bring Immke home. Second, in the morning you leave for Switzerland, my plane; you're going into the Lucerne spa we own. Our plastic surgeon is going to give you a new face.'

'You always plan everyone's life?'

'No. Sometimes I plan their death.' He chuckled. 'The surgeon says he'll try and keep you good-looking so you can get plenty of action. Shit, maybe I should go with you. Your new passport is with the money in your safety deposit box.'

'I suppose you included the photo too?' Butler yawned.

He never really heard the answer. The next morning he was shaken awake on the couch by two Red Berets. Half an hour later he was airborne to Lucerne to start his new life.

4
A Year Later, Chance Meeting –
Key West

Sunset at the Mallory Square docks is always a celebration in Key West, the end of another day in paradise. Jugglers tossing multicolored bowling pins, fire-eaters inhaling and spitting flames, a trio grinding out chamber music. They entertain their hearts out, then pass the hat.

A big crowd was gathered, all facing west, maybe a thousand people, mostly tourists, to watch the sunset. A glowing red-orange blaze filled the western sky, slowly sinking into the Gulf of Mexico to be swallowed up and extinguished for another day, a final last flash of green and then the purple afterglow. A hearty round of applause came spontaneously from all gathered, a standing ovation tonight.

Butler had been living at the Oceanside Marina for almost six months, ever since he took delivery on his Hatteras long-range cruiser. He bought her used in Fort Lauderdale with the intention of slowly cruising round the world. He had completed the work on her months ago, but he just couldn't seem to cast off. Key West held him in big, warm arms that made it easy to settle in. A pair of cutoffs, a T-shirt, and a way to get around was all that was needed. Butler usually used the tender, a fourteen-foot Boston whaler. It took him all over, including the flats on the Gulf side. He loved exploring the shallows and hunting for bonefish. For shore, he drove his 1,000cc Kawasaki.

He hit the kick start on the Kawasaki and headed for the Pier House Hotel.

He had stayed underground in Switzerland for almost six weeks, getting a series of operations at the spa and looking like someone had been beating the shit out of him on a constant basis, black and blue from the shoulders up. He had patiently waited for them to finish their work; his life depended on it.

He spent another month hidden away on the north shore of Eleuthera in the Bahamas in a tiny cottage, waiting for the bruises to heal and the swelling to go down. Intertel had provided every-thing, even a kind old black nurse to see him through. One night she and Butler got into the Anejo 151 and stayed up trying to wait for sunrise, sitting on the edge of the ocean. She left around 3 a.m. He stayed, meditating about the last fifteen years of his life – all of it, the good and the bad. Light slowly started to show in the east around six, an orange glow. Then the warm rays appeared on the horizon, shedding yellow light on the pink sand.

He wandered back to the cottage, walked into the bathroom and stood staring in the mirror.

He started with his chin. It was a little squarer and his lips were thinner; they covered a dozen recapped teeth that would have been okay for a Colgate ad. There were no scars. His nose was straight, no longer broken in three places. His eyes were the biggest shock; they were wider, fuller. His hairline was shaped almost into a widow's peak. He was looking at a stranger.

He liked his old face better. They had been together for thirty-six years. Still, better a new face than dead.

Butler had done a little checking. He was a wanted man worldwide, with two hundred thousand dollars on his head, dead or alive. Immke had even sent out flyers with his fingerprints. His old fingerprints. Harry had thought of everything.

Butler left Eleuthera for Lauderdale. He began checking with the Lauderdale yacht brokers and scouring the *Miami Herald* ads for the boat he wanted. He finally found her – a Hatteras cruiser. Privately owned, she was stuck in the middle of an estate battle in Key West. The boat was on the rough side but just what he wanted. It was a good deal, but it took almost half the money he had got from Harry. He rationalized that she was going to be his home from now on. He fired her up and headed straight for Bradford's Boatyard where he had her overhauled.

He refitted the interior and made some modifications in the fuel tanks, giving them an extra five-hundred-mile range – two thousand miles altogether, enough to handle the longest leg across the Pacific. He overhauled the two diesels and sprayed the fiberglass hull with Awlgrip paint, then sent all the electronic gear into the shop for a check: radar, sideband RDF, loran, satellite navigator, even the marine radio and phone.

He spent three months in the yard. It was therapy for him. When he did hard physical work, his brain cleared and things fell into perspective. He worked out every morning, then sweated in the hot tropical boatyard sun every afternoon. Gradually the poisons and the demons started to exorcise themselves. He was shocked at all the furies that were still screaming in his brain; they faded a little more with each rub of sandpaper and piece of brass polished. It was the first time he'd had solitude in almost ten years. He functioned best on his own. He needed some peace now and was determined to get it.

The great thing about physical work was seeing the end result. She looked beautiful sitting there on the fifty-gallon drums: proud new bottom paint, thin red waterline, glistening white hull, polished fittings, new carpet, new upholstery – ready for a long odyssey. Just like Butler – brand new.

Butler's family had always owned boats, sail and power. Every spring they got them ready in the yard, then dropped them into Long Island Sound. He and his brother worked like slaves, waiting for their father's final inspection and the nod to launch.

After Butler dropped the Hatteras cruiser into the water, he journeyed to Pier 66 in Fort Lauderdale. Met a few beach bunnies. Played a little. Got bored and eventually set off for the Keys, stopping at the Holiday Isle in Islamorada, just below Key Largo, for a few weeks. Finally he headed down Hawk's Channel to Key West, where everything went from slow to stop.

He was having trouble moving off dead center, getting started. He just couldn't seem to make it very far out of the harbor. Life in Key West was too sleepy and easy.

He pulled the Kawasaki into the parking lot of the Pier House and headed for the Chart Room, one of the world's great bars, frequented by a motley collection of the most fascinating characters in the Caribbean: smugglers, soldiers of fortune, business people, military types, drug addicts, beautiful women, tourists. If there were still pirates on the high seas, this was the bar they would come to when they were on land. It was a small bar. Thirty people made a crowd. The bartender asked you your name once. If he liked you and figured you were going to be a regular, he would remember it.

It was busy tonight; a lot of locals who had been to the sunset were there for a drink before dinner. Butler squeezed onto the last available bar stool.

She was sitting next to him, but he could only see her from the back. Smooth olive skin, long, shiny black hair, she was leaning with her elbow up on the bar, talking idly to a charter captain he knew and running her forefinger in bored circles round the rim of her glass, going steadily in one direction, then reversing. Her face was framed in the dusky mirror by whiskey bottles. She had beautiful green eyes, a fine nose, high cheekbones, like a high-fashion model without the affectations. She was Eurasian, maybe Cambodian or Vietnamese. He had to concentrate on looking away.

Susie was standing on his other side. He felt her tapping a rhythm on the top of his hand with her coke spoon. He turned on the bar stool to look at her; off to her right was black-eyed Rachel, the beautiful, coked-out Raven. They both smiled at him.

'Wanna toot?' Susie asked, smiling.

'No thanks, kid. I'm allergic, remember?'

Butler had many allergies and his reaction to coke was one of them, so he was never tempted.

'What's happening with you ladies?' he said to Susie.

'Nothing, that's the problem. We're partyers looking for a party.'

'How about a moonlight cruise out to Sand Key and a nature swim?' asked Raven.

'I've had too much nature already today,' Butler said. 'I spent the afternoon up in the Bay Keys.'

He couldn't get his mind off the girl sitting next to him.

'Anyone I know?' Susie winked.

'Lefty Sawyer. The blind guide.'

'How can he be a guide if he's blind?' Rachel asked, eyes so black you couldn't see the pupils.

'He's retired. The sun and cataracts finally got to him, but he's got a good memory and he still loves to be on the water. He tells me stories.'

'You like stories? I got lots.' She smiled.

'I think I've heard most of your stories, Rachel.'

'You probably have,' she said, refocusing on Buddy, the barman. Rachel tended bar at the Full Moon Saloon. Bartenders always knew when one of their own was broke. Buddy slipped her one on his tab.

She wandered over to the backgammon table and sat down with Captain Earl – Airborne Earl, as his friends called him. When he got drunk he always

Richard Smitten

shouted, 'Four Marines can't kiss the ass of one paratrooper.' He was quiet tonight; he was out on bail, awaiting sentencing. He'd probably pull hard time at Raiford Federal Prison for the four kilos they caught him with in a dingy hotel room in Miami – just Airborne Earl and three grisly DEA agents. He didn't seem to care. He gave Rachel a big smile and waved her into the seat opposite him.

Butler had no real moral objection to coke. To him it was like alcohol; if people wanted to ruin their lives, it was their choice. And if they wanted it bad enough, they would find a way to get it.

The Oriental girl was looking full face into the mirror now, directly back at him. Butler thought he had grown out of the heart-racing, throat-tightening, dry-mouth symptoms of adolescence. His mind was screaming for something to say. He thought of letting it slide. Maybe he'd talk to Susie or join Raven Rachel and Captain Earl. The girl kept staring in the mirror – maybe she wasn't looking at him.

'Hi,' he heard himself say.

'Hi.'

'Want to go round the world?'

She turned away. Why the hell did he say that? Street talk for a 69. Her back was to him now. How could he be so fucking stupid?

'I mean, would you like to sail round the world?'

She spun round, staring at him with those pale

58

green liquid eyes. She spoke with a light French accent.

'I don't like sailboats.'

'It's a motor yacht.'

'So why you say sail?'

At least she was facing him now. He could see the buttons of her nipples through her white cotton T-shirt. He was no stranger to pretty ladies, but she was in another category.

'I just meant travel. You know, travel around the world.'

'Your name?' When she smiled, one end of her mouth curled down.

Butler still missed a beat when someone asked his name. He hesitated. She extended her hand, very prim.

'Mitch. Wayne Mitchell, but just call me Mitch. Yours?'

'Mai Linh.'

'So you think you might like to come for a cruise?'

'I might. First I would like to see the boat that will make this journey.' She seemed to be going for it.

They made the trip to the boat with her on the back of the Kawasaki, her arms tight round him, the wind blowing her hair straight back.

She loved the boat.

For Butler, the next morning was like a slow-motion dream sequence in a movie. He had a slight hangover. Nothing serious, just couldn't seem to get his mind to focus. The sandals were visible first, then the white cotton T-shirt in a heap in the corner. He was alone in the bed in the main stateroom. He peeked out the porthole. It was a beautiful day, maybe seventy-five degrees. Where the hell was she?

He stepped out into the passageway and tripped over two big aluminum suitcases, the kind the film people use. He moved them out of the way; they were very heavy. Christ, she moves fast, he thought. Maybe he was only kidding. But who cared? If he could get a repeat of last night, he'd take her anywhere.

Butler never had much trouble getting women. It was wanting to keep them that was his problem.

He sidestepped the bags and shuffled up the three stairs to the main salon. God, there she was, in a black bikini, standing on the small rear deck, the sun shining through her hair. She turned with a start and smiled.

'So you are awake.' That same little down-curl of the lip.

She was standing there with one of his spinning rods in her hand, fishing, holding it right, comfortable with it, like she had done it many times before.

To Butler, her body was perfect: long legs, not too tall, slim waist, and nice full breasts – not big, just right. But it was those eyes. They seemed to change color in the bright sunlight, like the pure emeralds he had seen in Colombia. She smiled when she spoke. There was something very fragile and vulnerable about her.

'I put my bags on board. I took taxi to the Pier House early this morning. You mean it about the cruise, *n'est ce pas?*'

'You're wasting your time,' he said, ducking the question. 'There are no fish here at the dock, only little grunts.'

'We see. You like for me to cook breakfast?'

'Sure. I'm taking a shower.'

He took his time in the shower, trying to analyze his feelings. Did he mean it in the bar, about her coming with him? Was his subconscious trying to tell him something? He still didn't know why he blurted the invitation. Life was simple now, uncomplicated, the way he wanted it. He stood under the steaming hot water for a long time until finally he heard a bang on the door and a female voice.

'Breakfast, *monsieur. Le chef est fini prêt, maintenant.*'

The table in the main salon was decorated with a centerpiece of purple flowers. There had never been flowers on his boat. The table was set with his only two linen napkins, a full plate of scrambled eggs, English muffins, bacon, and, in the center, a two-pound snapper, baked. There was enough food for six people.

'You like? The flowers, bougainvillea de Madame Nature, the fish from Mai Linh.'

They never finished the fish. They finished the morning down in the main stateroom with a cold bottle of champagne.

That became a ritual for them for the next few weeks. He would wake up and she would either be fishing or preparing them breakfast for six. She loved to fish. She made him inflate the Zodiac that he used for a lifeboat and put the spare twenty-five-horse Evinrude on for her. She called it her rubber porpoise. She would hunt out the waves from the boat wakes so she could jump them.

It was the third week they were together that he absolutely made up his mind to take her with him. They were in the Marquesas Keys, anchored safely in Moody Harbor, the whaler beached in front of them with a picnic packed with enough food for two boatloads of people.

It was the end of summer, the best time in the Keys, with prevailing southerly trade winds, nice flat days when the ocean became a beautiful blue-green mirror, a sea like the Ancient Mariner must have sailed, hypnotic and mystical.

He was sitting on the beach with a Budweiser. Mai Linh was snorkeling in the bay wearing only a mask and a snorkel, a child of nature, free to run naked, strong and healthy. He could see her long, black hair floating in waves over her dark skin, shimmering in the bright sun as the water rolled over her back. He watched the light contrast of her buttocks as they rose in the air, followed by her long, slim legs pointing skyward just before she dove down, and saw the great smile on her face when she re-surfaced waving a conch at him, her prize, just before she slipped it into her goody bag. He could count on conch chowder tonight, spicy conch chowder. She swam in like a brown torpedo, very comfortable in the water, her bag almost too heavy to lift, full of conchs and urchins, even a big starfish that he threw back.

She had no fear of the water or nature, but somehow he felt she was deeply afraid. She had told him she was Vietnamese, but that was all. It was impossible to get her to talk about herself.

She set up the beach for them. She loved little ceremonies. First she laid out the sheet, then the plates, the side plates, even soup bowls, the wine bucket filled with ice, the knives and forks wrapped in paper napkins. Butler put out the main dishes: chilled gazpacho, smoked marlin, cold meats, potato salad, fresh Cuban bread, and plenty of strong spice, hot sauce, mustards, and horseradish. Mai Linh liked it hot.

She told him it was the way her mother used to prepare things. It was the first time she had ever mentioned her mother to him. The gazpacho burned in his mouth. He almost spat it out, too spicy. He put it to one side. She noticed but didn't say anything. The rest of the lunch was wonderful. Afterward they had a long snorkel together around Moody Harbor and a sleep on the sand in front of the whaler. They hadn't seen a soul all day, just a few light-tackle guides in flats boats taking a shortcut through the harbor back to Key West, twenty-seven miles away.

They made long, slow love on the sand when they woke up; afterward a swim to wash the sand off. Then they made their pact.

'Are you still up for our trip?' Butler asked.

'When do we leave?'

'Well, we should take the boat for a shakedown cruise first for a day or two, return to Key West, and then go for good.'

'Okay. Can we fish on our way?' she asked.

'Yes. Where did you learn to fish?'

'Everywhere – Vietnam, Los Angeles . . .'

'How long did you live in Los Angeles?'

'A few years.' She was starting to get uncomfortable. She changed the subject. 'You ever been to Vietnam, Mitch?'

'No. I got a deferment. My father had friends in high places.' Almost true, he thought to himself. His brother got the deferment. He had jumped in with both feet. He really thought there was an enemy to fight over there, or maybe he just wanted to impress his father.

'How long were you there?' he asked her.

'Till I was twenty-three.'

'The green eyes, from your father?' he guessed. Most of the French had mistresses.

Her eyes started to fill up. One tear ran down her cheek, leaving a little track of salt that glistened in the sun. Butler took her in his arms, her head on his shoulder like a little girl. He felt her body shudder slightly. She was afraid to raise her head. She buried it deeper in his shoulder and whispered.

'Have to make a deal, Mitch.'

'What kind of deal?'

'A treaty between us that our lives begin from this minute. No questions about before. Okay?'

It suited him.

She squeezed him so tight it almost took his breath away. He knew then that they both had their horrors and demons. Maybe they could help each other to bury them.

The return to Key West took them until sunset. They meandered, trolling and diving two of the big coral heads on the way in. They bagged some lobster and she caught a ten-pound grouper, trolling. At midnight they had a candlelight dinner of their catch up on the bridge. A full moon lit up the night, casting a soft light on them. He hoped it was a good omen.

5
Shakedown Cruise – Dry Tortugas

Mai Linh was too excited to sleep. Mitch often found her at the table in the salon with all the charts out and a big map of Central and South America spread on the carpet at four in the morning. She read Chapman's from cover to cover, even tried the section on celestial navigation and wanted him to show her how to use a sextant and read the log tables. She whistled all day, sang little French songs to herself, and dragged him to the library to take out all the books on the South Seas. She loved details and had an endless curiosity about new things. When he would tell her about the ocean and navigating, even the way the diesel engines worked, she would shake her head, smile, and say, 'Mitch, you are one smart son of a bitch.'

Oceanside Marina had about two hundred slips and was the only deep-water marina in Key West for larger boats. The boats southward-bound for Central and South America stopped here for fuel, a layover, or refitting. The people who lived aboard boats were a separate breed. It was like they knew a secret. The secret was about life on the sea and how it washes away the hustle and grind of landlocked life. When it's tasted for a long time, it's hard to go back to living on solid ground.

Mai Linh owned the docks where they lived. She seemed to have no idea of how beautiful she was, and her funny way with words charmed even the hardest heart. The women all loved her and found her openness wonderful, no threat to them. The men made no passes because she set up the rules at the outset. She was with Mitch. There was no need to waste time and wind up getting rejected. She had told everyone who would listen about their upcoming journey, and they all had wished them well. Many of the ocean-lovers had lived similar odysseys of their own.

Mitch put her in charge of food and supplies. She took it very seriously. Finally he had to stop her. She had hoarded enough food on board to outfit them for six months on a desert island. All the extra storage areas had food squirreled away in them. She had even suggested they use the extra space in the engine room.

Two days before their scheduled shakedown Mitch returned from Fausto's supermarket with the last load of supplies in the borrowed marina pickup. He eased the pickup into its spot near his pier and commandeered two marina shopping carts to carry the groceries down the broad cement pier. He was trying to navigate the two at once.

They almost ran him over. Three six-door Mercedes limos in a row. In his haste to get out of the way, he pushed one of the carts into a concrete abutment and half the groceries spilled out. Assholes. They must have come down from Miami, he thought. There was nothing like these cars in Key West. They looked like armored versions to him.

They had passed him in one big blur, looking like they were going to run right off the dock, but they came to a screeching halt at the gangplank of the *White Lady*. Mitch left both carts and stormed down the dock almost at a run. These people needed straightening out.

The *White Lady* had arrived that day and dominated the entire end of the pier. She was well over one hundred feet long, of Italian design, futuristic, with a swept-back flying bridge and long, low lines that made her look like she was doing twenty knots just moored at the dock. Two speedboats were suspended on davits in her stern section. They were centered by a Bell jet Ranger two-seater helicopter tied down to the bull's eye on the landing pad. Four covered motorcycles were lashed to the railings a little forward of the tenders.

Mitch got there just as the first car was unloading. He saw the puppies first, Ike and Tina, then the lynx coat; finally Lynx and his two mammoth bodyguards stepped out. He looked Mitch's way and smiled as if to say: 'Got something on your mind?'

Mitch walked away, back to the carts to pick up the groceries. His heart was pumping like it was going to burst out of his chest.

Had they recognized him?

He wanted to get out of there. But he bent over and methodically put the groceries back in the carts, taking his time so he could see what was going on.

He spotted the Bear right away. He was up in the flying bridge with his glasses trained on Mitch. He had seen the whole thing. He lifted them when the Colombian put a hand on his shoulder. They conferred for a minute, then walked below. 'Shit,' Mitch mumbled.

Billy Siegal slinked out of the third limo like a little ferret, took two fast looks around, one in Mitch's direction, then walked quickly up the gangplank. Chico and Sweet and Low were in the middle car. Chico believed he was a lady-killer. If there was a killer in that car it wasn't Chico. They didn't glance in any direction, just headed straight up the gangplank.

Mitch walked the rest of the way to his boat pushing the carts. The front wheel on one of them had almost fallen off, so it was no easy task. His boat was twenty feet from the *White Lady*. When he got there Mai Linh was below.

He quickly loaded the groceries into the salon, cast off the stern lines, climbed the ladder, and started the engines; then he slipped over the bridge and tossed the two bow lines on top of the pilings.

Mai Linh appeared from below, her inventory list in one hand, a small Texas Instruments calculator in the other. She lifted her head from her list and asked, 'Where are we going?'

'Dry Tortugas.'

'We leave now, Mitch?'

'Now's as good a time as any.' He tried to make it sound casual.

'But we haven't—'

'Watch those bow lines, Mai Linh.' She gave him a quizzical look but did as she was told.

Thirty minutes later they were over the reef, into the Stream, and headed south. The night was clear, the sea calm, with two- to three-foot swells. Mai Linh had prepared a light dinner of lobster, stone crabs, and a salad. She brought a tray up to the flying bridge. They ate in silence.

'You okay, Mitch?' She gave him a smile with that same lip curling down. She flung her head to one side; her hair followed in a long, flowing black mane. Then she filled his wine glass.

'Just got a little antsy at the dock. Cabin fever. You know.'

'No, I don't know. Why you say cabin fever?'

Mitch had to smile, lean over, and give her a kiss. She put both arms round him and gave him a big hug.

'Cabin fever, yellow fever, dengue fever, who cares?' she said, mumbling to herself as she started to clean up.

Mitch notched back the throttles and cut off one engine. It backed them down to six knots; an eighty-mile run would take them about thirteen hours.

He needed to stay up all night and think, to clear his head. The throaty rumble of the engine sounded good to him, like soothing music.

Mai Linh stayed up on the bridge with him till ten; then she went down to the main salon to read and study her charts. Mitch had promised her she could captain them into the harbor at Loggerhead Key near the park ranger station.

Seeing Immke's people again . . .

In one moment time had seemed to wash away. It was like he was back there with them. He had told himself that if he ever saw them again he would have control of the situation. Some control. He'd been sure they were going to come over to his boat and finish him.

72

By midnight they were finally starting to leave his mind. The ocean had a wonderful calming power. He thought of his youth on Long Island Sound.

Their family home was in Darien, Connecticut, a quarter-mile from the Sound and the club. His dad would always show up around noon and take his two slaving sons out to lunch. If the boat was in the water, Mitch and his brother would have to have it ready for the afternoon sail or race. Mitch's brother was two years older than he was, and the club Laser Class champion. There were people who thought his brother was good enough to try out for the Olympics, but he was never interested. All he wanted was to be an investment banker on Wall Street, like his dad. All games came easy to the family. Their father was murder on the tennis court, their mother was a scratch golfer, and Mitch excelled at any game that involved a ball.

He found himself thinking about all of them a lot lately. His dad never got over Crawford's death. Mitch was home on leave after his second tour in Nam. The family was supposed to meet at Delmonico's down near the Battery, then go up to Broadway to see a show. Mitch and his mother arrived minutes after it happened. No one really saw the accident except the driver of the meat truck. The driver was trying to beat a red light.

Crawford stepped off the curb only a block from Delmonico's, and it was over for him.

His mother took it badly, but his father was worse. Mitch had never seen a person so full of grief. Two of his father's partners had to stand on either side to steady him at the funeral. He looked up only once, and it was at Mitch, as if to say, 'Why Crawford? It was you who spent the last two years in the jungle, and now you're going back.'

Mitch put on the automatic pilot and went below. Mai Linh had fallen asleep on the couch. He covered her, made some coffee, and returned to the bridge.

The night air was a little cool now; it felt good to him. He could feel winter sneaking round the corner. The prevailing winds would switch to the north sometime in the next thirty days.

He saw the splash first; then dark gray figures broke through the water, coming straight up near the bow pulpit. There were two of them, walking on their tails, showing off. Porpoises. He heard splashes from the stern. A whole school was nosing along in the white wake and then turning and jumping over to the opposite side. The phosphorescence from the ocean glimmered like an electric sheen on their bodies. They started playing with each other, darting ahead of the boat and then shooting back up through the wake, bounding along, showing him they were perfectly equipped for their environment, happy to cruise the oceans of the world, foolishly afraid of nothing, not even man.

The first signs of light came at six, gray streaks, then white, then gold, finally the sun. Mitch went down and woke Mai Linh. She was restless, wrestling with some bad dream. She woke and saw him; she pulled him down for a hug and nibbled on his ear.

'You want we make a little passion?' She bit deeper on his ear.

'Yes, but who'll take us into Loggerhead Key?'

'My God, Mitch, are we there already?'

She kicked the sheet off, bolted out the salon door, and climbed the ladder to the bridge. He followed her after he made them both some coffee.

Mai Linh had turned the automatic pilot off, taking the helm securely in her hands. She had on nothing but his yellow-and-black peaked cap that said Cat Diesel.

The Tortugas were dead ahead less than three miles. Mitch reached down to turn the second engine on.

'Mitch, what is that floating?' A small white dot was bobbing in the ocean three hundred yards ahead of them. As they approached he recognized it.

'A kite. A fishing kite, probably from one of the guides.'

'How you use a kite to fish?'

'With live bait. You use it to swim the bait to the spot you want. With the kite you can even control

75

the depth the bait swims by the amount of slack line you let out.' He dropped both engines almost into neutral so they could creep up on it.

'What you do, Mitch?'

'We are going to get our first sea salvage.' He took the boat hook and went up to the pulpit in the bow. He reached down into the water and caught a corner of the kite, lifting it dripping wet onto the deck. It was in good shape; it even had the line attached.

'Mitch, you crazy? You throw it back, please. Now, maybe it's already too late, maybe we should burn it.'

Mitch carried it to the stern and set it on the chair to dry. She came down the forward ladder and through the salon, slipping into her T-shirt and shorts. She went right for the kite and started to throw it overboard. Mitch stopped her.

'Just a minute. These kites are expensive. We can use it to fish.'

'No. Bad karma. Kite bring all misfortune of former owner with it. Terrible bad luck. Bye-bye to this kite.' She reached her arm back to throw. He gently pulled the kite out of her hand.

'Mai Linh, that's nonsense. Now get up to the bridge and get us into Loggerhead Key before we run aground; that really would be bad luck. You are your own luck. Now get going.' He tapped her on the behind.

She climbed the ladder; looking back over her shoulder, she snapped, 'You not one smart son of a bitch now, Mitch. You see.'

'Have to have the last word, huh?'

'*Oui*,' she said, disappearing up to the bridge. Mitch secured the kite in the forward hatch and joined her for the final approach.

Loggerhead Key was the main entrance and natural harbor for the Dry Tortugas, a state park now run by park rangers. Fort Jefferson sat on the main island. Built as a strategic stockade in the early eighteen hundreds, it wound up holding Civil War prisoners. Its high stone walls could be seen clearly from the small channel markers they followed in.

'Red right return. That's good, Mai Linh.'

The red marker slid past their starboard side as they eased into the narrow channel. Even with the markers they still had to navigate by sight. The darker water was deep enough for them; there was maybe ten feet of available channel on each side of the boat. The underwater visibility was excellent – over fifty feet of beautiful aquamarine Caribbean Sea.

'Sure, it's red right return, Mitch. I study the Rules of the Road for a week. Now I get a chance to show off.'

The channel opened into a small bay about ten

feet deep with a good hard bottom. Mai Linh found a big circle of white sand in the coral about a hundred feet from shore and eased one engine into reverse while she left the other in forward. The boat stopped; then the stern slowly started to swing round until it brought the bow directly into the wind. Mitch dropped the big Danforth sand anchor off the pulpit, yanking the chain until they got a hookup in the sand. He would drop the stern anchor later and dive down to make sure they both had a good bite of the bottom. Sudden wind shifts and storms were possible at this time of the year, and they might find themselves beached, with the waves breaking up their boat. Mai Linh shut down both engines.

'Good job!'

'Yes, for sure, good job . . . I think so, too. The chart was right.' She beamed over at him.

'It's always good to use your eyes and the depth finder too.' He smiled. The shadow of the Cowboys still lurked in his mind. He needed rest.

He secured the anchor, then went below to their cabin and sprawled out on the queen-size bed. He hadn't slept in twenty hours.

Four hours later there was someone biting on his ear.

'Mitch, I'm lonely. You wake up now. We swim and shake down the boat, okay?'

'Okay, but what happened to the passion?' He started to slide his hand down her smooth stomach.

'Passion is for tonight. The day is too beautiful to waste.' She smiled and ran up the stairs naked.

In one smooth motion she dove right over the transom, cutting a clean splash into the water. He followed. He got over his sulk the minute he felt the warm caress of the water. It took all the tiredness out of his bones.

After the swim they had breakfast at the dining table in the salon and another swim. Then he got down to business, boat business.

Everywhere he went Mai Linh was his shadow. She wanted to know every detail. There was nothing too technical or minute for her. She didn't understand everything, but she gave it all a try. They started with the engines, a pair of GM 671s that gave them a cruising hull speed of eighteen knots. The Onan generator provided a day's supply of 110-watt electricity on five gallons of diesel fuel. They inspected all the lube levels, fittings, hoses, clamps, filters, and fuel lines. It took them about an hour.

Next they went to the lower wheel station to check all the electronics: radar, single-side band, RDF, marine telephone, and satellite navigator. The navigator would set a course if told where to aim and even provide an estimated time of arrival if the hull speed could be supplied. It took into account the wind, the ocean currents, and speed of the boat. Mai Linh was fully checked out on it. She loved to dial up for their position, then seconds later check the co-ordinates on the chart. She checked out the Loran last and went to the bridge and did it all over again with those topside terminals and screens.

She had the stores under control. After a half-hour of checking, Mitch stopped, sure that they had plenty of everything.

Finally they checked the safety equipment: the life jackets, extra bilge pumps, the Zodiac, the first-aid kit. Mitch was very fussy about first aid. He had seen too many people die because the medic couldn't make it in time. He had a fully supplied medicine kit, better than the one the Special Forces medics carried. He had bought it on the black market in Miami. It had everything: morphine, syringes, sulphur, bandages, an intravenous hookup, four bottles of saline, Percodan, tourniquet applicators, even cough syrup. Mai Linh just shook her head.

'This yachting, Mitch, very dangerous, huh?' She handled the morphine but never mentioned it.

'No, baby, but if it comes I would like to be ready. I've seen too much trouble caused by careless preparation, like guys not doing up their flak jackets.'

He couldn't catch it before it came blurting out.

She closed the medicine chest slowly and put the

morphine back in its secret compartment. Then she looked up at him, just staring, not blinking. She knew what a flak jacket was.

She let a minute go by. 'Don't call me baby. I'm no baby, okay?'

Mitch changed the subject, telling her there was one more thing he wanted to show her but that he would have to do it on the high seas. He went aloft to start the engines.

They were well out of sight of the Tortugas when he took her up to the V berths in the bow. He had stopped the boat and they were drifting. The wind had come up a little so there was a small swell that set the boat rocking, making their footing a little unsteady.

He sat her on one of the berths. When he was in the boatyard he had redone the two forward fiberglass inner walls, making them into secret compartments. There were no seams visible, but the panels were hinged to swing out. He pulled the first one open. Mai Linh let out a slow catcall whistle. He asked her to rearrange herself a little as he opened the one on the other side of her.

The arsenal came into full view.

'What you expect? Another war, Mitch? You got enough here to start your own.'

'Pirates.'

'I feel sad for poor pirate that picks this boat.'

She stood up now to examine carefully what she

81

saw. She ran her hand over some of the pieces: the M-16, the Uzi, the M1, the forty-fives, the long-barreled .44 Magnum.

'I don't like this, makes me sick, like bad memories of Vietnam. Throw these overboard. Just keep this shotgun with the pretty handle and the pistols. Please.'

Mitch took out the Uzi, the M-16, the silenced Ingram, and a bunch of clips and motioned her to go to the stern deck.

He had saved a case of empty Budweiser cans. He threw half of them overboard.

'I want you to learn to use these, Mai Linh.' He put the Uzi in her hand. 'Don't lean on the trigger; just short bursts, and watch that it doesn't pull up on you.'

'Why you got all these weapons on your boat? Where they come from? They look military to me.'

'No questions. Remember our deal. There're plenty of drug runners and smugglers where we're headed who would love to get a boat like this, with the range it has.'

'I hate drug runners. They are scum of the earth.' Her eyes got very hard, her mouth became a slit. 'They eat cow dung and fuck their own mothers . . .'

She whirled round and opened up on the cans. She zipped off the first clip and clicked in the second clip before Mitch could say anything.

When she finished there wasn't a Budweiser can

to be seen. This girl could shoot. And she wasn't too fond of drug dealers.

But that didn't explain why she had lost it.

'You want to talk about this, Mai Linh?'

'Talk about what?' she asked, thrusting the Uzi at him and walking off to the galley.

Mitch stayed on the afterdeck, deciding to check all the ordnance, clean the weapons and put them away up forward for good. He would not bring any of it out again unless he had to. He fired all the guns and even tossed one of the shock grenades to make sure it was okay. It went off underwater. He had a little silent laugh. If there were any sharks around they would have one hell of a headache.

It took three hours to finish the job. The last one was the .44 Magnum, a Ruger that Lynx had given him for flying him from La Guardia Airport in New York to Nassau and back. Lynx had come aboard with ten million in green and had gone home a happy man. He loved the long-barrelled model. Lynx had seen too many Clint Eastwood movies, tooted too much coke. He saw his death lurking in every shadow.

Mitch picked up Fort Jefferson on the radar and took a heading; an hour later he was back swimming in the lagoon with Mai Linh like nothing had ever happened. He let it go, but it bothered him a little.

They spent the rest of the afternoon exploring

Fort Jefferson, a monument to man's stubbornness. In the early 1800s it had been built as a military deterrent to enemy ships and pirates entering the Florida Strait, but all the bad guys had to do was sail out of gun range.

Nevertheless, it was an engineering marvel, with a complex aqueduct and cistern system modeled after the ones built by the Romans. Mitch explained to Mai Linh it was where they had sent Dr Mudd after he was convicted of giving John Wilkes Booth medical assistance, right after he shot Lincoln. He finished the story. 'So that's where the expression "His name is Mudd" comes from.'

'Why was it a crime if he was a doctor? Shouldn't he help?'

'It's a little more complicated than that. Anyway, a yellow fever epidemic hit the fort here. Dr Mudd worked at great risk to his own life and saved many lives. President Grant gave him a full pardon. They never had a real case against him anyway.'

'I like happy endings,' she said. 'I like for us to have a happy ending.' She looked preoccupied as she sat in the shade of the stone guard tower, her brows furrowed, a faraway look in her eyes.

'Now how about us catching dinner before the sun sets?' Mitch said. 'You snorkel. I'm taking the Whaler out a little to try out our new kite.'

'Your new kite. Don't mention no more to me,' she said.

He caught a stray kingfish with the kite. Mai Linh had done well – a conch for the salad and three stone crab claws. She wouldn't touch the kingfish and only picked at her dinner.

'Maybe we can just go to bed. Okay, Mitch?'

'How about tonight we sleep on the beach under the stars? I'll bring the sleeping bags in the Zodiac.'

She smiled and nodded, then dropped her clothes and, slipping over the side, swam in to shore. He followed in the Zodiac.

It was a magic night. The moon was almost full, and the beach was completely private. They made love on the sand with a hunger that consumed them both.

Mitch drifted off into his own gray world with Mai Linh next to him, breathing in slow, even breaths like a child.

Running. He was running full speed, tripping, slipping, bouncing off the rough bark of trees, branches slapping him in the face. He finally made it to the clearing that opened onto the long, broad farmer's field. He had a shotgun in his hand, the over-and-under his father had given him the Christmas before. His father had brought it back with him from England. It had a hand-carved stock.

He saw his brother first at the far end of the field, sitting still in the duck blind with their father, with Long Island Sound behind them in the gray dawn light. Corn had been left in the field by the farmer to pull the ducks down. Mitch ran across the field, sliding on the mud furrows, falling on his knees, the cold autumn air filling his nostrils, constricting his lungs, making his breath short. They both stood up at once, waving Mitch frantically back into the brush. He could hear the ducks coming in over his shoulder as he ran. He didn't care; he wanted to be in the blind with them. He kept running. When he got there they both reached out at the same time, pulling him in, jamming him in between them. They looked at him like he was a madman. Looking back over the field Mitch could see the estates on the shores of Oyster Bay, black and white through the gray overcast.

They started blasting; their father worked the Remington pump, cascading ejected shells as fast as he could. He never put the plugs in to make it legal, always loading the full nine shells into the chamber. Mitch's brother, with the double barrel, let loose at the same time.

Mitch stood up with the over-and-under, firing as fast as he could, his cold hands fumbling through the reloads. Ducks fixed in their landing patterns started to spin in mid-air, falling like rain. They only had two or three minutes to fire before the ducks figured it out, regrouped into a new flight formation, and continued their perilous journey south.

The silence was broken now only by Mitch's fire.

He couldn't stop. His father reached over and put his hand between the open barrels and the stock as Mitch was reloading. The other hand he laid on his son's shoulder, turning the boy toward him. His father stood squarely in front of him, blocking his vision.

'Enough, son. That's enough.'

Mitch woke up in a cold sweat, huddled in the sleeping bag, the warm Tortugas sunrise pouring over his head. The sleeping bag next to him was empty. The Zodiac was still where he had left it beached. He did a fast reconnoiter of the island. Empty. Where the hell could she be? He noticed some movement on the rear deck of the Hatteras.

Mitch tossed both sleeping bags into the Zodiac and tugged so hard on the starter cord he almost pulled it out of the engine. Seconds later he was tying up to the dive platform.

Mai Linh was calmly fishing off the rear deck. She had her Cat hat on. He heard the marine phone ringing in the main cabin.

He opened the transom door, gave her his worst look, and grabbed the phone out of its cradle.

'Yes!'

'Yes? What the hell is with the yes?' It was Harry. 'I've been trying all morning to get you. Don't you answer the fucking phone?'

'Harry, I'll call you back.' Harry could find anyone anywhere.

'When? It's important.' Mitch could hear the computers humming in the background. He wondered what kind of uniform Harry had on.

'Soon.' He hung up and disconnected the bell. Mitch knew Harry would call back in seconds.

He stormed back to the aft deck. She was baiting her hook, the morning sun shining on her naked body, on that little curl of the lip that was almost a pout.

'Mai Linh, don't do that again!'

'What?'

'What!' he said. 'Just leave like that. Christ, you scared the hell out of me.'

She put her rod down and came over to him very slowly, like a wary animal, to see if he was really angry. She reached out and took his hand in hers, then she slipped her other arm round his shoulders, pulling his head down so they could kiss. He held her. They stood for several minutes just holding each other.

'Why didn't you let me know you were going?'

'You were asleep like a baby. I didn't want to disturb you. I hate outside sleeping. I had to do it many times. I can't help it, it makes me scared. So last night after we make love I come back to the boat.'

'Why didn't you answer the telephone?'

'Bad news. I hate the telephone, always bad news.'

'Not always.'

'Yes, always for me. Someday I will have no telephone anywhere near me.'

Mitch saw it clearly as it came into view on the horizon. It was right over Mai Linh's shoulder in the Gulf Stream, far out in the shipping lanes. The Dry Tortugas was where the ocean-going vessels made the decision to go west or head south. It was the *White Lady*, and she was definitely headed south. He could see the rotor blades of the helicopter on the rear deck. It gave him the shudders. He was glad when Mai Linh distracted him with a little yell.

'Mitch, look over on the beach. What is that?' He didn't see it at first; then he noticed it sunning on the sand.

'A turtle. Tortuga is Spanish for turtle; this island is one of the few natural breeding grounds they have left,' he told her. 'The rest have been turned into condos.'

'Condos? What are condos?'

'Condos are not important, Mai Linh; they're just big, ugly buildings they put on the beach.'

'Oh, Mitch, I'm so happy to see the turtle.'

'Why?'

'He's good luck, always strong good luck. Maybe enough to wipe away the kite.'

'I have to call Harry back.' He noticed that the *White Lady* was almost out of sight, slipping over the horizon.

'You forget Harry. We go now and make the passion from yesterday, *oui*?'

'*Oui*.'

It wasn't till after noon that he called Harry back. Mai Linh was right. It was bad news. The next thing he knew he was in Harry's office.

6
Blackmailed – Peacehaven, Georgia

Harry let Mitch cool his heels in what Harry called the Games Room, his way of reminding Mitch who was important.

The Games Room was full of war memorabilia: miniature warships on papier-mâché oceans, fighter planes and bombers hanging from invisible ceiling wires, artillery pieces of all kinds, tanks and armored personnel carriers in brass and glass showcases. Harry was rumored to have the largest collection of toy soldiers in the world. Every Intertel office was on red alert from Harry to buy any metal soldiers that came up for sale. If anyone missed a good collection he could kiss his job goodbye.

Harry had a dozen full battles raging on giant tables, which changed whenever he was in the mood. The story went that the entire basement was also set up this way, with five full-time craftsmen restoring the tiny soldiers and positioning them according to Harry's battle plans..

One table had the Maginot line, showing the Germans overrunning it from behind, with the Panzer divisions pounding the immobilized cannons into dust.

The Normandy invasion was in the center of the room. It included a big fleet lying offshore. The Battle of the Bulge was in one of the corners, timed for the spring when the Allies finally broke through the awful trap the Germans had set for them.

Harry was very patriotic in his own way. He hated to see the United States not winning, so sometimes he took poetic license with the battles. Like the one at the Cho-sen Reservoir in Korea, where he had the Marines beating the hell out of the Chinese Communists who came flooding over the 38th parallel, instead of the other way around.

All the major battles were encased in Plexiglas so they couldn't be disturbed. Harry wanted them his way, and it was best not to discuss their historical accuracy.

Mitch was at Hué. He was trying to find his helicopter LZ in one of the tabletop battle scenes when Harry strode in through the double doors.

He was wearing his Israeli commando outfit today: black beret, desert camouflage jacket, and the matching pantaloon pants, the ones that slip into the top of a pair of black paratrooper boots. He was a big fan of the Israelis. He marched over to

Mitch, grabbed him by the shoulders, stared at his new face, smiled, and strode over to the battle in progress on a table in the far corner with no explanation of why he was late. Mitch followed.

'Surprise!' he said. 'First day of the Six-Day War, Butler . . . er, Mitchell. It was surprise that gave them the edge.' He looked down at the miniature desert war in full force.

'Hitler, too,' Mitch said, 'when he surprised Poland and Czechoslovakia.'

'Don't talk nonsense. No comparison.' Harry reached up toward the ceiling wires from which hung a squadron of Phantom F4s with tiny Star of David insignias on their wings and gently hit them; the motion set the planes swinging like five little metronomes, back and forth, over the desert battle scene.

'Action. The Israelis are all action, no talk. That's why the world shits every time they pass gas. Like you, Mitchell, action.'

'No more, Harry. I'm retired.'

'Yeah, sure.' He took Mitch by the arm, leading him out of the Games Room toward the office. He stopped in the doorway and turned to look back at his armies of tiny soldiers waging the fierce battles that had changed history. Mitch swept his arm in a gesture that encompassed the room.

'Why these particular battles, Harry?'

He paused before he answered. 'Sometimes when

I'm in this room I feel like Hannibal must have felt when he crossed the Alps with those fucking elephants. They said it couldn't be done, and he fucking did it. That's what I admire, Mitchell, the challenge beaten. Know what I mean?'

He turned and flicked out the lights, casting a moonless night on all the wars.

They walked slowly down the hall, both lost in their thoughts. They passed the computer room, packed with people and flashing terminals. There were twice as many on staff as the last time Mitch had seen it.

Harry held open the door to his office. The huge Plexiglas world map was a mass of blinking red battle lights. Things were heating up worldwide.

Harry sat down behind his desk. Mitch didn't like it; it meant that they were going to talk business sooner or later.

'Rum?' Harry lit up a cheroot, took a few deep puffs and swung his big swivel chair round, not waiting for an answer, and pulled Australia out of the map. He turned back quickly as always to check Mitch's reaction.. Mitch tried to look impressed. Harry smiled as he filled the ice bucket.

'Mitchell, you look good, like a movie star.'

Mitch wasn't going to ask Harry how his love life was going. He wanted to get back to Key West some day soon.

'You still work out?' Harry asked.

'Not as often as I should.'

'Me neither, although I got a new exercise room and a running track on the course outside. I try to stay in shape for the young broads. Maybe we'll go for a walk later. We got some new toys we're working on now that you might get a kick out of.' He handed Mitch his drink. 'These young broads, who knows what's in their heads? I got one now, Christine, nineteen years old, so crazy about me I practically have to put my own security on her to keep her from bugging me. Only two dates and she wants to get married. Can you believe it? Christ, I'm not interested in getting married. Shit, if Brooke Shields were asking I'd still say no.'

'I wouldn't worry about Brooke Shields, Harry.' Mitch smiled.

'It isn't funny. You know, I had this Christine kid checked out, and she's got a two-gram-a-day coke habit. Nineteen years old, can you believe it? She thinks I'm rich, connected in the right places with the right sources, so I can supply. Fuck that noise.'

'Cocaine.' Harry was finally getting to it. Mitch could always tell. There was something in the timbre of his voice, the way he avoided looking a person in the eye. 'What about cocaine, Harry?'

'It's serious, sixty billion big. You know how big the whole cigarette market is?'

'How big is it, Harry?' Mitch smiled.

'Quit the kidding. Fifteen billion dollars for

cigarettes, that's retail sales, Mitchell.'

'Impressive, but who cares?'

'Yeah, I'll tell you who cares. Uncle Sam. And you know who's the king of the cocaine business?'

'Immke, right?'

'Good guess.'

Harry stood up with his back to Mitch and studied the giant Plexiglas map of the world with all its little flashing lights.

'Never seen so much trouble in the world. All these stupid little skirmishes, religious wars, any one of them could end up with the big one going off. These madmen scare the shit out of me, like this fucking Gaddafi.' Harry slammed Libya hard with the flat of his hand, sending a loud, hollow sound echoing through the room.

'Christ, if they want him taken out, all it would cost would be around five mil, and I got just the team in Paris to blow his ass away. I tell you, he's starting to bug me. If he wasn't so good for business I might take him out for free.' Harry fell back into his chair. He was working himself up to something.

'You didn't fly me here to talk about Libya.'

'No. How about we take a little stroll around the grounds?' Harry suddenly got up, strapped on the webbed belt that went with the uniform, adjusted the forty-five on his hip, and strode off toward the door. Mitch followed. Harry wanted to show off a little.

The leaves were turning. They added just enough color to the green, rolling Georgia hills to remind Mitch of Long Island Sound in the fall. The fifty acres of Peacehaven had been carefully laid out in five sections: hand-to-hand combat, small-arms training, planting and disarming explosives, surveillance techniques, and industrial espionage.

This training was open to anyone who could pay the tariff: soldiers of fortune, multinational corporation personnel, government agencies, groups from third world countries who were for or against their current governments, and anyone who wanted to use high-tech weapons, even police forces. All these groups were welcome; the only rules were no Commies and payment in cash, in advance.

They walked through the hand-to-hand section and Harry nodded at Frank Delamo, the head instructor. He smiled and gave Harry a little bow. He had been Mitch's teacher. He had consistently beaten the shit out of Mitch for three weeks until Mitch finally nailed him once or twice near the end of the course. Mitch still wasn't sure Delamo hadn't let him win to boost his confidence. He wasn't about to challenge the man again to find out. Harry studied Frank to see if he recognized Mitch, but he didn't. Mitch was starting to see why Harry wanted to take this little tour.

They walked toward the small-arms training

grounds, about five acres in all. They passed the target areas and headed straight for the large concrete, soundproof building. Harry inserted his code card and then slapped a palm print on the glass. The steel door slid open to a large indoor firing range.

'Flashless powder, Mitchell. We already have that figured out. But we've gone a step past that.' Harry motioned to Carl, the trainer, to come over. Mitch knew him. He was tall and thin, with frameless glasses that made little orbits round his eyes. Carl was a great shot, good as they come, but his eyes were going. Even so, with a handgun he could outshoot anyone Mitch knew. He nodded at them and stuck out his hand; there was no sign of recognition.

'Carl, would you demonstrate our latest development?' Carl walked over to a table and slowly loaded a .357 Magnum. He walked up to the target station and squeezed off six, all dead center. There was no noise, not even a whisper of sound.

'Noiseless and flashless – think about it. No silencer. Regular muzzle velocity. Fucking awesome.' Harry handed Mitch two full boxes of shells. Sometimes Mitch tended to forget how deadly Harry really was.

'A .44 Magnum load and a box of .45s, a hundred cartridges in each box,' Harry said. Mitch tried to hand them back. Harry pushed his hand away.

'Put 'em away for safekeeping. Consider it a little present from Peacehaven.'

Mitch slipped the boxes into his pocket. For the next half-hour Harry walked the grounds, showing Mitch his hardware and telling him of all the high-tech advances they were making in the war business. They finally wound up back in Harry's office at sundown.

Harry poured them each a drink and swung his size twelve paratrooper boots up onto the corner of his desk. At the same time he delicately flipped two toggle switches with his heel, cutting off all but emergency calls. He stared at Mitch with those cold blue eyes and twirled the ends of his mustache for a few seconds; then he spoke.

'There's a certain somebody in the Oval Office who wants to hang onto his desk for another four years. The polls are bad, real bad. So he needs something big to be done that will prove he's straight and smart, give him a lot of free media coverage, and tell the middle-American voters that he's undertaking a never-ending vigil to keep them safe from harm. It would be even better if it's something the Silent Majority can all hate.'

Mitch didn't like what he knew was coming.

'Drugs. The Man needs a major international drug bust that he can personally take credit for. A big one, a mega-bust, biggest in history, maybe up to six months' worth of most of the world's cocaine supply. So he hired me to help him.'

'He has the DEA and he wants to use your services?' Mitch asked.

'He also has the FBI, the CIA, and Customs, but they all hate each other and spend most of their time playing politics or taking payoffs.'

Harry was puffing away at his cheroot, sending up clouds of smoke, starting to enjoy himself. He continued: 'There's a huge deal going down in the next six weeks. They're shipping the fall harvest, supposed to be the biggest harvest ever.'

'From?'

'We think Panama. Somewhere in the Canal Zone, so it can be transshipped to both oceans and easily stored.'

'And banks to handle the money?'

'Yes. Major laundromats. They're as big as the Bahamian banks now.'

'They have the government.'

'His code name is "Pineapple Face" and he is the government. He's deep in Immke's pocket, up to his Panamanian tits in white powder. Has been for years.'

'So what do you want from me? The Cowboys?'

'They're all involved, Mitchell, and they're big now, real big. We need to know exactly how large this harvest is, where they plan to warehouse it, and when they intend to ship.'

'Harry, you have a short memory. It was you who told me to retire permanently. You went to all the expense and trouble of giving me a new face.'

'True. And now I'm saying you owe me a little, tiny favor. I don't want any rough stuff – all I want is info. The real bottom line on the problem is they're afraid the price is going to drop like a stone to thirty bucks a gram – cheaper than grass. Then everybody is going to be tooting their brains out: blacks, truck drivers, college kids, waitresses, secretaries, everybody.'

'The Cowboys know me.'

'They didn't recognize you in Key West.'

Mitch stared at Harry, shocked. It meant that somehow he had been watching the whole scene on the dock. Probably had it on video cassette somewhere. It must have given Harry a big laugh, he thought.

He stood up and stretched, trying to figure a way out of this.

'How ya doin' for money? You got about a hundred gees left in the bank, right?'

Mitch sat back down.

'Yeah. And that's just fine for me for the next few years. I can always charter out the boat.'

'How about a quarter of a mil? Half up front and

half when you get the info I need.'

Mitch knew that all this fencing was Harry's way of being genteel. They both knew all Harry had to do was feed Mitch's whereabouts to Immke. Mitch would be dead in forty-eight hours and Harry would pick up the reward.

Still, that wouldn't solve Harry's problem or get him Mitch's services, which must have meant something or he wouldn't have been working so hard.

Harry was holding up a small mirror, using it to adjust his black beret. When it was the way he wanted it he dropped his feet off the desk with a thud, spun dead center in his swivel chair, and sat ramrod straight, elbows planted, looking at Mitch.

'Well, we got a deal or what?'

'Maybe, if I get some guarantees,' Mitch said, dealing from weakness, still trying to negotiate. 'I need to have access to everything, the whole Cowboy file. If they make me, I want to know when you know. And I want a time limit of thirty days. I'll give you what I have when I'm through. But no more than thirty days in Panama.'

'Okay.' Harry started to stick out his hand, then withdrew it. It was his bond; no contract was necessary. No matter what, if he shook on a deal it was a done deal.

'There is one more thing.'

Harry picked up a thick, yellow, legal-size folder

from his desk and walked over to sit in the overstuffed chair next to Mitch's. He dropped the file on the coffee table, knocking over a small display of British soldiers charging up the Khyber Pass.

'Don't say a thing until I finish.' Harry flipped open the folder. There were two eight-by-ten photos, blank sides up, stamped 'Los Angeles Morgue'. He turned one over.

It was Mai Linh.

'Your girlfriend's dead.' Harry sat still, waiting for it to sink in.

Mitch thought he was going to be sick, the photo was so cold and final. Whoever took it had shot a thousand like it. It was without any feeling or compassion. The eyes were open . . . empty. They were Mai Linh's eyes. Harry flipped over the second picture, full body shot, stretched out on a slab. It was worse: a gaping bullet wound behind the ear, a large open wound in the chest.

Mitch had to get up out of the chair. As he rose he turned both photos over and walked to the bar.

He couldn't get his hands to work. Harry came over and poured them both a stiff one. He put his arm on Mitch's shoulder and continued, 'We got this photo from a friend of mine who's connected with the Los Angeles police. We don't know the whole story, but whatever it is, it's bad. This photo was taken almost six months ago in the morgue.'

'Then it's not Mai Linh,' Mitch blurted.

But the picture was of Mai Linh, there could be no doubt.

'I'm following up with the Los Angeles Intertel office.'

Mitch slunk down in a chair and looked away.

'It's obviously not the girl you're with, but . . .' He let the 'but' hang in the air. 'There was no other way to show you.'

Of course there was another way. Harry was a master at shock and psychological games. Mitch had to struggle to get his mind working again. It was like those other moments when something awful had happened: the door gunner hanging dead in his straps, the wounded screaming for God or their mothers, the napalm sucking the air out of the lungs of a whole living village.

His way was to think of something else, quick. He tried to think of Long Island Sound in the fall, but it didn't work. All he could see were those innocent dead eyes and that beautiful face.

Harry kept right on talking, his voice slowly starting to filter into Mitch's brain. Harry was many things, but he wasn't a liar. The photos had to be real.

It was almost as if he was reading Mitch's mind.

'I don't know either. The body has never been claimed. There's no fingerprint ID. The LAPD says they are about to call it quits on the case, that it may

104

be drug related. But they say that about anything they can't figure out.'

Mitch just wanted to get out of there.

'You've got a pile of trouble there, Mitchell.' Harry was too smart to tell Mitch what he should do about it.

Somehow Mitch found himself on the Intertel Lear jet with the unopened Cowboy files in an attaché case on his lap. On top was the folder with the photos of Mai Linh. He slipped them into the case. He'd be landing in Key West after midnight, but he hadn't called Mai Linh. He dreaded seeing her. He had too many questions.

Mitch was suddenly grateful he had an assignment from Harry. It wasn't until later that he realized Harry had never shaken his hand.

7
Dead and Alive – Key West

The taxi Mitch took from the airport let him out at the marina. It seemed like a long walk to the boat. It was Friday night and there were two parties in full swing on his pier, both on big sailboats. He knew most of the people. A few yelled for him to join them, waving their drinks at him. He forced a smile, waved back, and shook his head no. Where was his carefree life now? The whole idea was to be mobile and free and stay away from trouble.

His boat was dark except for a small light in the galley. He swung over the stern railing and quietly entered the salon, tossing the attaché case on the couch. He heard the door open in the master stateroom, feet padding along the hall carpet.

'Mitch, that you? Better be you.' She was half running as she cleared the top step into the salon. She had on a pair of black bikini briefs, the same color as her long hair. Her body shimmered in the pale moonlight pouring through the starboard windows. Her eyes, still misty from sleep, flashed green as she turned on the cabin light. In a second her arms were round his neck. She curled up and rubbed against him like a cat, almost purring.

'Mitch. I have missed you like anything.' She gave him a squeeze and sighed. 'So you tell me everything now. I have slept myself out.'

Mitch procrastinated, asked for coffee.

She went into the galley for it, smiling at him with that lip curled down in the corner. She brought the tray in and put it in front of him on the chart table, setting it right down on top of Colombia.

He couldn't wait any longer. If this was going to finish them, it might as well be now. He reached for his case and slipped out the legal file folder, taking the two photos out face down, just as Harry had done with him. He placed them on the charts next to the little coffee tray.

'Mitch, you look extra serious.'

'I am extra serious, Mai Linh.' He flipped over the first photo, the full-face one. Both her hands shot to her mouth.

He heard the backward scream as she inhaled; her body started to tremble violently. She snatched at the second picture and turned it over in one fast motion; then she let out a real scream that came from some dark nightmare. Tears streamed down her face, her mouth moved, but no more sound came out. In her desperation she swept the table bare, sending photos, coffee, tray flying, trying to make the images disappear.

He went to reach for her but she pushed him away, running for the door to the stern deck, fumbling with the door handle, trying to open it with both hands. He lifted her and carried her over to the couch. First she tried to hit him with her fists, then she buried her head in the pillow and cried. He let her be for a few minutes and went to pour them both a drink.

Then he waited. He had to know.

It took almost an hour for her to come around. She had finished her third drink when she finally started to talk, slowly at first.

'Mitch, I tell you this. But I have never told anyone.'

She sat straight on the couch, took a sip from her drink, and looked over at the chart table. He had put the photos away. She wiped her eyes with a cold towel and began.

'We lived always in Saigon. My mother was Vietnamese and my papa was French. But they never lived together. My papa was a baby doctor in the hospital, and he also had a private practice.

'His car and he were blown up outside of his house early one morning by the Viet Minh. Mama went crazy. She was his nurse; they had a big love affair all their life, but he was married. Now she was left with me and my twin sister to look after, and we were young, only twelve years of age. It was 1965, just when you send the CIA advisers to help us. Mama had worked for years with my father, although we hardly ever saw him.

'She died six months after Papa died, of a fever, they said. For three years, maybe four, we live with relatives all over Saigon, until we are maybe sixteen. Our relatives are all poor with problems of their own.

'One day my sister says we are ready to live alone. And we move to a nice apartment downtown. Somehow my sister is able to pay the bills and she gives me money for school. She is no longer going to school. She works late hours, never home at night. But always there when I come home and in the morning. She is acting like Mama now.'

Mai Linh's eyes were filling up again. Mitch went below to get her one of his sweatshirts. She slipped into it and curled her legs under her. It looked like a little gray tent with only her head showing.

'My sister and I were identical twins. She never would say what she was doing. But one day an American officer with birds on his shoulders comes up to me on the street. You know?'

'A colonel?'

'*Oui*. He says to me, "*Bonjour, Liu*," and gives me a big kiss on the lips, I break from his arms and run.

110

When I look back he is just standing there smiling, with his hands on his hips. Later, when I tell my sister, she says: "These foreigners are all crazy, don't worry."

'But I do worry. So one night I follow her. She goes to fancy hotel, then into bar where she meets the colonel and kisses him, and they go off together. It was only then that I knew what was going on.'

'How old were you?'

'By then eighteen, and Saigon was in big trouble. The army is going over to Viet Cong. The city is surrounded and helicopters are landing on your embassy roof. The whole embassy is surrounded by screaming people who want to be taken to the aircraft carrier. Marines were beating them off the gates. As the helicopters take off, people are hanging from them, with other people inside kicking them and stepping on their hands so the helicopter does not fall to the earth from the weight.

'My sister and I go right past the embassy in the colonel's jeep, flags flying on each fender, two black Marines with a big gun in the center of the jeep. Everyone clears a path for us. We are taken to a secret field only a few miles from the embassy. But there is only a few minutes to board the helicopters before the people find the field and break in through the wire fence. The colonel has arranged everything for us. My sister shows the paper and we are taken right away to the aircraft carrier.

'The deck of the aircraft carrier is awful, packed with thousands of people. They are shoving all the other helicopters into the water so there is more room for the people. When we land she shows the paper again, and we are taken very fast down below the deck to the crew's quarters; we are put in a cabin with an American family from the embassy. The colonel never comes. Liu fears he may be dead.

'Now we are in New York City with only one thousand dollars, no passports, no green cards, no nothing. Liu finds us a hotel and calls a number in Los Angeles. The next day we are on a midnight flight to California. When we land we are met by two men who have a limousine. They take us to a hotel and say they will be back for Liu later.

'We have only one small bag, so while Liu is in the shower I look in the bag. Inside is a bag of white powder . . . No one has to tell me what it is. I have heard plenty in Saigon.

'The men come back and take Liu with them. Several hours pass. I am scared, but Liu comes back finally. I ask her where she has been, she says for me not to worry. She is carrying the bag on her shoulder. I rip it off, open it, and now there are two bags inside. I ask her to tell me what is happening.

'She says it can hurt me if I know. But I demand. She tells me it is none of my business. I am to go to school and start the family over again. She will provide the money. She always promised Mama she would take care of me no matter what. I make her tell me.

'She finally admits that she smuggled this bag of heroin in on the carrier for the colonel. He knew no one would search her after she was on board. She decided to steal it from the colonel, who was bringing in plenty from the Golden Triangle and shipping it to the US in body bags of dead Marines.

'She says she has hated the colonel always. Even though he saved us, he is still a scumbag person. She says she traded this one bag for two bags of what people like better in the US.'

'Cocaine?'

'*Oui*. So now she has two bags, she says, which is better than one bag. She says that we must never talk of this again. I'm hungry now, Mitch.'

He got up. 'I'll make us something. Talk to me in the galley.' He got out some bacon and eggs. She eased up onto the edge of the counter. He nodded for her to continue.

'So I never bring it up again and I go to school in Los Angeles, learn to speak English. One day I start to see Liu is acting funny, shaky, paranoid eyes, looks funny. And I start to think, maybe she is using what she is selling.'

'Was she?'

'She is doing freebase all the time, spending all her money, even sometimes the rent didn't get paid. I try to talk to her and she only nods and smiles, then

113

tells me to mind my own business. You know, gives me the lip service all the time. And then . . . and then . . .'

Mitch served the eggs and bacon, but she pushed her plate away and stared off into space, her bottom lip quivering, tears welling back up into her eyes. The bravado was faltering and the fear was creeping back.

He had known it many times before from men telling their stories. How they were in stride, kicking ass, winning, then how it swung against them and the roles reversed. They were fighting now for their own lives, running, buddies falling all around them, screaming, kicking the air. And finally they would break down, crying, sobbing so hard they could talk no longer. He had done it himself.

He took her back to the couch and made another drink for each of them. He decided to ask her a question to get her started again.

'What did you think she was doing, Mai Linh, all the time you were going to school?'

'I knew she was dealing the white powder, but she was also modeling and actress a little. I thought she was just doing a little side dealing for extra money. Plenty of people were doing the side dealing, even at school.

'She was very careful with me – she even had two cars, one for herself and one for me. Every time we go out she uses her second car and always takes me to fun things like the zoo, the art museums, the movies, sports events.

'She was very strong about the boys, does not want me to get involved with any one man who will pull me away from school by giving me a pregnancy.

'So I do as she says for several years. One day she says to me to pack and get ready to leave, that we are going to go on a long vacation, that we will not have to worry about money any longer. She has a wild look in her eyes all the time now; she is my twin, so I feel lots of times what she feels in her heart, but I can never explain it. I know she is not happy. She tells me she wants to travel and together we will build a new life and have fun.

'I ask her if she is using the white powder a lot. She says yes, but she will stop when our new life starts. We will be able to go out together and live a normal life like she always wanted.

'So that night I pack. I have a final exam the next day; it is my last one for the semester. When I arrive home that evening I park next to her car, the red Fiat convertible, and the roof is cut. I look in the car and all the seats are slashed and the trunk lock has been broken. I run up to the apartment and the door is not locked. I burst in, and the apartment and everything is ruined, all clothes piled in the center, the kitchen spoiled, couch torn and turned upside down. Then I go into the bedroom and . . .'

115

Mitch thought this part was going to be too much for her to go through, but she persisted. 'The mattress is torn off the bed and slashed many times. Then I see a pair of feet and I struggle with all my might to move the mattress. Maybe she is just hurt, I say, maybe I take her to the hospital. But it is too late, she is gone, gone.'

She was like a person in a dream state as she told this part of the story.

'Liu had drilled me about emergency happening and what I should do: she says that always the awful could happen, I should be ready to run. She says that if anything happens to her, because I am the twin, I must protect my safety. By dawn I am starting to remember what she tells me, so I go and pack my bag and then at nine I go to the bank. She has told me how to imitate her signature, and so I clear out the bank account and then the safety deposit box. I am surprised, there is much more than I thought, enough to live for maybe five, six years if I am careful.'

'How did you come to pick Key West?'

'I wanted to go as far away from California as I could and I wanted to stay south in the sun, so I came to the most south place in the USA, away from those terrible people that could do such a thing to my sister.'

'How long ago did she die?'

'About six months now, but I am still frightened.'

'You drove here?'

'No, I flew. I sold both cars that afternoon. The used-car man was not happy with the Fiat, but he took it anyway. That afternoon, for the sake of my sister, I called police from the airport and left for Key West.'

'So when I offered you a cruise around the world it worked well with your situation,' Mitch said bitterly.

'Mitch, I get plenty of offers from the yacht men. I never consider them once till I met you. Don't you say such stupid things to me.' She started to cry now like a dam bursting, a release after her story. He believed her. Anyone that looked as good as she did would get all the offers she needed.

'I'm sorry, Mai Linh, I didn't . . .' She didn't wait for him to finish. She crawled across the couch cushions on her knees and fell into his arms. He held her tight to him for a long time.

'So you think we have enough food for our journey?'

'You mean we still go?' She looked up at him.

'Yes.'

'Well, then, maybe you stop kidding about the food, huh?' She smiled, wiping her eyes and sitting up.

'Maybe.'

'Maybe you go hungry if not for me, what you say, Mr Wise Guy?'

'I say it's time for bed, that's what I say.'

'Mitch, I missed you real terrible.'

They went below and made love, passionate, ferocious, violent, like they were condemned.

8
High Seas – The Gulf of Mexico

The next day started with a long, solitary run on the beach. He had a lot to think about.

Did he believe Mai Linh because she was telling the truth or because he wanted to believe she was telling the truth? The truth – always a constant, shaded mystery to him, changing as new information came to light. He decided to leave it alone for now. Besides, he had some secrets of his own.

They didn't discuss the night before, silently agreeing to bury themselves in the details of their trip. He went to the bank and withdrew some cash, then finished provisioning the boat by topping off the diesel tanks. By five that afternoon they were ready to set out.

It was five thirty when they cruised past the Sand Key light and headed west toward the Yucatan Channel. Mitch wanted to give Cuba a wide berth, so he had decided against the Windward Passage. At ten knots average speed it would take almost four days of steady plodding until they saw landfall. Once they passed the Yucatan peninsula they had Guatemala, Honduras, Nicaragua and Costa Rica to put in their wake before they hit the Canal Zone. Mitch set their course using the automatic pilot and the sat nav.

After a light dinner Mai Linh took over her watch on the bridge. Mitch went below and took out the briefcase that held the Cowboys' file that he had hidden with the ordnance. It was thick. They had been very busy.

He started with Lynx, who had the thickest dossier of all. He would read each report and then destroy it, as he had promised Harry.

Lynx had told Mitch that he hated Harlem, but he couldn't seem to leave it. He operated out of a rundown, rat-infested apartment building near 125th Street. He had gutted the top three floors to create an apartment that rivaled any layout on Park Avenue or Sutton Place. The other nine floors he left alone but kept empty except for the floor on which his security was housed.

Immke had first met Lynx at the villa in Colombia. Lynx had twenty thousand dollars in cash and a plan to control the market in the major cities of the United States.

According to the report, he had achieved his objective. Lynx was the major supplier to blacks in the US – over five hundred million in sales. He only sold wholesale and in keys, at thirty to forty thousand a key. His cost was less than ten grand, delivered to New York.

The street dealer, by the time he hit the stuff with Manitol, vitamin B complex, or inositol, might get up to half a million for each key. Lynx delivered 90 per cent pure, but by the time it reached the street it would be down to 12 per cent. Lynx didn't care. He made a good profit on a fast turnover and he was out of it, with only a small chance of getting busted.

With his income he could buy his way out of most problems. According to Harry's file, Lynx's business had doubled every year for the last three years. With a lower street price his business would soar.

Lynx was also a user, with a habit estimated at two to three grams a day, according to the report. He was paranoid, with violent fits of temper – dangerous, basically without conscience or feelings of remorse.

Mitch didn't need to read the report for that information. Lynx had been one of the biggest pimps in Harlem before he went into the white-powder business. A lot of his girls met violent ends; he was proud of the fact that none of the girls in his string left unless he told them to go.

Mitch set Lynx's file aside and opened the Sweet and Low dossier. She had a smaller business than

Lynx, but on a percentage basis it was growing faster. She operated out of Washington, DC, with a warehouse and packaging operation in Virginia, somewhere near Alexandria. She constantly moved it to a new location – at least once a month. She did it all: brought in the pure, hit it for the street, and packaged it in Sweet'N Low packets. Her delivery boys ranged from Senate pages to assistants in the White House.

Her real name was Randie Taylor. Vassar-educated and homecoming queen, she had married a lawyer who eventually became a Congressman. He turned gay. She divorced him and started to live the Washington high life. She saw a strong market for coke. Her theory was, the more pressure, the greater the need for coke. So she took thirty thousand of her divorce-settlement money and flew to Colombia and Leonard Immke. He wanted a Washington distributor badly, so he took a chance and set her up. He liked her legs and her attitude.

Mitch was there the first day she arrived. He had picked her up in the Miami airport and flown her directly to the villa. She had sat in the co-pilot's seat, so nervous she couldn't stop talking. He could tell then she was hooked on the buzz, the danger, the lure of cocaine and all that easy money. She had a great way with men, promising everything, delivering nothing.

She was well established now. There wasn't a lot that went on in Washington that she wasn't aware of. Rumor was that she also paid Immke in information, and that was how he stayed one step ahead of his enemies. Her psychological profile indicated that she was potentially dangerous, but no acts of violence could be directly connected to her.

The report estimated that she controlled eighty per cent of all the coke that was consumed by the Washington political community. This included people in the Department of Justice, the Pentagon, the CIA, and most other official agencies. She was a sporadic user, with no known steady habit.

At eleven fifteen Mai Linh came into the salon, looking dismayed and upset. Mitch slipped the files back into the briefcase.

'Hey, Mitch, we have big problem with our course.' She was waving the major chart of the Caribbean at him, pointing at the Yucatan. 'I have checked it seven times and each time the same – we are headed for the Yucatan, not Venezuela. Big difference, you know, Mitch,' she said, hands on her hips.

'Yeah, I know. Leave it alone; it's right. We're going to Panama for a few weeks. I have a little job to do there.'

'So how come I have to find out like this? I don't

like it.' She threw the chart in his direction and slammed the door behind her as she left.

Five minutes later he joined her on the bridge, handing her a mug of tea as a peace offering. She made a sweeping gesture and offered him the captain's chair. Slipping into the pilot's chair, she spun round to face him, her head tilted. Finally she spoke.

'Well? You tell me or not? What is going on?'

'Sure. When I went to see Harry, he asked me to do a small job for him in Panama. He's got some land on the coast he picked up when WOS fell, and he's thinking about making it into a resort. He wants me to check it out and give him a report,' he lied.

'Mitch, I thought you were retired from jobs.'

'I am. This is more of a favor, but I get paid too.'

'So why you didn't tell me?'

'I was going to last night, but . . .' He never finished. She looked away. He decided to change the subject.

'Have you ever heard of WOS?'

'Sort of – maybe is a bank robbery or something.'

'A little worse; it's the World Overseas Securities fund, the biggest Wall Street rip-off in history, two hundred and twenty million dollars.'

'Interesting. You get those pictures from this Harry?' She was looking directly at him now.

'Yes.'

She shook her head and looked away. 'He is a busy man, *non?*'

'Yeah, he gets around. You want to hear the story?'

'Maybe someday you tell me about this man Harry?'

'Maybe,' he said, not meaning it. For now he would tell her about Immke.

'It's a long, complicated story, Mai Linh, of broken dreams and broken bank accounts. A story of Leonard Immke, one of the world's great con men.'

'Good. I like long stories,' she said, humoring him.

'Immke hit the street at sixteen and discovered his gift. Selling. He found he could sell anything he wanted. He bounced around his neighborhood selling encyclopedias, raffle tickets, and used cars. He was eighteen when he decided to start selling insurance. He loved big-sounding names, so he named his company the Greater National Chicago Life Insurance Company. He found an old New York Life policy, took it to a printer and had the name changed at the top. Then he hired an answering service to handle any inquiries.

'He went door-to-door, asking for only one-third down, payable in his name, since he was the agent. The rest would be financed; remember, this was before anyone was financing insurance policies. He worked the suburbs of Chicago. In the first three months he made twenty-seven thousand dollars.'

'So he did good, young man like him with a good new idea for insurance,' she interrupted.

'Sure, until you tried to collect and found there were no assets. He was going great until the police bunko squad set him up for a big sale and let him talk himself right into a pair of handcuffs.

'He was released because the legit insurance companies didn't want the bad publicity. But Mayor Daley's best scared him right out of the insurance business for ever. He spent the night in jail and vowed it was the last night he would ever spend like that. So far he's kept his promise to himself.'

'How you know this tiny detail? You know him, or something?'

Mai Linh was very sharp. He would have to be careful how he told her.

'No. Harry had a full report on Immke and his group that I read as background for this assignment. Now be quiet if you want to hear the rest of the story.'

'Okay. I will be silent as a mouse.'

'Good.' She could always get a smile out of him. She sat with her legs tucked up under her and her long hair folded and stuffed into her peaked Cat Diesel hat. She was wearing a gossamer-thin white T-shirt that pressed against her body every time the wind blew over the bridge. Mitch continued.

'The insurance business taught Immke one important lesson. People will believe in a piece of paper, and pay cash for it, if it looks official and institutional, like stock certificates or letters of credit, bank drafts, even bank ledgers showing the balance. You know people want to believe, so the most they will do to verify is make a phone call or drop a small inquiry into the mail. Immke covered that possibility with phony answering services or by using a post-office-box mailing address. He learned to spare no expense on printing or on his offices.

'He went straight, or semi-straight, and by the time he was twenty-eight he had put together a conglomeration of different, unrelated companies that did almost a hundred million in annual sales. He pyramided the companies on paper by giving the owners stock in his parent company in return for stock in theirs and by promising them fresh capital, which he never delivered. Even with creative bookkeeping and constant juggling, he was always on the verge of bankruptcy.'

'How he get that stupid Immpy name?'

'It was Immkowski, but the immigration officer couldn't spell and had no time to waste on a Polish immigrant, so his father wound up with Immke and a fast escort out the door. Immke hates the name because it ends in a vowel, or so I'm told. No class.'

Mai Linh shrugged her shoulders, looked away, and yawned. She wanted him to get on with the story.

'Finally he got bored and sold his company to an even larger conglomerate, only he sold for cash, four million dollars in hard currency. He was thirty at the time. He decided to find out what he had been working for. He spent the next year traveling to all the great watering holes of the world: St Tropez, Marbella, London, Paris, Gstaad, St Moritz – all the hot spots.'

Mitch took a short break and went below deck to do a routine check of the engines. He walked around the two big GM 671 diesels. They were hard at work, spinning the shafts that turned the bronze propellers that were pushing the boat across the surface of the ocean. Everything looked fine. He climbed back up to the bridge. Mai Linh had made some fresh coffee. It smelled strong in the open air.

'So what the WOS got to do with Immpy?' she asked.

'Okay. The story began at a wild party in St Tropez where Immke met Justin La Pierre. A Frenchman, the opposite of Immke, he was cool, urbane, well dressed, from a very good French family – just a brilliant bad seed. At twenty-two he was arrested and sent away to prison for selling stolen stock certificates. He went gay in prison, according to his file. Immke generally hated fags, but he was fascinated by La Pierre.

'La Pierre worked for Manny Rothman, king of the mutual funds. He actually called himself King of Kings, a name that has stuck with him. Rumors were flying all over Europe and the States that Manny was over-extended and looking to bail out of World Overseas Securities fund. He had big personal gambling debts, a bad image from playing with too many bunnies, and the Swiss police were about to kick his door down and spirit away his files for a closer look. Zurich was not a good head-quarters location for a worldwide bankruptcy.'

'Explain mutual fund to me.'

'A mutual fund is a company that buys shares of other companies. When you invested a hundred dollars in WOS you got a small share of many listed companies. The idea was that it was more secure than putting all your money in any one stock.

'Manny Rothman was a genius at marketing and selling concepts. There were five separate funds with over two hundred million in total assets.

'Mutual funds became trendy, the press got behind them, and people started to believe the fund was solid, like a CD or cash in the bank. Meanwhile, because of his excesses, Rothman was strangling to financial death in his best Gucci silk cravat, with the law breathing heavily down his neck, ready to move in any second. But Rothman had heard that Immke was a player and that he had some ready cash. So he sent La Pierre to talk to Immke about selling him fifty-one per cent of the management company.'

'How come he no sell to some big company?'

'They would do an audit, and that's the last thing Rothman wanted; it would turn up all the problems inside the management company. At first Immke laughed when La Pierre came to him with the deal, saying he was only mildly interested.

'Rothman kept getting squeezed, until he finally offered La Pierre ten per cent of the selling price as a commission if La Pierre could close the Immke deal.

'La Pierre was smart and capable; he came up with a full plan that was complex and thorough. He caught up with Immke in an elaborate whorehouse in Morocco, one that specialized in all the baser sex acts, only they served them up in elegant, opulent settings. He grabbed Immke between perfor- mances and outlined his plan. Immke had started to burn out in the world's fleshpots. He knew himself well enough to know that his first love was money. In particular, cash money, green US dollars that you can fold and spend. La Pierre showed him how he could have it all. Immke knew he would never in his lifetime have another chance at controlling two hundred million in cash, in one liquid lump. After two days of talking, Immke's mind was off sex and onto cash. He knew more about himself than most men do. He knew why he loved money. Money was power. Pure, clean, unrestricted power. With enough, you could do any thing; without it, you were defenseless. He told La Pierre to solidify his plan and meet him in London.

'A week later, Immke and Rothman had come to terms. Five million in all, two million on closing and three million in a bank draft cashable in thirty days. The draft was on a Canadian bank in the Bahamas. Rothman called to verify the draft and they closed. La Pierre got his full commission up front from Rothman, five hundred thousand. Before he left for parts unknown, La Pierre planted the seeds of a plan so outrageous it had to work. He outlined to Immke the full plan for the total liquidation of the fund, how to rape the fund – take the money and run.

'The financial world stopped spinning on its axis for a few minutes when it came out in the press that lowlife Leonard Immke had full control of the largest mutual fund ever assembled. Investors, the smart ones, started selling their WOS positions almost immediately; it wasn't long before the money being redeemed by investors exceeded the new money coming into the fund. The funds were dropping a million a week in net assets. This only accelerated Immke into executing his secret plan as fast as he could.

'It was a race to see who could clear out faster, the smart money or Immke. Immke won. It took less than three weeks to put the plan in play.

'In the meantime, Rothman went to cash his second check. It bounced, a forgery. No one at the Canadian bank had any record of the account. It seems the phone number Rothman had originally called was not the bank but a disconnect, from a one-room office on Bay Street in Nassau. When Rothman called New York on the bad check, there was only the shattered, empty shell of the WOS mutual funds. Rothman knew there was no jurisdiction that would apply to prosecution and extradition against a Swiss company and a Bahamian bank. Besides, that was a small crime now in the Immke lexicon of criminal activities.

'It was to become the most famous criminal Thursday and Friday on Wall Street. Immke started out first thing Thursday morning, selling WOS assets all over the world. They sold casinos in the Bahamas, a huge shopping plaza in Dallas, enormous blocks of DuPont, IBM, General Foods, Barclay's Bank, General Motors, Shell Oil, Eastern Airlines. The stocks all hit the street at market prices. In one day the Dow Jones dropped eighty points. From the real estate trust, valuable properties and land in Las Vegas, California, Florida, Colorado, New York, and Spain were sold at bargain-basement prices to anyone with cash. By late Friday all the WOS funds were completely liquid, cashed out.

'The cash then exited on the books as fast as it had entered. Sixty million went for a thousand-acre swamp in Nicaragua. Forty million went for three over-the-counter stocks with no assets and that no one had ever heard of. Twelve million went for a hundred-acre farm in Arkansas; thirty million, for a small strip shopping plaza in a depressed part of Ohio. Friday, when the bell rang at four on Wall Street, all the accounts of WOS were empty of cash; it had all been spent on these empty deals.

'Immke was the veiled owner of all the companies that had received the money. He had assembled two hundred and twenty million in the process.'

'How they carry all that cash?'

'They wired most of it out to numbered Swiss, Bahamian, and Cayman accounts as fast as it came in. Immke carried the rest in suitcases out to La Guardia and the waiting WOS 707 they had acquired after the Rothman deal. I heard it was fifty big suitcases full of cash thrown into the belly of the plane.

'Their first stop was Nassau for the weekend. Three Nassau banks opened up specially for them on Saturday to accept the cash.'

'Why the police not stop them?'

'They tried, but they were too late. The SEC had a cease-trading order out first thing Monday. The New York police and federal marshals armed with warrants burst into the trading room inside the

New York offices and found them empty – no employees, no files, no clues. It was the blatant simplicity that the bankers and WASPs of Wall Street couldn't believe, even when they saw it happening. At first they thought it was some brilliant new strategy that the fund was employing. It wasn't until late Friday afternoon that a few of them twigged to what was going on; by then it was too late. Besides, half of Wall Street was on its way to the Sound or the Hamptons for a nice summer weekend. Immke knew their habits and weaknesses.'

'So he was pretty smart, huh?'

'And it's getting late.'

Mitch thought it was time for Mai Linh to get some sleep, and he told her so. She pouted but finally went below. He could hear a lot of rattling around and mumbling in the galley.

He had set up four watches a day, with eight hours on, four off, four on, and eight off. He had volunteered himself for the twelve-to-eight night watch; it was almost three now.

He loved this watch; the conversation had stimulated him, but now he was enjoying the solitude. The engines were purring and there was no other sound, just his own breathing. Yellow, hazy moonlight silently bathed the boat, then disappeared quietly behind the clouds. He heard shuffling footsteps at the foot of the ladder in the cockpit below. A small voice came wafting up.

'So you should finish this story, Mitch. It's not fair you get me interested, then you send me to bed. It's like coitus interruptus. You know what I'm talking about?'

As she talked she climbed up the ladder so her foot was finally on the top rung. She stood there on the bridge, smiling with that corner of her lip turned down. He didn't know any man who could have said no to her.

He gave up and patted the chair next to him, motioning for her to sit down. She smiled and jumped into the seat. He continued.

'By noon on Monday every newspaper in the world had headlines like "WOS Raped – Over Two Hundred Million in Cash Missing", with pictures of Immke on the front page.

'He stayed on the run another four months, never in one place for more than five days. He believed he might be betrayed in any of the countries he visited: Libya, Algeria, Saudi Arabia, Brazil, Costa Rica, the Bahamas. The engines of the big, black 707 were never cool. Then he found Colombia.

'Immke knew that Juan Perez, the president of Colombia, was looking for expansion capital for his personal coffee-exporting company. Immke had tried to sell Perez mutual funds, so he knew Perez well. It was arranged for Immke to provide Perez with a five-million-dollar unsecured loan in return for an unlimited visitor's visa. Perez also included a verbal promise of Colombian citizenship and a full passport within two years if Immke invested a further ten million in land and other Colombian businesses, mostly Perez's businesses.'

'Expensive passport,' Mai Linh said dryly.

'Not really; it represented less than one year's interest on the money. Immke built an estate in record time. Two thousand acres of patrolled private property. He was allowed special duty-free permission to import American labor and products for "Immke's Palace of Impulses", as it was referred to by the American help.

'He was still mostly in cash except for the Colombian investment. The world markets were unpredictable, the Arabs were getting stronger, inflation was just starting to run away, gold was on the rise, the dollar was soft. And Immke never liked his money to sit around for too long.

'Besides, he had a plan: he would become the World Bank of Cocaine by financing the grower, the wholesaler, and the retailer. Immke saw a great future in cocaine and he knew they needed funds for equipment to process the coca paste, advances to the street people, boats, planes, and a myriad of other things. The idea was to organize where there was chaos and stay a long way away from the action – and jail.

'Just like any good banker, Immke was to provide the money and take a cut from everyone. The standard fee for use of the money was one hundred per cent for every thirty days the money was needed. The margins in the business are so high that the fee was acceptable to most operators and smugglers. If the deal went bad for legitimate reasons – a real bust, for instance, or a storm at sea – well, then there was room to negotiate, even get more money. But if Immke found out it was a scam, then the principals were executed, quickly. That's how it got the name, the "Bank of Death".'

'So, Mitch, I still do not understand this Harry. Is he a drug person, too?'

'No, he has nothing to do with drugs. He and some other investors bought the land in Panama from the WOS receiver, and now it may have value as a resort,' he lied.

'So where is Immke now?'

'He is fighting to stay in Colombia. Perez is gone and they have a new president who is trying to throw him out of the country, and there is tremendous pressure from the United States to get him. They are still trying to nab him and bring him back to the States to stand trial.'

'That I find hard to believe, Mitch. They never make the rich pay for their crimes – only the poor, you know?'

'Yes, I know. But Immke has hurt a lot of people.'

'You mean he hurt important people.'

'Yes.' Mitch paused. 'Well, that's enough about Immke. Why don't you do what you were told and hit your bunk?'

'What do you mean, hit my bunk?' She jumped over into his lap and gave him a big hug. 'Why don't we put on the automatic captain and hit my bunk together?'

'Not at night. We're in the shipping lanes, and if you don't get some sleep now you'll fall asleep on your watch. Got it?'

'*Oui*, I got it. So when we make love? Your watch, my watch, your watch, real boring; maybe I make love with the automatic captain, huh?'

She flashed him by raising her T-shirt up to her chin and smiled, then scooted down the ladder. He heard the marine telephone start to ring as she entered the main cabin. A few minutes passed and it kept on ringing.

'Mai Linh, answer that, will you? Mai Linh!' She was standing in front of the phone, Mitch could just feel it, waiting for it to stop. Finally she answered it.

He heard her mumbling as she walked through the cabin, 'Stupid phone. Who calls at three in the morning? Stupid phone.' She yelled up the ladder, 'Hey, Mitch, it's for you. Your friend Harry says it's important.'

'I'll be right there.'

When he entered the cabin he saw that Mai Linh was at the refrigerator door, fiddling with a chicken wing. He knew she wanted to listen when he saw that the speaker switch was on – not too subtle – but he left it on. Harry spoke first.

'So. Having a nice cruise, Mitchell? Hope you don't mind the late call, but I figured someone would be up. I know you're not going to anchor out there.'

'Not and get to Panama in the next few days. Any changes in that situation?'

'None. But I just got a call from my friend, the LAPD connection – they're three hours behind us, you know.' Mai Linh was standing stock-still now. The door of the refrigerator was swinging like some ominous pendulum, back and forth, rocking with the gentle sway of the boat. Harry continued.

'I hear you still got Miss Vietnam with you. Someday you'll listen to me, Mitchell.' Mai Linh was staring at Mitch.

'Harry, what's on your mind? We're on the speaker phone. Why don't I call you tomorrow?'

'So turn it off.'

'It's okay. Mai Linh and I have talked about the WOS deal in Panama.'

'That's nice. But I got some bad news, buddy. I found out some new info. I told you there was no fingerprint ID. Well, now I found out why. There were no fucking hands on the body, that's why.'

139

Mai Linh bolted from the galley, down three steps, right into the head. Mitch could hear her gagging and choking all at the same time.

'Harry, I hope you don't stay a prick all your life. This could have waited.'

'Don't worry about my life, Mitch. You should thank me and start worrying about your own. I'll keep you posted.' He clicked off the line.

Mai Linh was still in the head. She had the dry heaves. Mitch tried banging on the door and got nowhere. He felt it was better to leave her alone, so he went back up to the bridge. About thirty minutes later he heard doors open and close as she left the bathroom to enter the master stateroom. The porthole was open and he could hear her muffled sobs. She must have been crying into her pillow. Finally there was silence from below. About an hour later the sun started to rise. It emerged in the east as a brilliant red-orange fireball, as if it had been asleep in the deep all night and was finally coming back to do its job of providing light and heat. It was going to be hot, that nice, complete, tropic kind of warmness that permeates the whole body, makes a person feel safe and secure all day long.

Mitch took in the full sunrise and decided to extend his watch so Mai Linh could sleep, but she surprised him by showing up on the bridge at exactly eight o'clock. He stood up away from the captain's chair. She gave him a level gaze. Her eyes looked red from crying as she slipped into his chair and took over the helm; no words were spoken.

He poured himself some coffee in the galley and headed for bed; he needed sleep. He was bone-tired, and long ago he had learned to keep his mouth shut whenever he was in that condition. There was hardly anything that couldn't wait. He would think about last night when he awoke.

But sleep wouldn't come. What the hell was that call from Harry all about? Well, he would get to the bottom of it sooner or later. After an hour of tossing and turning he snapped the light on. He got up and sat in the chair at the small desk. He opened Billy Siegal's file.

Siegal's business was growing at the fastest rate of any of the Cowboys. He specialized in the entertainment business, which also included sports. There was hardly a movie made anymore that didn't include a hidden cocaine budget. They all came to Billy. He had the best product, a fair price, and unlimited quantities.

He lived in Bel Air behind a stone wall twelve feet high, with dogs and twenty-four-hour security guards. It didn't look a lot different from the other Bel Air mansions. His massive den had six big-screen TVs for the sporting events: football, baseball, basketball, hockey. He picked them up on his satellite dish every weekend and sat in front of the screens cheering and yelling at all his clients.

He bet the games based on the buys. He believed in coke, so he bet heavily on the players who were his biggest clients. He felt that coke numbed the pain and gave them more energy. Besides, whatever he lost gambling on the games he would pick up on their next purchase.

Siegal stood only five foot five. He was originally from the Bronx and had been a gopher for a rock-and-roll band for years. He started with them, buying coke for them in quarter ounces, hitting it hard, and selling to other groups in a small way until he found out about Immke and Colombia. Mitch flew him in the first time from LA in the 707. Siegal was too nervous and jumpy for Mitch. He made Siegal sit alone in the cabin for the whole trip.

Immke wanted a distribution network in Hollywood, so he took Siegal's ten thousand dollars in cash and extended him a quarter-million in credit. Immke also put two men on him twenty-four hours a day until he paid it back. It took him only six weeks; then he was back for more.

Siegal used to drive Immke crazy with his stories of starlets and wild Hollywood parties where people would do just about anything for coke, especially if they were out of work. El Hombre would brush it off with, 'A coke whore is just a coke whore, no matter where she is.' But Immke didn't agree. He promised Siegal a free key if he would bring just one star down for him. Siegal never delivered.

Siegal was a heavy user – between two and three grams a day – very dangerous and unstable. Any violence was usually carried out through emissaries, with Siegal staying as far from the scene as possible.

The next file was on Chico Gonzales. He lived in Coral Gables and spent most of his time fighting the major Colombian families for control of the Hispanic market. The report indicated he was losing and that eventually the Colombians would overpower him. They were starting to bring it in directly from Colombia, in competition with Immke. Wars were raging on the streets of Miami. 'War wagons', bulletproof vans with armed Colombians, roamed the palm-treed drives looking for Cubans and trouble. So far Chico had been able to give them what they were looking for.

Chico had come over from Havana in '58 with the giant exodus of Cubans who were fleeing the new Castro regime. He started out selling grass in Little Havana until he was able to finance a shrimp boat full of the stuff from Colombia.

The shrimp boat was caught in the Florida Straits and towed into the Miami River. Chico stood and watched his cargo being loaded into sheriff's vans to be incinerated along with all the profit he had made in the ten years he had been dealing. He scraped up fifteen thousand dollars from friends and relatives and went to see Immke. His plan was to sell coke only, to the Hispanic market in Florida, Texas, and California – a potential market of over twenty million people.

Immke liked the idea and bankrolled him for ten keys of pure cocaine. Chico never looked back. And he never dealt grass again: too bulky, less money per sale, less profit margin, and less repeat business. So why bother?

He fell in love with Sweet and Low the day he laid eyes on her. It was 1977, the first full convention of Cowboys at the villa. She was everything he wanted in a woman – blonde, beautiful, well educated, and sexy. The problem was she was as macho as he was. She had no interest in him, but she played him along anyway, thinking maybe he would be of some use to her later, and he was good for her ego.

Chico was a hard worker, only slipping away in his Magnum ocean racer for the occasional decadent snowy weekend in Nassau or Bimini.

A steady user, he was considered very dangerous, with over ten deaths directly attributed to him. His habit was at least two grams a day and growing.

Mitch closed the file and snapped off the desk lamp. Immke was bright, some thought brilliant. He had put together a tight, solid marketing plan aimed at target groups, with skilled people who knew their customers' wants. He isolated big, growing markets that would continue to prosper through the eighties. He controlled the money and the source, with no risk to him.

Mitch took the files to the blind side of the cockpit so Mai Linh couldn't see and slowly ripped each one into eight pieces, scattering them to the wind, wishing his assignment would be that easy. Then he went into the galley; he was hungry.

Mai Linh was studying the chart when he got to the bridge; she didn't look up. He had a roast beef sandwich in one hand and a can of Budweiser in the other. She reached for a sip of the cold beer. The satellite navigator was on, with a display reading of their exact position. Mitch could see by the chart that Mai Linh had also calculated their position by dead reckoning, using their speed, the wind, and the currents. She was close in her calculations. She learned fast.

For the next three days, Mai Linh slipped into a deep depression, picking at her food, hardly eating anything. A blackness seemed to settle into those beautiful green eyes. She looked away whenever she caught him looking at her, as if she had a secret that was eating away at her soul.

Several times he tried to talk to her or put his arm round her, and each time either he was met with a grunt or she would leave him to be alone with her sorrow. She performed all her sea duties, showing up exactly on time for her watch, checking all the electronics and navigational gear, cooking, and cleaning. It was as though she needed the menial tasks to forget about the things that were preying on her mind. They didn't make love once during the whole trip. It was easy for both of them to avoid sex because of the alternating watches: they were never in bed at the same time. It was the afternoon of the fourth day that it was finally mentioned; she brought it up. There was no preamble.

'I think maybe you will want me to get off and leave the cruise in Panama. You do not make love with me, I do not make love with you.'

'I need to be able to trust the one I'm with.'

'We all have our secrets, *non*?' She looked at Mitch in that quizzical way, as if to ask: 'How about you? Are you telling everything?'

'The body had no hands, Mai Linh,' he said gently.

Her shoulders began to move in rotation as if she was going to start sobbing. He went to reach for her, but she pushed his hand back.

'No. I finish what I start with you. I could not tell you because it is the worst thing that ever has happened to me, and when it comes as a picture in my mind it is as if I will go crazy if I think one more moment about it, like a spring in my mind that will pop and my mind will be no good anymore, like I will have to throw my mind away and I will die thinking about that thing. You can understand, Mitch?'

He had to look away from her and get hold of

himself. He knew she was telling the truth about her feelings. He had the same kind of images buried in his own brain. Things that he had seen himself in the Asian war, things that the shrink had revealed to him. Long ago he had told himself that he would judge no one again, and here he was doing it to someone he cared about. Maybe they were just happy being together and that was enough. He hoped so. He looked back at her. Her head was down and there were small tears running down both cheeks. He squeezed her hand and held her.

'Forget it, kid. Tell me when you can.' He lifted her chin and kissed away her tears; then he went below and had a stiff belt of Anejo. He looked out of the cabin window and saw a vague outline of landfall.

It was Panama and the Canal Zone. The wind had picked up and a heavy groundswell was beginning to form.

9
Reunion – Panama

The Canal Zone is only fifteen miles wide and fifty long. Down the length of it is a thin thread of water that joins the Atlantic to the Pacific, with Colombia to the south and Costa Rica on the northern border. It is a lush tropical swamp that the US Army Corps of Engineers tamed after Dr Walter Reed isolated the yellow fever mosquito. Teddy Roosevelt created Panama and fulfilled his dream, against all odds, of building a canal that would cut months off the journey between the great oceans, bypassing Cape Horn and all of South America. He prevailed by sheer willpower and temerity in the use of power. He carried a big stick.

There were over two hundred slips in the marina. It was American-run, with all the conveniences, including a 220-volt electrical hookup and a clean source of fresh water for every boat that was moored. Mitch took the center slip in an end finger pier. He had radioed ahead for the mooring and for directions from the dockmaster for Customs and Immigration clearance.

He eased the boat into the slip, using only the engines to back it in. Mai Linh handled the lines like an old salt now. She moved fast, with no talk, easily securing the bow line and the spring line, almost in one motion. But she was still depressed.

He decided to check them into a hotel, get her off the boat for a while. A new setting might get them back to where they had been. He chose a small place about three miles from the marina that had been recommended by the dockmaster as charming, clean, and inexpensive. He sent Mai Linh to the room while he placed a call to the local Intertel office from the lobby. It was almost six, but there was still some staff hard at work. He was put right through to Jose Santiago, Harry's head man in Panama. Jose gave Mitch directions and they set an appointment to meet at ten o'clock the next morning in a cafe near the Intertel office. Then Mitch joined Mai Linh in the room.

It was clean and inexpensive, all right, but not charming by any stretch of the imagination. The linen was threadbare and the furnishing ugly and utilitarian. It looked as if the hotel management was expecting some wild rock-and-roll band and didn't want to leave anything of value in the room.

When Mai Linh and Mitch started to make love, one of the legs on the bed broke, spilling them both out on the floor. Mitch laughed, but it upset her badly. She curled up in a chair and wouldn't get back into the bed. He had them back on the boat in twenty minutes. They made love again, but it wasn't the same; there was nothing Mitch could put his finger on, but it felt a little strained, as if a part of her was missing.

Afterward she fell into a fitful sleep. Mitch was restless, so he showered and then went up to the bridge with a brandy. An hour later Mai Linh appeared, bleary-eyed and wrapped in his big terrycloth robe.

'So you can't sleep, Mitch. What's the matter with you?'

'I'm concerned about us. Are you unhappy about anything?'

'No, Mitch, I . . .' She drifted off without finishing the sentence.

'Do you want to go home, Mai Linh?'

She looked at him and said quietly, 'I have no home.' She turned away; the wind caught her hair just slightly, hiding her face. 'Do you want me to go?'

'No,' he said. 'If you go, who's going to cook me

dinner for six?' That finally got a smile out of her.

She took his hand. Together they went back to the bedroom. This time there was nothing missing.

Mitch took an early jog down the finger pier and out onto the road that led into town. He ran for close to four miles, trying to put together his plan for the next few days. He wanted to get Harry his information safe and fast and be on his way. He returned to the boat, showered, and dressed. Mai Linh was still asleep when he revved up the Kawasaki to leave for the Intertel meeting he had set up.

The ride to the cafe took him down a long dirt road that began just outside of the Canal Zone, weaving in and out of donkeys, chickens, roosters, and roadside vendors selling fruit, vegetables, and any other items that were even slightly edible. He could smell the open-slit trenches that were used for sewage and shuddered for the children who were playing along the side of the road.

Once he got onto the tarmac things got better. There was a little more prosperity. A few trucks were pulled over to the side of the road with their hoods up, steam rising in hisses from the hot engines. Sometimes only the worn soles of the driver's shoes could be seen hanging over the radiators. The men swore and waved their arms in exasperation, fighting valiantly with engines that had already been recycled through at least one full life. But somehow Central America made Mitch feel good – lots of action. By ten fifteen, he had finally figured out Jose's directions and spotted the cafe.

It was an open-air restaurant, crowded with office workers, taxi drivers, a few tourists, and boat people. All the tables were full, and there was a lot of jostling and good-natured yelling as the local people recognized each other with hearty waves and slaps on the back. Jose had a table in the rear near the espresso machine under the red and white Coke sign.

Mitch recognized Jose at once from the description Harry had given him. Jose weighed about twice as much as he should. The man overflowed his chair; his sides seemed to slip over the slim wooden arms like lava. He tried to rise when Mitch approached but gave up. Mitch was sure he would have risen chair and all. He had an attractive grin, a perfect set of white teeth framed by a huge mustache, and a full head of wavy black hair that he tried hard to slick down, with no success.

'*Buenos días, Señor* Mitchell.'

He waved Mitch into the seat next to him with a sweep of his mammoth arm. Jose was dressed in a white suit of light cotton that only seemed to emphasize his bulk. A Panama hat lay on the table. He pushed it off to the side when the coffee came. At the same time he undid the top button of his shirt and yanked the knot of his tie down a few inches, as if to say the formalities were now over and they could carry on. The tie was black, matching the band on his Panama hat. It looked brand-new and pressed, like the rest of his clothes. He crossed his legs with great effort, showing size fourteen brown sandals. They didn't seem to go with his suit. Mitch inadvertently glanced at them. Jose noticed and changed legs in a wide swinging arc, as if by changing feet it might make a difference. Mitch liked him immediately.

'*Señor* Mitchell, we can talk here if we keep our voices a little low. The bartender and the manager are slightly on our payroll.' He finished this statement with a big wink; it almost made Mitch laugh. Jose had seen too many movies. It's hard to be inconspicuous when you're over three hundred pounds and dressed completely in white.

'I'm assuming you have been briefed on my mission here.'

'*Si*. They are here now, in the big yacht. They have a special wharf only up the road from you, in the Canal Zone. It is designed to give them the utmost privacy.'

Mitch wondered why Harry had ever selected Jose for an assignment like this. Jose must have been reading his mind.

'I am an expert with *Mama Coca, señor.* All the details. You know?' Mitch nodded and smiled. Jose continued.

'The problem I have predicted all along is when the year will come for a huge crop, a giant harvest. I think this is the year. All my sources say so.'

'How big?'

'We don't know exactly – over billions of dollars on the street. And we think the US street price will drop to under forty dollars a gram.'

'Almost as cheap as grass.'

'*Si.* We know it is still in Colombia, yet to be shipped. But we don't know exactly where it will be stored in the Canal Zone.'

'How come it's so big?'

'It is a crop, *señor*, like wheat or corn. This year all the conditions on the steppes were perfect: not too much sun, never above sixty-eight degrees, plenty of humidity. And there are more big growers in Peru and Bolivia operating under El Hombre. There is more acreage than ever before, all high up on the eastern slopes of the Andes, the best side, facing toward the jungle and the Amazon.'

'Has it been sealed yet?'

'We think no, because all the Cowboys just got here and they have stayed here.'

'Immke – have you seen him?'

'No. He is like your second cousin twice removed. You only see him at weddings, wakes, or when he wants money.' Mitch smiled. 'I tell you, *Señor* Mitchell, he is a man whose presence can always be felt. He comes here twice a year, and we always know the minute he arrives. The Canal Zone is a small place, and word of him travels like the bad weather that gets to you before you can close the windows.'

'Is Lynx here, and Chico Gonzales – and Sweet and Low?'

'Yes.'

'Billy Siegal?'

'He is most certainly here, *señor*, and El Hombre with his huge bodyguard, the one that never leaves his side. Sometimes I wonder, do they sleep together?' Jose showed a big mouthful of teeth he was obviously proud of. He thought he had made a good joke. Mitch knew the truth – the Bear did sleep in the corner of El Hombre's room, curled up on his sleeping blanket. If a tiny lizard, on padded feet, crossed the room, the Bear woke up. He was the reason El Hombre was still alive. Jose changed the subject.

'Harry called me this morning about the

woman you are with, Mai Linh by name.' Jose almost whispered her name.

'Yes, Jose.' It was already starting to rankle Mitch. 'Go on.'

'He asked me to assign her a bodyguard while you are here in Panama, for her protection.'

Mitch studied Jose for a minute and decided that that was probably what Harry, devious as ever, had said to him. Harry really wanted a shadow on her to watch her movements, not to protect her. What was there to protect her from? She should never be in any danger, but Mitch couldn't really say no.

'Behind you, *señor*.' Mitch turned. Sitting near the door at the first table in the bar area were two well-built men. They were casually dressed, idly chatting to each other.

'There is another team as well, but these two are the main team; each will take a twelve-hour shift.' He finished his glass of water in one fast swallow.

For some reason Mitch trusted Jose. He didn't know why, but he had stayed alive a long time by following his instincts.

'So how about we order a rum punch?' Jose smiled.

'Sounds good to me.'

Jose ordered two *grande* rum punches, served up in large, chilled glasses with beads of sweat running down the sides. It took two hands to lift one.

Jose carried on: 'I know that time is very important in this mission, so I will tell you what we know, which is very little. We own the madam in the number-one whorehouse, just outside the Canal Zone. It is frequented by the Cowboys, and the girls are very pretty. They come from the Dominican Republic, Argentina, Peru; they are some of the best in this part of the world.

'This woman will have some information. Maybe tonight you could go there. Harry wants all source information to be given to you. He trusts no one else except me, and I am too well known in certain quarters.' He winked again. 'She expects you at eleven. She is a blonde woman, with big beautiful breasts.' Jose made a gesture of grabbing his own chest, as if he was holding two coconuts. Mitch laughed.

'You laugh, *señor*, but you will see I am right.' He had a good smile. He continued: 'We need reliable information on the size of the shipment, where it will be stored in Panama, what vessels and planes it will leave on. Harry wants to do the bust on the ocean for the boats and track the planes on our satellites. If they do it in the Canal Zone he is afraid it will open the Pandora's box. You know? It can be very bad politics if the United States points out to the world how deep in the white powder some of these Panamanians are.' Jose stood up abruptly, shrugged, then polished off his rum punch and paid the bill. He motioned Mitch with a fast wave of his arm to follow him to the Intertel office. Mitch nodded at Jose's men as he walked by their table. They both looked him right in the eye and slowly nodded back.

Jose was a terrible driver, but Mitch thought he didn't seem any worse than the rest of the Panamanians. From the time he entered his tiny Ford Escort until they reached the Intertel office he was leaning out of the window yelling, punching the horn with both hands, scattering clusters of children and chickens, leaving a trail of dust. Mitch could see fists shaking in the air when he looked in the mirror. When they got to the office, Jose told Mitch to wait outside for twenty minutes, then come in.

It was a dingy, crumbling office building near the edge of the slums. Harry had all his offices assume the lowest profile possible. When the twenty minutes were up, Mitch reached for the handle on the front door. It was loose and almost came off in his hand. Inside, he had to sidestep quickly to avoid tripping over an old woman on her hands and knees monotonously rubbing a rag back and forth, trying to get the ingrained dirt out of the gray tile that had once been black and white. She looked up at Mitch and smiled. Immke flashed through Mitch's brain. One night in Colombia Immke had told Mitch his mother had put in thirty years with the night clean-up crew in the Mercantile Mart building in Chicago. Mitch took time to smile back at the old woman.

The Intertel office door was on the second floor. It had no sign, but it was shiny stainless steel, brand-new. It stood out like a flag against the peeling plaster walls. There was just the number eight painted on the polished metal. It was Harry's lucky number. Inside, everything was new and clean. There were two small offices and a big computer room, with floor-to-ceiling microfilm files. There were five terminals; the screens of two were lit up and full of data. The operators turned them off the minute Mitch walked in.

He saw the small Plastique-explosive boxes on the righthand sides of the terminals and the sulfuric acid nozzles suspended above the files. It could all be detonated from Peacehaven if Harry fed the Panama code numbers into the main computer. Mitch had to wonder at Harry. The least it must have done was to keep his people sharp, knowing they could be terminated at any time along with their machines.

Jose was in the smaller office. The rum punch must have gotten to him, along with midday tropic heat. He seemed to be dozing, feet up on the desk, completely filling the large tipped-back desk chair.

One of the computer operators stopped in the doorway and coughed loudly to wake him up. Jose's feet fell and he lunged forward, eyes popping open as a surprised smile crossed his face.

'A mini *siesta*, very good for relieving the tension.' Mitch sat on a steel-frame chair facing Jose, who continued: 'We should keep in very close contact, *señor*—'

'Jose, I hope what I have to say next doesn't hurt your feelings,' Mitch interrupted. 'I work alone. If I need help I'll always let you know; otherwise I want to be left alone. I don't like groups, and I don't like meetings.'

'*Si. Comprendo.* What else do you need from us?'

'Survey maps of the entire Canal Zone that will show all the major warehouses. The Coast Guard and geodetic survey charts for the canal and ten miles of coastline in all directions.'

Jose was very co-operative. He scurried off to get what Mitch needed. Twenty minutes later he drove Mitch back to the bike. Jose put his huge arm round Mitch and smiled, saying, 'You watch those ladies tonight, huh? Many have entered and not come out for days, and when they did they were shadows of the men they once were.'

'I'll watch it, Jose.' Mitch packed his briefcase on the back of the bike and returned to the marina.

The marina was full, a bustling place with yachts and smaller commercial boats on their way to all the ports of the world, Atlantic and Pacific. When Mitch got to the boat, Mai Linh was in a much better mood. She had started a major lunch for them of lobster bisque, Caesar salad, and a big loaf of garlic bread that she had purchased fresh at the marina supermarket.

She told him she had sunned on the bow for a few hours and done lots of thinking. Her fishing tackle was spread out on the galley table, the reels apart for lubrication. She moved gracefully between the tackle maintenance and making lunch, talking all the time. She handed him a large Anejo on the rocks with lots of ice, the way he liked it, a big slice of lime floating on the surface.

'A drink for you, Mitch, with my apology for acting like a foolish girl.'

'You okay now?'

'Yes. Very okay. I was just having a moody time; it happens to women.'

'Men too.' He gave her a little kiss.

'Your meeting was good?'

'Yes.' At the last minute he'd had Jose slip in an extra set of coastline charts that Mitch had marked up in red to show Harry's land. Mitch gave her a second kiss and went down to the forward V berths. He opened one of the fiberglass panels and eased the briefcase in with the ordnance.

He returned to the galley with a handful of the coastline charts. She was putting her tackle away when he surfaced.

'I have to go out again at eleven tonight for a meeting. I won't be long.'

'I can come?' He shook his head, no. 'I would like to see a little of this place,' she said, persisting.

'Not tonight, Mai Linh. But after lunch I have to get some gear for the boat. Want to come then?'

Mitch started to eat the lobster bisque; she turned just enough to look at him out of the corner of her eye.

'Why can't I come tonight?' He took a big bite of bread to avoid answering. 'It isn't another woman?' She started on the Caesar salad. 'Better not be. It was only once when we did not make love, and it was that terrible tacky motel you find. Next time I pick the hotel.' She was smiling now. 'Sure I want to come.'

She darted downstairs to slip on a dress. She was back in minutes, wearing a white cotton dress that contrasted with her dark skin and green eyes. It created a beautiful, simple elegance.

Mai Linh knew what worked for her.

'So I look okay for the marine store?' She twirled round the cabin, the white gauze dress floating up like a silk web as she spun.

'Yes. We'd better go now, before I carry you down stairs.' He took the dishes to the galley sink.

'You carry me anywhere you want, Mitch.' She gave him a fast kiss, then slipped out the salon door to the aft deck. In one liquid movement she was on the dock.

'Come on, Mr Slowpoke.' She was halfway down the pier swinging her straw purse over her arm when she looked back for him.

The marine store was wall-to-wall people. It took Mitch almost an hour to get what he wanted. Finally, the clerk filled two plastic bags with their gear and handed them to Mitch. He headed for the door while Mai Linh waited for the change.

A man yanked the door open and looked over Mitch's shoulder into the packed store. It was Billy Siegal. Even with the Panamanian sun he still had a pasty blue-white face. He turned paler after he looked inside the store. He muttered something and let the door go slamming into Mitch, knocking him off balance.

Siegal scurried down the dock as fast as he could. His little feet took short choppy steps, as if he was running for the bathroom to try and relieve himself before his bladder gave out. He was scared.

He made it on the run to the pumps at the end of the pier, where two of the crew of his boat were gassing up the tender, a Cigarette ocean racer. He reached down and pulled the pump handle out of the starboard gas cap, squirting high-octane fuel all over the dock.

The dockmaster was pointing at the spilled gas and waving the bill. Siegal yelled something back at him over the screams of 'Explosion! Explosion!'

He started the boat, threw the lines on the dock, and sped off into the dusk.

Mai Linh was putting away the change as she came out. The Cigarette was nothing but a noisy wake with a rooster-tail plume of white water ten feet in the air.

'What is all the trouble, Mitch?'

'Nothing important; just some jerk arguing at the fuel dock.'

Mitch walked the rest of the way in silence. He felt sure Siegal had not recognized him, but why had he run? What had frightened him?

Siegal had always been jittery, Mitch thought. Too much coke. Maybe tonight was no different.

10
Assault – Bordello, Panama

After dinner Mitch checked around the marina,
keeping his eyes open for the Cigarette or any sign
of the Cowboys. The area looked clean to him, so at
eleven he set out for his meeting. As he walked by he
nodded at the two men Harry had assigned to guard
Mai Linh. They were sitting near the end of the dock
playing cards.

The night was murky black, and it didn't make it
any easier to find his destination. It was twelve
when he finally spotted the house hidden away on a
quiet side street. Goats were grazing on the sparse
lawn. It was an old white clapboard structure, with
a sweeping veranda and an antique wooden swing
that could comfortably hold two people. At the
moment it was full. It squeaked as the occupants,
two girls in thin cotton dresses, glided back and
forth. They sat in the swing sipping drinks and
smoking. Mitch pushed open the heavy oak door
without knocking. A huge black stood inside. He

looked Mitch over and then walked with him into the foyer, where a fat Cuban woman with black patent-leather hair flashed a couple of gold teeth at Mitch.

'On one of the boats, *señor*? Such a nice tan. You came to the right place for fun. We have everything you could want in a woman.'

A gauze curtain blew slowly in the breeze from the open window. Behind a translucent wall were at least fifty women in the sheerest lingerie, sitting on couches, lounging on bar stools, talking to customers in big easy chairs. Mitch could see a parquet floor for dancing, with two girls gliding languidly in each other's arms. The smaller one had her head resting on her partner's shoulder. They looked as if they were in love.

'My name is Mitchell.'

'Of course, *señor*. We have instructions.'

The black had moved silently until he was positioned directly behind Mitch. Mitch had seen his move. He turned quickly as the black was about to put his hand on Mitch's shoulder. Mitch started slightly as the fat woman said, 'I'm sorry, *señor*, but we must observe security.'

The black frisked Mitch quickly like he knew what he was doing. He left his hand just a little too long on Mitch's ass. When Mitch looked at him he gave Mitch a little smile, winked, and said, 'Please to come with me, *señor*.' He led Mitch through the main parlor. The girls stirred; they weren't shy about displaying what they were selling. The black waved them away as if he was shooing flies. They went up a long staircase. There were at least twenty doors on the second floor. The black knocked gently on one of them and pushed it open. Mitch walked in. The black whispered a sweet nothing in Mitch's ear as he closed the door.

She was sitting in the shadows in a full-size white peacock chair behind a seven-foot wicker desk. It wasn't until Mitch got to the edge of the desk that he could see her face clearly. She hadn't changed.

'Hi, baby.' She had a way of smiling with her eyes that Mitch liked. It was Roxie.

Mitch stepped back out of the light so she couldn't see his face. He extended his hand to her, relieved to see it was steady. The thought of Roxie almost following her redheaded friend out the door of Immke's plane that night in Colombia flashed through his mind.

'I know you?' She withdrew her hand.

'No. I have a good memory, especially for someone as pretty as you.'

'Nice. Drink?'

'No, thanks.'

She motioned to him to sit on the couch facing her.

'Something about your eyes . . . You look familiar.'

'We've never met,' Mitch said firmly, maybe too

firmly. 'You have something for me?'

'Yes. But these goddamn walls have ears, so let's move over to the bed and pretend we're getting at it. Maybe you don't want to pretend.'

She smiled at him, getting up from the couch and starting to unzip her dress. He zipped it back up.

'We don't want you catching cold or me forgetting why I'm here.' He smiled.

She started to bounce up and down on the edge of the bed, the springs squeaking out a symphony of discordant music. Mitch sat next to her.

'Oh yes, give it to me, oh, oh, don't stop now, keep it right there, please. Oh my God, it's good, baby.' She stopped to light a cigarette and continued, 'Yes, baby, more, just like you're doing.'

She leaned over toward him and whispered, 'These Cowboys are a gang of vicious pricks. It goes back a long way between me and them. I hate them.' She pulled hard on her cigarette. 'There's a couple of them here right now.'

She handed him her lighted cigarette for a puff. He shook his head. She rode the bed to keep the springs squeaking and moaned a couple of times.

'That fucking Colombian, El Hombre, is one of the weirdest I've ever come across. He does it all night, comes maybe ten times, wears out half my staff, while all the time that thing he calls the Bear stands in the corner. He never even lets him take a turn.'

Mitch thought to himself it must have been a long journey from the glitter of Las Vegas to this strange bordello on the edge of nowhere. He wondered what Harry had on her, how much he was paying her. She brought Mitch back to reality by pointing at the bed and indicating that he should bounce.

'And that slimeball of a Billy Siegal – Christ, I knew him when I worked in LA.' She continued, 'He promised all the good-looking girls coke and stardom. He delivered a little coke, that's all. He comes here and wants to see girls do it to each other, then he gets in the middle, makes a sandwich, and snorts himself into oblivion while he jerks off. He gets real high and tells plenty, like he's got power, knows important secrets.'

It was a bizarre scene, the two of them bobbing on the edge of the bed. He could see their reflections in the mirrors.

'But they're not secrets now,' she said. 'Here's what I picked up. The goods are definitely still in Colombia, in at least four big locations near El Hombre's hacienda, ready for the pre-inspection. All the Cowboys will be flying there the day after tomorrow on Immke's 707, the black one. You know the plane?'

'I've heard about it.' For a minute he thought she was fishing, trying to catch him in a slip.

'They're planning to spend no more than two days down there at the coca labs; then they come back here. But we still don't know how many kilos will be in the shipment, – metric tons, is more like it.' She smiled. 'They'll seal their buys down there, then it will be El Hombre's job to ship the stuff into Panama.'

'Where?'

'Don't know exactly, just that it will be in the Canal Zone, probably in a restricted area.'

The ornate brass phone on her desk rang loudly, startling both of them. She got up and answered it. She said nothing, just slipped it back on its cradle and stood there for a second.

'Something terrible has happened on your boat. The girl.'

'Is she all right?'

'No.'

He ran through the house; the black at the door took one look at him and stepped aside to hold the door open. Then Mitch jumped on the bike, scattering the goats across the lawn and leaving a deep rut right down the center of the front yard. The ride back was a blur for him. The high-pitched whine of the bike rang in his ears all the way to the marina.

He was halfway down the pier when he saw Jose, a white apparition, running toward him. He was waving his arms and motioning with his hands to quiet the bike, to shut it down, so Mitch wouldn't arouse the attention of the other boats. They met at the stern. Mitch jumped over the transom onto the aft deck, almost landing on a canvas-covered form. He ripped the top part of the canvas sheet back, looking for Mai Linh. It was one of the bodyguards. His head hung loose, almost resting on his shoulder. Someone had snapped his neck like a matchstick. Jose was struggling to lift his leg over the gunnel. He finally made it, hitting the deck heavily.

'My God, *señor*, I still do not know what happened. I came only a few minutes ago to find out how your meeting went with Roxie, and I found . . . this.'

'Where is she?'

'Inside on the couch.'

Jose moved aside so Mitch could squeeze through the doorway. The boat was a mess. It had been completely tumbled. Charts, glasses, and dishes were strewn on the floor, and the liquor cabinet was open; the smell of booze from broken bottles was everywhere. There was a second body propped in a sitting position in the corner, covered by a sheet, with only a pair of leather Topsiders sticking out. There was blood all over the cabin. Mai Linh was lying on the couch in the main salon, shaking. She was covered up to her neck with a blanket. Mitch could see patches of red-brown bloodstains. Those pale green eyes – pleading like a little child's, confused, bewildered, filled with tears but not crying. She was trying to form words, trying to talk to him. Her mouth was moving, but no sound was coming out. Finally, she raised her hand and reached out for him. It broke the trance he was in. He could see where someone had belted her very hard on the jaw and pulled a hank of hair out of the side of her head. Jose knelt down with Mitch by the couch. She finally spoke.

'Mitch, oh my God, Mitch, I feel bad. They were awful.'

Mitch gently raised the blanket. She had only her bikini bottom on. There were small black marks on her breasts and thighs. He had seen them before on other people. They were cigarette burns. Jose had to look away. Mitch put the blanket back to cover her.

'Mai Linh, can you move? We're going to take you to the hospital.'

'No. Please, Mitch, no. I want to stay with you, please, please . . .'

She was in deep shock. Mitch did a simple check for internal injuries and broken bones. She seemed okay. He got up to talk to Jose in the far corner of the galley. Jose was on the verge of tears.

'What the fuck went on here, Jose?'

'I don't know. I got here only minutes before I called you. This is a real mess; thank God it's the US Canal Zone, where we have some influence.'

'Can you get a wet team?'

'They're on the way.'

174

'And him?' Mitch pointed to the corner.

Jose walked over to where the body was propped against the wall. He looked to see that Mai Linh was facing the other way before he pulled the sheet down. It was the other bodyguard. His throat was slit from ear to ear.

'I think your cover must be blown, *señor*. You should leave now, leave the marina, leave Panama.'

'I agree, Jose. I'm finished here, but I still don't understand how they could have made me so fast.'

Mitch returned to the couch and bent down to lift Mai Linh.

'No, Mitch, I am afraid. Please, I told you I do not want to go to the hospital. I will look after myself. Please, can we go from here to a hidden place somewhere away from these men?'

He checked her over again, then sent Jose down the pier to wait for the wet team. Mitch went up to the bow where he kept the ordnance and took out the medicine kit. He found a syringe and a vial of morphine and took them back to the couch with him. As he knelt to administer the needle he could see the figures of the wet team running down the pier. Mai Linh was drifting; as he injected the morphine in her arm she winced slightly.

'Mai Linh, I'm sorry. This is all my fault. If it wasn't for me, none of this would have happened to you.' He could almost see the morphine creep through her, taking effect slowly, caressing her body, relieving her pain.

'No, Mitch.' She was floating now. 'It was me they were after. It was Billy Siegal and his friends . . . he's the man who killed my sister.'

He watched her drift off, out of it. He had many questions that would have to wait. She would sleep for at least twelve hours.

11
The Decision – The Cove, Panama

Mitch covered her with another blanket and walked Jose to the stern, telling him that he himself would get in touch with Harry from wherever they ended up. Mitch watched Jose's huge white form waddle slowly down the dock, shoulders sagging.

Mitch grabbed the charts of the coastline that were lying crumpled in a corner, then cast off the lines and quietly slipped the mooring, easing down the narrow channel and putting on the power only when he reached open water.

He followed the beaches that make up the coast of Panama. It took an hour to locate the isolated cove marked on the chart. He had decided to lay over there until he could form a plan. It was high tide, so he managed to slip in over the sandbar. Even with the high water he could feel a thud as the boat touched bottom. They would be trapped there on low tide, but it was the best spot he could find.

When that was done he cleaned the blood from the boat as best as he could. In the short time before they had left the dock in Panama, Jose's wet team had arrived carrying two neatly folded body bags that looked like sail covers. The men were dressed in slick vinyl jumpsuits – easy to hose the blood from them. They stuffed the bags with the bodies and then slung them over their shoulders. They would have carefully eliminated all telltale traces of the struggle from the boat, but Mitch didn't have the time to wait for them to perform their gory janitorial duties.

He finally found a hole in the mangroves with the spotlight. It was a small stream running into the cove, covered by a clump of big royal palms that would hide them from the air. Mitch followed the stream a few hundred yards and then secured the main anchors off the stern and tied the bow line to the base of one of the palms so the boat lay parallel to the mangroves, invisible from the open sea. He got out his machete and spent the next hour on the beach cutting palm fronds for extra cover.

It was four thirty when he finally finished and turned on the alarm system, took a shower, and fell asleep on the floor next to Mai Linh, with his Ruger .44 Magnum under his pillow.

He woke up suddenly. The sun was streaming through the windows and the alarm system was

178

screaming in a high-pitched whine. He grabbed the Ruger and bolted up the ladder to the fly bridge. It gave him a panorama of the whole cove. A big, fat pelican sat on the bow rail. The bird had set off the electric eye. He was staring up at Mitch as if to ask what gave them the right to be in his cove. Mitch flipped the alarm off and checked his watch; it was ten thirty. He could hear Mai Linh moaning in her sleep, so he went below.

She looked worse in the sunlight. Mitch made her a drink of orange juice and placed it next to her in case she should waken. He decided to go for a swim, down the stream to the cove, to get his head clear.

The cove was shallow, about eight feet deep on the average, with a sandy white bottom. He swam out to the sandbar and stood in knee-deep water. It was low tide, so the bar showed in many places, with the white water boiling over the sand. Idly he walked its length until he found the deepest spot. It might be possible to clear the Hatteras over the bar at that point, but it would be close, even on high tide. He marked the spot with three co-ordinates to form a triangle; then he swam back to the boat from the far end of the sandbar. When he got to the boat he sat on the diving platform in the stern, his feet dangling in the water, thinking. He had just got to Mai Linh and Billy Siegal, first on his list, when he heard the unmistakable waruump, waruump of a low-flying helicopter. He scrambled up to the bridge and peered through the mangroves. An army Huey with a Panamanian crew was flying the beach-line, just out on the ocean side. They were looking for someone. Probably him, he thought. Evidently he wasn't the only one with friends in high places. They flew by without pausing. The cover must have worked. He went below to the cabin.

She was struggling to drink the orange juice, her face contorted. She turned round slowly, finally facing him. He had to stop himself from wincing – they had done a real job.

'I know I look bad, Mitch. You don't have to pretend. But I will fix myself. I will need aloe leaves for these burns.'

She started to lift her blanket to show him. He stopped her.

'How do you know Billy Siegal?' He had to ask.

'I know him before in LA. Once he came to our home.'

'I thought your sister never conducted business at home.'

'Only this once. Just before my sister was killed he came to our apartment. I hide in my room, but I could see him.'

'What did he want here on this boat? What was he after?'

'I don't know. He asked how come I am still

alive, did I pay someone to stay alive. But it was all happening so fast, I was sure he was going to kill me.'

'Why did he ransack the boat?'

'I don't know,' she said weakly.

'What was he looking for?'

'I don't know.'

'Why did he burn you?'

'I don't know. I don't know!'

The buzzer started to sound on the marine phone. Perfect timing, Mitch thought. It had to be Harry wanting to know what was going on. Harry could wait. Mitch got up and flipped the buzzer off. The red light continued to wink for a few minutes. Finally it stopped.

'Just calm down and tell me what the fuck went on here.'

'I was up on the bridge waiting for you, and he was suddenly there, the big one. He just seemed to come out of nowhere.'

'The Bear . . .'

'Those awful black teeth and sick yellow eyes... He grabbed me and carried me down to the cabin. I tried to resist, but he was very strong.

'Billy Siegal and the other one were waiting below. They held me on the couch. The big one was holding me, and the other one with the blue eyes that never blink, he held me too. Siegal was asking the questions. They had just started with the cigarettes when the door flew open and two men with guns came in. The guns did them no good. Before I knew it they were both dead.

'But first they had to let me go. I try to kill Siegal, we are fighting all over the cabin, rolling on the floor. I put a big scratch on his face. I would tear his eyes out if I could. The big man comes back and separates us like we are two small children. He then ties my hands with tape. They talk for a second and then decide to take me with them on their boat. As they get ready to carry me off they hear your friend, the big, fat one with the white suit.'

'Jose.'

'Yes. He is calling your name, but he is very nervous because he cannot find the two men he has posted outside. He has his gun out as he walks down the dock. They decide it is too hot now, so they go over the side into their own boat and speed into the night as fast as they can.'

'Did Siegal ask about me?'

'It's hard to remember.'

'It's important.'

'I remember that he asked who you were, why you were in Panama.'

'What did you say?'

'The truth. That we just met, that you had business here.' She gave him a quizzical look. 'But that's not the truth, is it, Mitch? You did not come here to check on real estate.'

They stared at each other for several minutes. It was a little before eleven. Mitch could tell that the morphine had almost completely worn off. He got up and went to the bow for another ampule. When he came back she was sitting with her feet on the floor, her hands folded in her lap. She held out a stiff arm to stop him.

'No, please, I will go through this without any more morphine.'

'Why suffer?' He bent to give her the shot.

'I do not want any needles, you understand?' She was almost shouting. He put the morphine back.

When he returned she asked in a tired voice, 'So will you tell me, Mitch, the whole story?'

He looked up at her and saw the red flasher blinking on the console. He had been ignoring it. He knew it would be Harry. It had been flashing all day. He flipped it on, picked up the phone. Harry started right in.

'What is it with you? Your brains get rearranged with your face? Why didn't you dump that broad?'

'You don't know the whole story.'

'I know that whatever happened on your boat moved those Cowboys. They left today for

Colombia, two days early. I want what I asked for, Mitchell. Information. I want you to go down there.'

'Look, Harry, I never agreed to go to Colombia.'

'As far as I'm concerned we made a deal. You don't stick with it, I don't stick with my end. I need to know the size of the harvest and the date of shipment.'

'That's all?' Mitch said sarcastically.

'No. I need to know where in the Canal Zone they are going to stash it. I'll have the Intertel plane ready tonight. You can pilot it yourself. Be at the airport at midnight.' Harry clicked off before Mitch could respond.

While he had been talking, Mai Linh had hobbled over to the chart table. She sat idly examining the charts of the Canal Zone. She had heard only Mitch's end of the conversation. He saw her put a big black X where the marina was located, a second X where they were now. He sat down directly across from her. He had decided to tell her more of the story.

'Harry wants me to get some information on the cocaine trade; the real estate was just a cover story. But that's all shot now anyway – maybe my cover is blown. I'm going to get out of here and follow my original plan, go on a long cruise. Our luck is bad here, I can feel it.'

'My luck has been bad for a long time. I'm tired

of running. Cocaine is an awful drug. My sister was hooked. It started slowly but finally she was a slave to the freebase. People don't believe you can get addicted, but you can. Lots of times when I came home she would be locked in the apartment, sometimes for a week or two at a time. When I came home from school there would be no lights on, only my sister sitting alone in the living room doing the freebase.'

'This was when she worked with Siegal?'

'Yes. Selling for him. I saw her often crying and mumbling bad things to herself. I tell her to stop; she says she can't and runs into her room slamming the door. The drug was like a devil that lived inside her, that controlled her. It was horrible to see.'

'We're going to leave in the morning.'

Her eyes narrowed. 'You only tell me tiny part of the real story. You have been trained in these things, haven't you? You wouldn't be here if they did not think you were the best for the job. I saw you, the way you looked the day we shoot the weapons in the Dry Tortugas. But that's okay, Mitch. You leave. They think they can kill my sister. They scare me, scare you, scare anyone until they are boss over everything. I hate these men. When I am well I will kill them. I should go to Colombia.'

She was shaking with rage and grief. Mitch

lifted her gently out of the chair and held her for a while before he helped her back to the couch.

'My sister was not a bad person. She had a hard life, but she was just trying to survive. She slipped so deep into the trap they set until they finally killed her. Someone must stop these men.' She looked up at him defiantly.

Mitch didn't answer her. He stayed with her until she finally dropped off to sleep, then sat in the salon for most of the afternoon, finally climbing the ladder to the bridge.

Revenge was always a mistake; it only made things worse. Mai Linh could never avenge her sister. Not with this group.

Mitch's friend the pelican came and took his evening perch on the bow rail. The bird studied Mitch for a while; then he got bored and tucked his head under his wing. Mitch had a lot to think about.

Harry wanted him to complete the mission. Mitch owed him, and in a way Harry was right. Mitch had fucked things up because of Mai Linh. But she was part of him now, inside him. He could feel her pain.

He didn't want to lose her.

Who was he kidding anyway? Harry was pulling the strings and loving it. Mitch had to get his life back into his own hands, but Harry held the final big card – Immke. All Harry had to do was let Immke find out about him, and he would be dead. Harry would be richer. And only a short time would pass before he found someone to replace Mitch. He had no real choice. He had to go to Colombia.

The pelican pulled his head out from under his wing, flicking it from side to side. He checked Mitch over and took off for parts unknown.

Mitch envied him.

12
Into the Jungle – Colombia

The takeoff went smoothly. In less than ten minutes the Gates Lear jet had lifted Mitch clear of the Canal Zone and out over the Gulf of Panama. He would follow the gulf into the Pacific and then into western Colombia.

The boat was secure. He had powered it even deeper into the mangroves and placed more cover topside so it couldn't be spotted from the air. He promised Mai Linh he would be gone no more than three days.

It felt good to be flying again, with no co-pilot and no passengers. He wondered why it was at times like these he always thought of his father in his den, the smell of books and tobacco permeating the room, his father pacing back and forth talking philosophy, morality, ethics like a professor, until the lecture ended with the same message about Mitch's shortfalls, his impulsiveness. Mitch took a deep breath to break away from these thoughts and went over his weapons checklist.

He started with the worn attaché case belted securely in the seat next to him. Inside were the parts to his standard-issue M-1 carbine with the anodized stainless-steel barrel, which had been carefully re-rifled and modified in Austria by a gunsmith who worked for Mitch's former employer, the CIA. It was single-action, but at two hundred yards Mitch could empty a fifteen-cartridge clip into a silver dollar in less than three seconds. The scope had an infrared attachment that let him see in the dark. An assassin's rifle; he had used it many times in Asia.

There were no whitecaps on the ocean tonight. It looked like a huge, gray mirror. He was flying low, following a thin gold sliver of the full moon reflected in the water. Old habits were hard to break.

He was unsure about predestination or fore-knowledge, but he knew there were times when one thing was set in motion, completely removed from another thing, and it was inevitable that the two would collide or become intertwined. Sometimes these forces met more than once in the course of a lifetime. That's how he felt about Immke and the Cowboys. They had unfinished business to take care of. He just didn't like the odds. Maybe he could even them up a little.

He dug into his backpack. It held one handgun, the long-barreled Ruger .44 Magnum, a throwing knife, a survival knife, and four grenades: two incendiary, two shrapnel. He had tossed in five pounds of Plastique explosive with delayed fuses. He counted eight cans of C rations. He always ate very little on these kinds of missions. It kept the senses high.

He took the Lear up to ten thousand feet as soon as he hit the Colombian coast, clicked on the automatic pilot, and changed into his battle jacket and pants, mountain-terrain green. Then he slipped into a black jumpsuit that he would wear until he got up into the terraces. He took the top off the can of carbon black that he used to blacken his face and hands. It was half used. He checked his rain poncho and his money belt, giving it a squeeze to check the bills, then slipped in a few amphetamine pills in case he had to stay awake for a few days. He had packed the noiseless forty-five and .44 shells Harry had given him, so he didn't need silencers.

Mitch thought Bogotá was a beautiful city, sitting nestled in a deep valley, surrounded by lush green mountains that hid the crude labs which produce eighty per cent of the world's supply of cocaine. He knew the surrounding thick rainforest gave birth to some of the most beautiful trees and flowers in the world, and to some immense fortunes.

The wheels touched down with a small screech, then a slight bounce when the nose wheel grabbed.

Mitch taxied directly into the private sector. Bogotá was no stranger to private planes. A Customs and Immigration man did a cursory inspection and cleared him. The Intertel office manager for Colombia was waiting on the tarmac. He hustled Mitch and his gear over to the parking lot and a vintage jeep.

It was road-weary, with a cracked windshield, dented fenders, holes in the floorboards, and part of the grill was missing, but Mitch was sure it was mechanically perfect. It would draw no attention in the mountain area where he was headed. He threw his gear in the back and disappeared into the night, headed for Tingo Maria.

He didn't really have a specific plan. Jose had left him a sealed file in the Intertel plane; Mitch had requested additional maps and aerial photos as well as all the latest information on any major labs. He had been to El Hombre's heavily guarded hacienda only once, years ago. The first thing Mitch would do was check it out to see if the Cowboys were there.

In under thirty minutes he was out of the city and into the mountains. The forest was a verdant green, almost too green to be real. As he penetrated deeper, the foliage got thicker and more complex. The plants seemed to grow into each other, cutting off the life-giving sunlight.

Mitch passed a giant red hibiscus tree that reminded him of Mai Linh, the way she would slip the flowers into her hair. He wondered how she was doing today.

Last night must have been a tough one for her. He had found her crying because of the pain when he came down from the bridge. She tried to stifle the sobbing when he entered the salon. He stayed for only a few minutes, then left her alone and started to pack his gear. After a while he returned to the salon.

'So you go?'

'Yes. Tonight.'

'Mitch, I wish with all my heart I could come. I would help you.'

'You just get yourself better.'

He held her in his arms for a while. It was impossible even to kiss.

'I could help you, you know?' she mumbled into his shoulder.

'You could help by getting well.' He kissed her forehead, inhaling her perfume.

He had to smile to himself. It was hard to imagine her here with him, running a jeep full speed down a rough mountain trail, about to head up into the Andes.

He would skirt Tingo Maria and head directly for the hacienda. The maps had pinpointed only one big

193

lab about six hours from the hacienda. There were at least seven other labs, spread out like the spokes of a wheel, but their locations were not confirmed.

It was dawn when he reached Tingo Maria. He had been there years before when it was being built. It had sprung up suddenly, a village of tin roofs and tar-paper shacks. El Hombre controlled a big section of downtown. Most of the bars and whorehouses were his. The town's main commerce was the buying and selling of cocaine. It was a Wild West frontier town out of a movie. Most of the men carried guns and they had no problem using them. A lot of them were coked out on a permanent basis.

It took two more hours to reach the perimeter of El Hombre's hacienda. Mitch left the jeep in the bush and climbed high enough to look down into the compound. It was like a fortress – guard dogs roamed inside, and electric-eye systems criss-crossed the property. The main house looked impregnable for one man. Mitch climbed up a palm tree and hugged it to try and get a better view. The aerial photos taken by the DEA plane were very current. The entire hacienda was made out of solid stone, with small windows on the second floor only, too small for a man or child to fit through. One huge wooden door was in front, two in the back. Mitch had assaulted houses in his day, but this one was designed by an expert. He scanned the courtyard. All the jeeps and ATVs were gone. The Cowboys had to be at one of the labs, but which one? He gave up on the hacienda and slipped down the tree. He headed for the lab that was marked on the map.

The trail leading to the factory gave him a good chance to get used to the terrain. It was semi-tropical jungle and rainforest, not as rough as Vietnam, but it was going to be real tricky in its own way. The beauty of these rolling foothills could lull him, especially when he had a cut, well-beaten trail to follow.

It was almost five that afternoon when the trail narrowed, then instantly evaporated. He drove the jeep off the road and took some time to memorize the maps and photos, then disabled the jeep, hiding the distributor rotor. He wanted a vehicle there when he returned.

He followed a small donkey trail for an hour, fighting the heat and mosquitoes, until he came up on the lab marked on the map. It was a complete setup, with still, bunkhouse, and warehouse, but there was no sign of the Cowboys.

He dropped off into the brush to think it out, soaking wet with sweat. He pulled a T-shirt out of his backpack and hung his battle jacket on a bush to dry. The sun had almost set. He had no choice; he had to wait until dawn now before making a move. His chances were about one in eight that this was the right lab. Not very good odds.

So he decided to bring the Cowboys to him.

The mosquitoes woke him at dawn. He ate a can of C rations. He would eat only twice a day now.

The air smelled clean and pure; all the birds and small animals were beginning their discordant symphony. Mitch had learned long ago that violence must be fast and sudden. The planning can take time, but the action must be swift and unwavering, and once set in motion, it must be carried through.

He would circle the lab and come out of the jungle in the rear. This would place him directly behind the main bunkhouse. He stayed quiet where he was on the edge of the clearing for almost an hour, waiting and watching the Indians.

The Indians were generally very short, like jockeys, slight and wiry. It was the coca leaf they chewed all their lives that kept them feeling young and strong. Then one day, before they were thirty, they would gaze into a mirror to see an old, wrinkled face, the parchment face of someone a hundred years old.

He was fascinated watching them. Even at this hour they were heavy into the leaf, moving like steady, mindless drones.

The camp was quiet, almost sleepy. Mitch circled it until he found the small river that fed into the clearing. He followed the river down to the edge of the camp near the bunkhouse, keeping a careful eye out for sentries.

The still was next door to the bunkhouse. It was the largest building, with five four-hundred-gallon cauldrons, giant metal vats, each with its own propane tank underneath to heat the aviation fuel. The tanks were lit; the relentless blue propane flames were licking the base of the vats.

The still was square and made of wood, with its floor raised about two feet off the ground. It was open on all sides and surrounded by a dozen lean-tos for the Indian workers.

Some men were loading donkeys with empty five-gallon fuel cans, while other men strapped the cans directly onto their backs. They were all high on pure coke or leaf. They would never notice if their loads were full or empty. They wandered off down the trail like worker ants with backpacks.

Mitch had decided to blow the still with Plastique and a silent quartz timing device. It would make one hell of a bang and a lot of black smoke. Someone would come to investigate and lead him back to the Cowboys and the main stash.

The high-octane, kerosene-based aviation fuel would help. They used it to boil the paste, which was later purified with acetone into cocaine. The fuel was taken to a slow boil but kept just below the flash point. Most of the Indians chewed the leaf or snorted. If one of them got too high or didn't keep his eye on the temperature gauge, his life ended in a big orange flash that looked like napalm. Explosions occurred on a regular basis; a job hazard, but nothing worked as well or was as readily available as aviation fuel. No one thought much about the danger until a still blew. Then it took some fancy talking and a lot more coke to get the Indians back to work.

The security around the still was minimal. The opposite was true of the warehouse, another wooden building somewhat smaller than the still, located twenty feet away.

Mitch made his way over toward the warehouse to check the inventory, staying well inside the cover of the rainforest, until he could get a clear view.

The coke was neatly stacked in transparent heat-sealed plastic bags with little red embossed seals in the corners. Every Cowboy had his own seal. Like royalty, they stamped their signet rings into hot liquid plastic for the seal and attached it to the bags. Later, the bags were sent to the central warehouse and finally reinspected in Panama. They were one-kilo packs, worth at least twenty-five thousand dollars each at wholesale prices. Like the still, the warehouse was an open building, but it had a heavily armed guard at each corner. It was packed solid, the little seals shining crimson against the pure white cocaine. This was a big warehouse but not the major stash. Mitch estimated it held about twenty million dollars' worth wholesale.

It was noon when he finally slipped into the

campsite, covering the ten feet of hard-packed earth on the run and then rolling into the crawl space below the still. It was very tight and hot. He had to move slowly, pulling himself along on his elbows, looking for the best place to plant the charge.

A few rats scattered out, startled by him. He held his breath, hoping they wouldn't arouse the guards.

He spotted a loose beam almost in the center of the building and laid the Plastique on top in two mounds, one smaller than the other, setting the fuse for five minutes. It would be tight, but he should have enough time to get out.

As he was setting the charge, he could feel the heat from the propane flames through the floor above him. The constant gurgling and bubbling of the boiling aviation fuel was the only sound. He was soaking wet, almost blinded by his own sweat.

There were cracks between the planks on the floor where he could look up and see the calloused soles of the Indians' bare feet as they padded around the still. He hoped they wouldn't look down. He was easy pickings, trapped. A quick spray under the building with an Uzi and he was dead.

There was some movement where he had entered, so he decided to take a different route out, slipping along on his elbow and exiting about fifteen feet to the right of where he had gone in.

He emerged face to face with two Indians. They

were squatting five feet away from him, surrounded by a haze of smoke, puffing away on big bazookas, cigarettes made with unrefined coca paste, the kerosene still in it.

They were fucked up to the limit, eyes glazed, but the grins on their faces turned into masks of hate when they saw Mitch. They moved like lightning, both coming at him at the same time, their machetes poised over their heads. No sound, like wildcats before they strike.

Mitch was trapped under the still, squirming and sliding to get out. He had left the Magnum with the backpack. He had only his throwing knife in his belt. He was barely on his knees when he hurled it full strength. It caught the first little Indian in the throat, raising him right off his feet. The Indian dangled in the air like a puppet, mouth open in a silent scream, flashing the same rotten brown teeth as the Bear. He fell in a lump.

The impact of the knife distracted the second Indian just enough for Mitch to dive forward and roll. The machete whistled by Mitch's ear. He was on his feet now. The Indian charged straight for Mitch, but his timing was bad. Mitch stepped to the side and did a one-foot takeout, sweeping the Indian's feet out from under him. The Indian hit the ground so hard Mitch could hear him deflate. He grabbed the Indian's hair and broke his neck with the side of his hand.

There had been no noise. The whole thing had taken less than a minute. Mitch quickly pushed both bodies under the still and ran headlong back into the forest, with only seconds to spare before the Plastique went off.

Bent over double, out of breath, panting, almost hyperventilating, he steadied himself against the base of a thick banyan tree, watching the camp through the gaps in the twisted roots that formed the trunk. He had set a short fuse, with two ounces of the Plastique, to go up first. It would give the men in the camp a sporting chance to find cover before the big blast.

The first explosion sounded like a tire blowout. It set the camp on the run. No one had to tell these men they were working inside a dynamite stick. Mitch checked his watch and counted thirty seconds. The full blast came right on schedule, shaking the jungle floor.

But it wasn't one blast, it was two, about ten seconds apart.

The still went first, sending up a huge orange flash. In seconds, the entire building was consumed in flames and black smoke.

The fuel dump with the ether and acetone went next. The four guards from the warehouse dove off their stations into the jungle as the fuel compound exploded in a thundering roar.

The temperature kept rising after the explosion,

to the point where the wooden lean-tos just burst into flames. It was the ether and acetone. The bags of cocaine seemed to melt together into a thick lava paste, a molten, seething liquid that flowed through the wooden floor. At least half the cocaine was a total loss.

Patches of jungle foliage on the border of the campsite instantly turned charred black. The heat was so intense Mitch was forced deeper into the rainforest. Scared wild animals were screaming in the trees, birds flew off in confused, cluttered circles, little jungle creatures collided, brushing his ankles as they headed for cooler regions.

He climbed a palm tree and positioned himself in the top foliage, out of range of the flames and heat. Thick smoke spiraled skyward, like heavy black refinery smoke, choking and darkening the clear afternoon sky. He settled in to wait.

No one made even the slightest attempt to try and put out the fire. The acetone added a blue hue and acrid smell to the flames. The column of smoke rose even higher, like a murky cobra hanging in the air at least a thousand feet over the camp.

It shouldn't take them long to arrive.

Mitch found himself remembering all those missions in Asia, all the innocent people killed. A war that had trained him to be able to slide under a building and plant explosives when he should have been in his father's office on Wall Street. He forced those thoughts out of his mind and got back to watching the burning lab.

In less than an hour the Bear arrived with four armed men. He was furious, pushing and shoving the men who worked at the still. He cuffed two of the guards, and they tumbled off into the jungle like small dogs. Then he gave them each a good kick as they scrambled out. He suspected sabotage.

He spent less than ten minutes watching the fire. It was a total loss. He slung his shotgun over his shoulder and headed back down the trail in a half run.

Mitch amused himself by sighting the Bear in the crosshairs of the scope on the M-1. It would have been an easy shot, no more than two hundred yards. With silent cartridges, he would have fallen stunned, bewildered, looking aimlessly for his killer. A silent, swift ending for him. It took all Mitch had not to squeeze off half the clip. That's what it would have taken to bring him down.

Instead Mitch slid down the tree, grabbed his backpack, and ran a path almost parallel to the Bear's until he reached the main trail. Their vehicle was a little further up the trail than Mitch's, so he had to wait for them to turn round and head back down. When they had cleared the trail, Mitch headed for where his jeep was stashed.

They hadn't stolen it, but someone had stripped off everything of value, including the spark plugs and carburetor. Mitch sat down and leaned against the wheel hub to catch his breath. They had even taken the tires.

If too much time went by he would lose the Bear, so he got up, strapped on his backpack, and started down the trail in a slow run, carrying the M-1 at port arms.

He had run at least five minutes before he heard a spitting, coughing noise. It had to be a small motorbike.

He found a curve in the road and waited on the blind side, pulling his watch cap down into a mask. He knelt in the center of the road with one knee in the dirt and the M-1 tucked into the notch of his shoulder.

An Indian rounded the corner at full speed, with two five-gallon cans of aviation fuel strapped to his bike. He saw Mitch and hit the brakes so hard that he flew right over the handlebars. Mitch had to roll off to the side to keep from getting hit.

The Indian fell with a grating, scraping sound as the bike flew off into the jungle, wheels spinning. Mitch gave him a small chop behind the ear to make sure he would sleep for a while longer and then pushed his body into the bush.

The bike was okay. Mitch cut away the fuel cans and started it up. Now he had to pick up the Bear's trail. He figured the Bear was about two to three miles ahead of him. The dust on the trail hadn't settled, so each time Mitch came to a fork in the road he followed the dusty side.

Fifteen minutes passed before Mitch heard the noise of their engine, clouds of dust billowing up behind them. The Bear was driving, with the four men sitting in the back of the pickup. They were hanging on with both hands. It was a rough road. Mitch had to concentrate on missing the deep potholes and staying out of sight.

The Bear suddenly swung a wild left off the road into the jungle, bursting through a light cover of brush onto a well-camouflaged, hidden trail. Mitch drove right past the entrance. He felt there would be sentries behind this manmade jungle wall.

He went almost a mile further down, found a clearing, and drove off the road to study his maps and photos. The satellite photos showed an abandoned airstrip and some strange building configurations less than two miles from where Mitch was.

It was almost four now, with no more than two hours of daylight left. Mitch checked the gas tank on the bike; there was a quarter of a tank of fuel left. He hid the bike and started up the main trail, entering the bush about ten yards from where he had seen the Bear crash through.

He was right. Two armed guards sat on old rickety wooden folding chairs playing cards on one of the fifty-gallon drums they had placed back in the middle of the dirt trail. The drum had fresh metal scars. The Bear must have driven right through the barrels at full speed.

Mitch eased past the guards, found the airstrip, and followed it up toward the base camp that had been carved out of the thick tropical forest. Strewn along both sides was the wreckage of small aircraft, one- and two-engine planes that had missed the runway. These were the planes that brought in the coca paste from Peru and Bolivia. Colombia grew very little coca leaf. The Colombians specialized in processing the paste into cocaine, shipping it, and collecting the money.

Mitch reached the end of the runway and found the Bear's pickup and five other new vehicles parked in front of the largest wooden building. It looked like the main warehouse. He skirted it, staying out of sight.

This was a full-blown operation, with warehouse, still, and several bunkhouses. There was accommodation for at least three hundred men. But there were only about thirty there, all heavily armed Indians. They were a lot more alert than their friends up the road. Especially after the Bear delivered his report.

There they were, the main borrowers from the Bank of Death, large as life, standing on the veranda of the warehouse, talking among themselves. Mitch had to take a deep breath and drop into the bush for a second. The sight of them still chilled his blood and stirred his anger.

Billy Siegal was pointing to the column of black smoke that was drifting like a haze over the jungle; then he pointed toward the Blazers and Jeeps as though he wanted out of there. But the Colombian pulled him roughly by the arm into the warehouse. Seeing Siegal made Mitch think of Mai Linh's sister and the photos Harry had given him. Siegal had killed her or had had her killed. Mitch thought about blowing them all up while they were inside the warehouse and being done with it.

Lynx followed Siegal in, his bodyguard carrying the lynx coat neatly folded over his arm. Sweet and Low was the only woman present. The heat didn't seem to bother her a bit. She sauntered into the warehouse with Chico Gonzales in tow.

A few of them stopped in the light of the entrance before going in, to scrub their signet rings, scraping the sealing plastic out of the signet crevices so the rings would make a clear impression.

There was no easy way to get a look inside the warehouse from where Mitch was. It was a solid wooden building with only a front and a rear door, no windows.

He worked his way slowly past the warehouse to the still. There were two vats working, the blue propane flames flashing against their bases, causing the aviation fuel to swirl in slow circles as it boiled. They were just processing the scraps of paste that were left over from the main harvest. It would be at least twelve more weeks until the new harvest would start to appear.

Mitch noticed a second still at the far edge of the camp, a little smaller than this one. It was positioned out of danger in case this one went up in a flash of fire. The warehouse was in the best position of all, at the apex of the triangle, far enough away from both stills to be safe. He made his way back to the main warehouse and eased himself into a clump of banana plants and waited.

The Cowboys were in the warehouse for at least two hours. Lynx was the first to emerge onto the veranda. His white silk shirt and white linen pants clung to his body as if he had been doused with buckets of water. It was a sultry ninety degrees outside, over a hundred in the warehouse.

Chico Gonzales was next. He couldn't wait to rip off his purple-and-white polyester shirt. Buttons flew in all directions as he popped them open and pulled his thick arms out. He threw the shirt in a corner in a soggy heap; three Indians casually eyed it and sidled over next to it. They would fight over the shirt if Chico left it behind.

Sweet and Low was next. She was damp, but not soaking like the others. The Bear followed. He filled the doorway as he looked around uneasily; then he motioned for El Hombre to pass.

Billy Siegal straggled out into the light, a mess, soaking wet with sweat. He looked around furtively, then almost ran to the waiting vehicles and the cool air conditioning inside.

The rest of the Cowboys followed. They sped off down the trail, leaving little brown motes of dust suspended in the hot tropical air. By the time the last vehicle had passed out of sight it looked like a desert storm had hit. The dust filtered back, a thick brown fog over the camp, causing some of the Indians to cough and cover their mouths.

It was dusk now, almost dark. Mitch had to see inside the warehouse to get an accurate fix on the size of the crop.

He decided to make his move before the fog settled. There were two open hatches on the roof. They were there to let the air circulate, to keep the moisture level under control. Excess humidity was bad for cocaine.

As the sentry made his rounds and reached the far end of the veranda, Mitch moved – out of the banana trees, across the clearing, and onto the porch, where he jumped up for the edge of the roof, using a beam for leverage to get his feet up so he could swing onto the roof. He crawled along the roof to the open hatch. He slipped in through the opening feet first. The drop was close to ten feet, but there were pallets of cocaine stacked off to the side that he could use to break his fall.

Swinging like a trapeze artist, he was hanging down inside the warehouse holding onto the edge of the hatch with his hands when something grabbed his ankles in a viselike grip and ripped downward, tearing him away, pulling him with such force he could actually hear the nails of the hatch edging groan as they popped loose.

Mitch fell at least seven feet through the air before hitting the ground, part of the edging still in his hand, with a nail sticking out. Mitch swung it as hard as he could in a low arc. It hit something solid and stuck.

It was the Bear's thigh. He just stood there grinning like a toothless monster. His mouth was black in the darkness.

The Bear pulled the board out of his thigh and threw it at Mitch, catching him in the left shoulder and driving him forward toward the rows of cocaine.

Mitch scrambled for the first narrow passage he could see, hoping the Bear would have trouble fitting between the stacks. The cocaine was piled almost to the ceiling in plastic bags on pallets packed so close Mitch had to turn sideways to slip between them.

The problem was the Bear knew the warehouse better than he did. Mitch moved sideways down the stacks for about twenty feet. The Bear's bulk slid into view, blocking Mitch's exit. Mitch fired two shots with the Magnum. Cocaine exploded in every direction. Missed him.

Mitch leveraged himself up the stacks, his hands ripping through the bags as he tried to get a grip, his feet kicking big holes in them. Mitch held his breath and closed his eyes to keep the shower of white powder from filling his lungs or blinding him.

From the top of a stack Mitch looked down at all the little waterfalls of white powder, thousands of dollars cascading onto the floor. He lay still, trying to find the Bear in the blackness. There was no escape through the open hatches: they were too high. The doors were the only exit.

The Bear knew it too. He was moving down there somewhere, slowly, calmly, stalking Mitch like an animal.

The moonlight filtering through the hatches was the only light. Mitch would have to stay clear of it to avoid being silhouetted. He jumped across to the top of a large stack of unrefined paste in a dark corner of the warehouse, with his .44 out but nothing to shoot at.

He leaped to another stack of paste. He was in the air when he heard the roar of the shotgun. Two loads of buckshot ripped into the middle of the stack he had just left. A shower of paste powder started to fill the warehouse.

Mitch had made a mistake. When he was on the

finished cocaine, the Bear wouldn't shoot. Every shot was at least a million dollars in damage as the little pellets tore into the kilo bags, but the paste was a different story. The Bear would unload freely now. Two more blasts tore into the stack Mitch was on. The Bear was spraying the whole corner.

There was so much cocaine and paste dust in the air Mitch had to stifle a sneeze, pulling his turtleneck up as a mask so he wouldn't inhale the dust. The room was filled now with a white, light, powdery snowfall. The shafts of light from the hatches were clearly visible as the white powder floated through the moonlight.

The gunfire would bring the other guards. Mitch had only seconds left before they came in with flashlights and plenty of firepower.

As the powder permeated the room, Mitch could smell the kerosene. It was a light, heady smell like the slight whisper of perfume.

He pulled off one of the grenades clipped to his battle jacket and lobbed it as far as he could toward the opposite end of the warehouse. It was short-fused, exploding with a thundering roar as it hit. The whole far-side wall blew out. Boards flew in all directions, while more paste and pure cocaine powder filled the air.

Mitch leaped from one stack to the next as fast as he could until he was close to the blown-out wall.

The two main doors flew open and guards streamed in with their flashlights arching the warehouse, causing pinpoints of light to shine and glisten in the raining powder and paste.

Mitch didn't hesitate. He lobbed the second grenade against the wall opposite. Lying flat on top of the stack spread-eagled, he waited. The blast shook the whole warehouse.

The guards ran toward the new explosion.

Mitch leaped down from the pile and out through the hole in the wall made by the first grenade.

On the edge of the veranda Mitch got hit with a fist, a mammoth club smashing into his back up near his shoulder blades. A second blow on the side of his head drove him off the veranda. The Bear stood on the edge of the porch, his yellow slitted eyes staring down at Mitch, no expression in them. The Bear stepped down and brushed away the Magnum with his foot as Mitch tried to raise it. The whole right side of Mitch's body seemed to be paralyzed.

The Bear gave him a kick in the stomach just to make sure he wouldn't move around. Then he kicked Mitch's Ruger into the jungle. The Bear had known the explosions were nothing but a diversion; he had just waited for Mitch to come out.

A giant paw reached down and grabbed the back of Mitch's battle jacket at the neck, lifting him like a rag doll. With his other hand, the Bear clamped onto Mitch's belt in the small of his back, raising him over his head. The Bear began to walk toward the still.

The still was open on all sides. The flickering blue propane flames had the aviation fuel swirling in little rivers on the surface. Three Indians were still working like zombies, steadily processing the last of the paste. It looked evil.

They looked up to see the Bear striding across toward them. They knew what he had in mind and scattered to the sides of the building.

He stopped, letting go of Mitch's belt, but still held his jacket by the neck. Mitch swung round in a slow arc to face him, his feet at least a foot off the ground. They just stared at each other. The Bear smiled, and in one angry heave he slung Mitch over his hip, his arm locking him against his waist.

The Bear mounted the steps to the still and stood looking at the two boiling vats. He chose the one at the far end. The iron of the vat glowed white-hot. One of the Indians came over to offer help. The Bear took a swipe at him with his foot. The Indian scuttled off and huddled in a corner, his eyes dead and expressionless.

Mitch was fighting to stay conscious, drifting in and out, dizzy and disoriented. He was facing downward, looking right into the boiling kerosene; the hiss of the propane and the bubbling fuel in the vat were all he could hear.

As the Bear stepped up to the lip of the vat Mitch felt him shudder, only a slight tremor, a trembling. Mitch summoned up everything he had and started to squirm and kick as hard as he could.

The Bear slipped backward, his step faltering as if he were drunk from all the powder he had inhaled. Mitch had an arm free now, pushing and swinging wildly, but the Bear still had a steely grip on him. Suddenly the Bear dropped to both knees as though he were praying, offering Mitch as a human sacrifice.

But then he started to pitch forward, releasing Mitch slightly. To catch himself the Bear grabbed the edge of the glowing-hot metal vat with his free hand. He screamed and let go of Mitch's waist. Mitch rolled down the back of the Bear's leg like rain falling off a roof, landing heavily on the platform.

The Bear stood up holding his wrist. He looked at his burned hand in utter surprise and then down at Mitch as he fought to stand up. All his hatred welled up as he lunged toward Mitch.

Mitch kicked for the groin but hit the Bear's hip. The Bear spun, catching his foot under the lip of the vat. It burned right through his sandal. He hung there in midair for a second. Then he fell into the vat. Mitch tumbled and leaped off the platform to avoid the shower of hot liquid fuel.

The three Indians were standing now, mouths

215

open, watching the rolling waves in the vat. The pattern suddenly quieted, then stopped. The Bear suddenly erupted straight up out of the seething liquid, arms raised over his head, mouth open to let out the most horrible scream, a sound summoned from the depths of hell.

He was looking straight at Mitch. Slowly he was swallowed back into the boiling fuel, arms still raised over his head, hands open.

It stopped everyone.

They looked at each other, horrified. It gave Mitch the few seconds he needed to run the length of the still and disappear into the rainforest. Gunfire followed him, bullets whipping through the jungle, tearing leaves and bouncing off tree trunks.

In the bush on the run there are only three choices: run, burrow, or climb. Mitch had no strength left, so he climbed into a notch of the nearest tree, working his way into the foliage at the top, cutting extra branches with his survival knife to make a nest, hoping it would blend in with the camouflage he was wearing.

He rested, breathing slowly, trying to get his adrenaline down. All night he heard them rustling below as they scoured the undergrowth looking for him.

It took until dawn for his thoughts to start making sense. The Bear must have had a heart attack from breathing in all that paste and pure cocaine. That would account for the tremor, the hesitation Mitch had felt in him. The paste was very powerful and poisonous when it was still laced with kerosene. It had added to his strength, but it had also revved up his heart until it burst. Ironic. He had been brought to his death by an overdose.

When sunrise came, Mitch was astounded to see he had only made it about two hundred feet from the encampment. He could look down and see the whole camp clearly.

The quiet was broken by a black Blazer as it tore into the clearing, going at least sixty. A few sleepy Indians dove off the trail opening to keep from being run over.

It was El Hombre.

He slammed on the brakes and slid the final thirty feet to the edge of the still. Two Indians got out with him carrying silenced Uzis and sidearms. El Hombre stopped to talk to a man who looked like the foreman. He pointed to the vats inside the still.

The Colombian took out his gold-plated forty-five and smacked the man in the face with it. The foreman fell to his knees and stayed there until the two Indian bodyguards dragged him away and left him sagging in a heap by the warehouse.

El Hombre started to yell, shouting for the men to form a wide, silent circle round the entire camp. He walked up to the veranda and stood, looking at each of the men, taking his time, measuring each man, trying to decide if any were involved. When he finished, he looked into the jungle.

Mitch felt those blue eyes burning. El Hombre must have stood looking into the jungle for several minutes. Then he turned and walked into the still.

One of the workers ran up to him, offering him a sledgehammer. He took it and started to break up the platform round the vat. Wood splintered and flew into the air around him. He was oblivious of it. The vat was cool now and calm on the surface.

When the platform was destroyed he jumped down to the ground. He took the sledgehammer again and with a mighty heave he knocked the support beam away, causing the iron vat to topple forward. At the last second he jumped aside so the liquid wouldn't splash him.

He watched the fuel soak off into the hard-packed earth. Bones tumbled out, bleached white. They glistened against the dark, wet earth. Finally the skull rolled out, black teeth grinning up at him. El Hombre bent double, fell to his knees, hugged himself, and rocked back and forth.

His dirge started low at first, the plaintive wail of a hurt animal; then it slowly built, higher and higher, until his keening filled the air. It was the grief of a man who had lost his father. The Indians looked away. Some shrugged, embarrassed, confused to see this man in this posture.

El Hombre was sobbing uncontrollably now. The

guards went to help him. He motioned them away and looked toward the jungle once more, letting out a shrill scream of grief and hatred that froze Mitch's blood. El Hombre would not rest now until the Bear was avenged. Mitch huddled into the notch of his tree and waited.

It took several hours to clean up the camp. El Hombre had them put the Bear's remains into a wooden box while he went to survey the damage done in the warehouse.

The men sat in little clusters trying to sift the cocaine up off the warehouse floor with Dustbusters or scoop the paste back into bags. Mitch estimated twenty per cent had been destroyed, about ten million dollars' worth. With Immke now acting as their banker, this was easily replaced – written off as an 'unforeseen cost'.

Pickup trucks had already started to arrive, piled high with more filled plastic bags, red seals in the corners, the produce of other factories being brought to this central warehouse to be flown to Panama.

About an hour later the fleet of Blazers and Jeeps arrived with the rest of the Cowboys. Lynx and his bodyguard were the first to step out, followed by Chico Gonzales, Sweet and Low, their bodyguards, and finally Billy Siegal.

They took one look at the warehouse and the expression on El Hombre's face and headed straight for the two-engine Apache that would take them to Bogotá and Immke's waiting 707. Siegal went up to say something to console El Hombre but closed his mouth in mid-sentence and scurried onto the plane.

El Hombre stood in silence as the small plane took off, then went over to see how they were doing with the wooden box.

Mitch decided not to wait for nightfall. He slid down the tree, found his Magnum, and headed deeper into the rain-forest to wait for dusk. He picked up the road at sunset but stayed out of sight until he passed the camouflaged trail that led to the airstrip. He gave it a wide berth.

The sound of an engine howling drove him off the road. El Hombre's black Blazer burst out of the trail opening, all four wheels spinning as it lumbered up the small embankment onto the road like a sluggish black beetle.

The Blazer passed so close to Mitch he could almost see the blue of El Hombre's eyes through the jungle foliage. The lights inside were on and Mitch saw the wooden box on the seat next to El Hombre. He had his arm cradled across the top to keep it steady, pressing it against his body as he careened along the road.

El Hombre turned suddenly to look out the rear window. It sent cold beads of ice down Mitch's back as El Hombre disappeared into the night.

What a mess. Mitch's plan was a shambles. Harry had sent him for information and he had left behind three dead men, smoke, and ashes. All for information that would become yesterday's news by tomorrow. The whole situation had escalated because of the Bear. Killing the Bear was a mistake. El Hombre would be consumed with revenge.

Mitch threw the half-eaten can of C rations he had opened into the bush and found the bike. He kicked the starter.

It was midnight, and a good six hours of rough road lay ahead of him before he would arrive at the Colombia airport.

13
The Hunt and the Hunted –
Canal Zone

Jose was mumbling to himself. He had asked for a complete debriefing; instead he got a vague silence. Mitch told him he would talk to Harry from the boat. He wanted to make sure Mai Linh was okay.

The battery had gone dead on the tender, so Jose took the battery out of his car, and finally they got the tender cranked up. Mitch sent Jose waddling down the dock with the battery pressed tightly against his ample stomach, the jumper cables swinging back and forth over his shoulder, leaving black marks on his white suit.

Mitch put the Whaler in gear and sped out through the marina entrance into the canal, then finally into the open ocean. The ocean air hit him like a wave of cold water. It had a feeling all its own, clean and new, like youth.

The ride up the coast was exhilarating, wild

white beaches, a few primitive sailboats, and local fishermen trying to squeeze a living out of leaky rowboats. Mitch spotted a couple of frigate birds circling, looking for lunch. Frigate birds were supposed to be good luck to mariners. He hoped it was so.

There was a slight chop, but the spray felt good on his face. He took his shirt off to let the sun seep into his skin. His body tingled, felt alive. He needed to see Mai Linh.

He spotted the cove, the sandbar showing pure white against the aquamarine shallows.

The Whaler sped full tilt over the sand spit; it drew only about eight inches up on a full plane. Mitch backed off on the throttle. The boat seemed to heave a sigh as it sank back down to the waterline.

He could hear a bleating, a faint wailing. It was the boat alarm. He revved the engine and ran up on the sand, grabbed the M-1 and the Magnum, and disappeared into the mangroves.

The tangled root systems were impassable. He finally gave up trying to scramble through them and waded out into the small channel that led to the boat. The water was waist deep near the bank and sloped down to five feet of mud at the center. He followed the channel for about a hundred yards until he saw the stern of the Hatteras fifty feet ahead. The palm fronds he had cut covered most of the white hull. The alarm was louder now, but it was still only a faint, tired whine, as if it had been on for a long time and the batteries were almost exhausted.

The hull was buried so deep in the mangroves, Mitch's only entry was from the dive platform. He slithered up onto the teak platform and rested on his knees, peering in over the top of the transom into the cockpit and salon; then he surveyed the bridge. There was nothing.

He leaped over the transom and into the salon, then rushed through the galley, the forward berths, the bridge. All empty. No Mai Linh. No note. No nothing.

The boat was abandoned. She was gone.

He found himself leaning on the bowsprit rail with his friend the pelican watching him from the mangroves, thoughts flashing through his mind like a high-speed movie. Where the hell was she?

He went back to the beach to get the Whaler and the rest of his gear and slowly navigated the small channel back to the Hatteras.

There was no sign of a struggle.

He boarded again, threw his gear into the stateroom, and headed for the radio on the flying bridge. He was so exhausted and upset it took two tries with the marine operator before he got through to Harry. Maybe Harry knew something.

'Nice to hear from you, Mitchell. Some friends

of mine tell me there's still smoke in the mountains. Nice going.'

'Look, Harry, things got a little out of—'

'I know. With you that always seems to be the case. Can't ever keep it simple, huh?'

'I'm back at the boat now and Mai Linh is gone. I've looked—'

'I don't want to discuss Mai Linh.' He wasn't going to help. Mitch wondered if he did know anything. There was a long silence. Mitch broke it.

'You want to know what I found in the mountains?'

'Yeah.'

'The crop is huge, at least fifty per cent bigger than normal. I didn't see it all, just two warehouses, but my guess is a quarter of a million kilos.' There was a long, low whistle from Harry. 'Over one hundred long tons,' Mitch added.

'At eight thousand a key, bottom wholesale, that comes to about two billion dollars cost to the Cowboys and net to the Colombian.' Harry was almost whispering. He added, 'With this much they could easily drop the street price in half.'

'Yeah, and I figure they will, forty to fifty bucks a gram.'

'Timing?'

'It's leaving as we speak. I'd guess at least two-thirds is in Panama already.'

'They sealed the whole crop?'

'Yes. They must have worn out their rings. That's a lot of imaginary money to count; greed is going to be way up there on the scale.'

'You got any idea where it's going in the Canal Zone?'

'No. I got rid of a little of it for you.'

'Yeah, and that's not all I heard you got rid of.'

'It was either him or me. He did it to himself.'

'I don't care how you did it, but count on one thing. You made yourself a primo enemy for life in that fucking Colombian, and he's a lot tougher than Immke. Maybe he's got your girlfriend.'

'I don't think so; there's no sign of a struggle.'

'I want you to leave Panama. We have enough to go on and you're a liability to the operation now. They know you, and they're going to do anything they can to take you out. If they see you again it could blow the whole thing for me. You fucked up down there in Colombia, Mitchell, tipped our hand, so I want you gone for sure, understood?'

'Harry, I wanted to be gone last month, but I'm not going without Mai Linh.'

'That's not for you to decide. Who the hell knows about women anyway? Maybe she found somebody with a bigger boat. I want you out of there today.'

'Whatever you say, Harry.'

'Don't "whatever-you-say" me. You don't want

to make an enemy out of me too, Mitchell.'

'What am I supposed to do, just forget I ever knew her?'

'I want the next transmission between us to come from a location at least three hundred miles from where you are now. I'm telling the Intertel people you aren't on our team anymore. See ya, Mitchell.'

The line went dead in Mitch's hand, giving out a low, ominous buzz.

He needed sleep. He thawed a steak in the microwave, broiled it, and wolfed it down, then secured the alarm system and tried to sleep. It took him a long time to get Mai Linh out of his mind, but he slept for eighteen hours, tossing and turning. It was six the next morning when he awoke.

He swam in the cove, speared a few fish, and ate a solitary breakfast on the bridge. His ex-employers had spent a great deal of time and money training him to think under the worst conditions. If you can't think clearly, don't think at all. Don't speculate. If your mind is hazy, lie low and rest, get centered, then put the pieces together. If you're going to react, get your adrenaline working with a clear mind. No random action.

Mitch was rested now, enough to start putting the pieces together. He started in her closet.

Most of her clothes were there; a few things were missing, enough for an overnight bag. The Zodiac was gone, and so was the spare fuel tank. It was more fuel than she needed just to get into the marina. He checked the cash stash. A thousand was gone, but over four thousand was left, untouched.

He went back up to the bridge to think about their last few conversations. Had he read her that wrong? Was she lying to him the whole time, was she hooked up with them somehow? Was it a setup from the start? If it was, they would have been waiting for him and he would have been dead now. No, it was something else. He believed her story about her sister, her hatred for Siegal. Then it struck him.

He slid down the ladder from the bridge and into the forward V berths, found the seam, and opened up one fiberglass panel. Everything was as it should have been. He closed it and opened the opposite side. The Uzi and the silencer attachment were gone. He noticed that a full box of 9mm shells was missing, along with the extra clip. He slammed the door shut. Goddammit, she'd gone after Siegal.

He went back up to the bridge and tossed the pelican a fish he had speared earlier that morning. At least he looked happy.

He lowered the motorcycle into the Whaler. He

had to swing it over on the davits and gently lower it into the bow. It was still covered. It looked like a big body, bundled up in green vinyl. Then he waited for nightfall.

As the sun went down, Mitch headed for the *White Lady*.

He stayed close to the beach just outside the white-water curl of the surf. The wind had picked up a little, so it was rough going the last two miles before he reached the entrance to the Canal Zone. He picked up the channel markers and followed them on past the marina for about two miles to the beginning of the restricted zone.

She stood out against the black dock, pure white, fully lit by floodlights.

Mitch shut down his engine and drifted silently past her sleek hundred and fifty feet. The Bell jet Ranger helicopter was secured to the landing pad, covered with a tight black shroud to protect it from the elements. There was very little activity on deck, only some crew drifting aimlessly around. The security guards were bored, smoking and idly talking to each other.

Mitch waited until he had drifted out of sight, then started the engine and returned to the far side of their pier where he found an opening in the seawall wide enough for the Whaler. He turned the engine off and pulled himself through the opening to the other side, weaving between the pilings; then he secured the bow and stern of the Whaler and wriggled out of his jumpsuit. He rummaged through his duffel bag until he found the snub-nosed .32. It slipped easily into a Ziploc waterproof bag and into his shorts.

Dropping silently over the side, he swam out through the small hole in the seawall, making his way underwater to the wide metal diving platform on the stern of the *White Lady*, hanging there until the security guard made his round, then up and onto the afterdeck just as he cleared the stern.

There was a large dining table and eight white wicker chairs. The table was clear. Mitch went through the main salon and down the hatchway into the aft staterooms. The boat was empty except for a skeleton crew. As Mitch went slowly back up the hatchway he could hear some crew in the galley, working.

Mitch's head was just clear of the top step when he saw that the starboard salon glass windows had been shot out. He could see the bullet-hole pattern across the salon wall, black spiders against the polished mahogany, right up to the entrance to the galley. They were rough, splintered quarter-sized holes, the kind 9mm shells make. It looked like the Uzi to Mitch.

Beneath the row of bullet holes, three large couches formed a U pattern. It was against the far couch that Mitch spotted her black scarf, ripped almost in half. She used it when she was seriously occupied, like while she was fishing. He scooped it up as he passed by and tucked it into his shorts. He made the length of the aft deck in two steps and dove over the side, passing underwater through the seawall into the blackness. He turned to look back. A couple of guards were looking over the side; then they shrugged and walked forward. They must have figured the splash was a tarpon feeding or a ray shaking off parasites.

Minutes later Mitch was in the Whaler again and had started to pull his way back through the pilings to the other end of the wharf and into the canal.

Where was everyone? And no blood – was she all right? If Siegal and the Cowboys had Mai Linh, what would they do with her? Maybe they would keep her alive and try to get her to talk about him. Was it all a con, a snow job from the beginning, a complicated trick with Mitch at the center? No; too many inconsistencies. He had to find out where they were.

He noticed a small, secluded beach and ran the Whaler over to it, slipping the bow high up on the sand. He lifted the Kawasaki upright, took off the cover, and fired it up. He jumped it right over the bow, the rear wheel spinning in the soft sand, almost spilling him. It gave an old wound in his side one hell of a pull and almost caused him to black out. He finally got the bike straight and snaked it up to the dirt trail, then hid it under a tree and returned to the boat.

He found a mooring for the Whaler at a commercial pier nearby, slipped the Panamanian dockmaster ten bucks, and eased back to the bike on foot carrying his gear, which he stuffed into the saddlebags.

He got the bike on the trail and found a paved service road that ran parallel to the canal. It was like looking for one grain of sand on a beach, but he had no other leads. If necessary, he would have to check out each restricted compound on both sides, going on his instincts until he found something.

The first one he reached was a free-trade zone where goods could be held in bond for transshipping. It was a large commercial enterprise with several bonded warehouses, too busy and too public.

So he moved on, coming to a US military restricted zone next. There were Marine guards on the gates protecting about six acres of military ordnance.

It was at the third spot, a Panamanian restricted zone, that Mitch picked up the headlights in his mirror. They hadn't been there before. He stopped at the armed gate, watching the lights in his mirror also stop. He nodded at the two guards. One of them started to walk his way, grimacing and motioning Mitch to keep moving. He put the bike into gear and slowly followed along the chain-link fence. It was a big compound, almost ten acres, with at least thirty buildings, mostly Quonset huts, given over to the Panamanians as part of the treaty agreement. The interior security was heavy, with several two-man patrols, each with a dog on a leash.

One team let their dog go when they saw Mitch cruising outside the compound. He hit the fence so hard he made it sing; he was up against the fence on his hind legs, teeth bared, barking, snarling, biting the fence. He was putting on a real show for his master. Mitch revved the bike and sped off. The guards laughed as they put the dog back on the lead.

The headlights were with him again. Now there were two sets. Mitch wasn't sure if the second set had come out of the compound or not. He took the bike up a little, to fifty. The headlights stayed steady in his mirror. When he hit the end of the restricted zone he picked up a third pair. But these were coming at him head on. And they were in his lane.

The oncoming car turned in a slide and spun lengthwise across the highway, blocking both lanes. Mitch hit the brakes hard, his front wheel almost touching their back door. Figures moved frantically inside the car and the passenger door popped open.

Jose grunted and fought his way out of the car, rising like a white mountain in the glow of Mitch's headlight.

The two following cars settled in right behind Mitch, side by side, their engines idling. There was only a small space of about four feet between them.

'I'm sorry, but you must come with me, *Señor* Mitchell,' said Jose. Mitch heard all the front doors of the black sedans open behind him. Four men stepped out, all dressed in suits.

Mitch casually backed the front wheel away from Jose's door. The four men from the sedans started toward Mitch. He dropped one side of the bike and twisted the accelerator as hard as he could. It brought him around in a slow, curving U. He aimed for the space between the two cars, betting they wouldn't shoot or react fast enough. The men scattered.

The front wheel of the bike smacked into the open doors squarely, slamming them shut as Mitch squeezed in between the two parallel sedans. He checked his mirror. They were all scrambling to turn round.

Both sentries were out on the road as Mitch

shot past the guard station. The chain-link fence was a blur; only the little posts that held the three strands of barbed wire at the top registered. Mitch had to concentrate on missing the potholes and washouts as he headed into Panama City.

All three cars were back in his mirror now, six headlights glowing in the blackness like cat's eyes. The nearest one was no more than thirty feet behind him.

He almost missed the main intersection. He hit the brakes, banking out onto the highway, tires screaming. Their lights blinked up in his mirror again, only now they were about half a mile behind him. The lights of the city were ahead now, so Mitch opened up the bike, slowing down only for a traffic circle. So did they. They stayed with him.

He finally spotted an alley next to the Panama Hyatt and sped down it, hiding the bike behind a huge garbage container. Out of the corner of his eye Mitch saw the first pair of headlights pop into the alley, just before he closed the service door into the hotel kitchen.

It was a huge, open room, with six or seven men in tall chef's hats and about ten prep cooks assisting. It was the dinner hour and the room was bustling with activity, waiters coming and going through the one-way doors. Busboys followed them carrying trays of dirty dishes, weaving and dancing through the traffic.

Mitch spotted the employees' locker room and slipped in. Freshly laundered waiters' jackets were hanging on wooden pegs. He took one that fitted and went back out into the main kitchen just in time to see the rear door slam open.

Jose and two men came bursting in, looking for Mitch. They fanned out as soon as they entered, but not fast enough to get round the head chef, a big Panamanian with a meat cleaver in his hand and blood in his eye. He grabbed the two outside men by the lapels, still managing to hold onto the cleaver as he herded them, together with Jose, back to the door. All the time he was screaming at the top of his voice.

The head chef pushed all three men through the doorway at the same time, forcing the door closed behind them. He then turned and started to yell at all the white hats standing behind him. They grinned at each other and went back to their work. They were proud of their head chef. He banged the lid down tight on a steaming pot of vegetables for a Chateaubriand. No one entered his kitchen and tried to take over. No one.

Mitch made himself scarce in the pastry corner. The pastry chef was taking a pan of hamburger buns out of the warming oven. Mitch looked over at the next table, where two prep cooks were folding Burger King wrappers over Whoppers. A second chef was sprinkling extra cheese on some Pizza Hut pizzas and putting them in the microwave oven. A third man was trying to bring the Kentucky Fried Chicken back to life.

Immke!

There were six big trays laid out on a long stainless steel table, with two waiters standing ready to take them away. Mitch got in line to take the third. The tall, thin waiter ahead of him gave him a strange look as he noticed Mitch's pants were not the regulation issue. Mitch had no choice but to look him in the eye and smile. The waiter didn't smile back, just turned away. The Intertel men and Jose would be searching inside the hotel by now. If they got hold of Mitch, he would be out of Panama and out of action, maybe for good.

A fourth waiter appeared and stood behind Mitch, then a fifth. By the time the sixth waiter appeared all the trays were prepared – Whoppers, Big Macs, Arby's roast beef sandwiches, Dairy Queen sundaes for dessert, pizza, chicken, two dozen bottles of André and Taylor champagne, and a tired tray of Taco Viva burritos. Mitch picked up the tray of Whoppers and followed the three waiters in front to the service elevators.

The button for the eighth floor was pushed. As they started their ascent, the tall waiter turned and started to say something. Mitch interrupted him with a palmed fifty-dollar bill. It was gone in the wink of an eye.

Mitch spoke first. 'I need to find a girl – an Oriental girl. Very pretty,' he whispered and handed over another fifty. It flew out of his hand.

The waiter leaned over and spoke into Mitch's ear: 'Room 813.' He seemed to like being part of a conspiracy. He smiled to himself and rubbed his open palm absently on the jacket pocket where he had put the cash.

The elevator stopped abruptly. Mitch had to steady his tray with his free hand; the other waiters were used to it and were undisturbed.

The doors sprang open. Two guards stood in the doorway. Each stuck his head in, looked around, then motioned for the waiters to step out, one at a time. Mitch was last out.

As he entered the hall, the larger of the two guards stopped him with an arm on his shoulder, while the other one walked over next to him. They both moved at the same time. In one smooth motion they each glommed two double Whoppers. They had already commandeered a bottle of champagne and some pizza. They laughed to each other and motioned for Mitch to carry on, giving him a little push.

The other waiters had disappeared down the hall into the last doorway. Immke had the whole floor rented. He was relatively safe in Panama.

Mitch looked over his shoulder. The guards had settled into their Whoppers and champagne and had their backs to him. Room 813 was halfway down the hall on the left side.

Mitch tried the door, slowly at first. It was unlocked. He pushed it open with the edge of the tray. The hinges were stiff, so it opened with a slight creaking noise. There were no lights on and the drapes were pulled shut. Candles were glowing blue and yellow on the coffee table.

He smelled it first; then he saw the bottle of ammonia, half used; the eyedropper stuck in the open mouth. A glass beaker stood alone, half full of cloudy water: cocaine and ammonia mixed, a chopstick for stirring leaning against the side of the beaker. There were a half-dozen used coffee filters lying flat and tired on the surface of the table, still slightly coated with the pure base residue that was left after they had poured the liquid through.

Two large lumps that looked like damp flour stood on a mirror, waiting to dry and be chopped with a razor, then mixed with pot. A small glass pipe was peeking out of a nearby ashtray, waiting for the freebase.

On the far edge of the table, away from the freebase, was another plate covered with two syringes, a pile of pure coke, and some crushed Dilaudid pills. Artificial heroin. A speedball kit.

A plastic tube circled the plate like a transparent worm.

Freebase and speedballs, a deadly combination.

It took a second for Mitch's eyes to get used to the dark. He decided not to turn on the light.

As he was setting the tray down he heard a moan, like that of a sick animal, the mewing of a small kitten. Impossible to tell whether it was pleasure or pain. Someone was curled up in the corner under the window sill, in the blackest part of the room.

Mitch closed the door gently behind him. The flickering light of the candles was casting wild, dancing shadows on the walls and ceiling. He moved closer to the huddled figure.

It was Mai Linh. Her green eyes reflected like cat's eyes in the candlelight.

There was no sign of recognition, only a blank, glazed look. He was a stranger to her.

'Mai Linh, it's . . .'

She pulled away from him when she heard his voice and seemed to want to squeeze even deeper into the corner, become part of the wall, evaporate from sight.

'I want you to come with me now. They've drugged you.' A glimmer of recognition passed through her eyes, and she reached an arm out toward him. She was on some strong stuff.

'Oh, hi, Mitch.' She tried to flash him her little

sexy smile; it looked pathetic in the shadows.

'We have to move. There are a couple of guards in the hall. Can you walk?'

Her eyes filled with tears.

'Oh, Mitch, my poor Mitch, you don't understand. It is very bad; you must go.'

'It's going to get worse. We have to get out of here.' He tried to lift her, but she pushed him away.

'Mitch, I'm so sorry. It's not how you think it is. I have not told you the whole truth. It was me. I am where I belong. Go away. You must go away now.'

'What are you talking about?'

He didn't hear the door open.

The lights went on as he tumbled forward, hit by a strong chop that landed between his shoulder and neck, numbing the whole side of his body as he slammed against the windowsill. He fell at Mai Linh's feet. She was weaving, almost standing, using the coffee table for support.

The Colombian stood full frame in the doorway, gold-plated forty-five swinging loosely at his side. The two guards hovered over Mitch like they wanted to make a play. The Colombian pushed them aside, glanced at Mai Linh, and kicked Mitch with all his might in the stomach. It drove the air out of Mitch; he fought hard to remain conscious.

Each of the guards grabbed an arm and started to drag him out of the room. As they did, a second team came in with a doctor's bag, one of them flashing a syringe in plain sight.

Mai Linh was standing now. She stumbled unsteadily against the corner of the table, her eyes connecting with Mitch's. The team bent over her. Mitch saw the plastic tube being wrapped round her arm and the tip of the needle on a direct line to a vein.

She said, 'I'm sorry, Mitch. I was the one. It wasn't my sister, it was me. I am the bad twin.'

14
Into the Ocean – The Flats, Panama

The door slammed shut behind Mitch. The Colombian led the way down the hall as they carried Mitch through the last door into a big, open suite. All the Cowboys were there, partying. Roxie and several of her girls were circulating, entertaining the Cowboys. Roxie's mouth fell open when she saw Mitch. Lynx sat watching in a corner with his bodyguards. Ike and Tina were asleep in his arms.

Immke was standing at the end of the room with Roxie. He pointed and waved toward a closed door at the far end of the room. The guards carried Mitch through the door into a bedroom. They heaved him toward the bed and missed. Mitch fell in a heap at its foot.

The Colombian came over, kneeled, and slipped a pair of handcuffs on Mitch's wrists, then paused for a few seconds, staring into his eyes. Mitch could feel his side throbbing where the Colombian had kicked him, the pain coming and going in regular waves. Mitch knew it took all the Colombian's will not to kill him instantly.

Immke and Roxie came in with Sweet and Low, who was doused in Opium perfume. The fragrance slowly filled the room. It made Mitch sneeze; the pain from his side almost made him black out. Just before Immke spoke, Mitch saw Siegal slide through the small opening left in the doorway and find his way unnoticed into a corner of the room.

'Is this the guy?' Immke asked, looking at the Colombian.

'Yes. He fits the description and goes with the Oriental. I'm sure it's him – *chinga su madre*.' The Colombian was caressing his gold-plated forty-five as he stared down at Mitch unblinking, like a mountain cat.

'There's something familiar about this guy.' Immke stroked his chin, musing. 'Anybody know him?'

Siegal wriggled out of the crowd and looked down at Mitch, his little gray ferret eyes boring through him. He shook his head and went back to his corner.

'Something about his eyes, build – something . . .' Immke walked round Mitch.

'I feel the same way.' It was Chico Gonzales. He bent over Mitch and grabbed his chin, thrusting it up toward him, his platinum coke spoon swinging in slow, hypnotic rhythm in front of Mitch's face. He pushed Mitch's chin down with his thumb, shaking his own head from side to side.

Finally, Sweet and Low came over. She stood above Mitch, her head tilted at a slight angle, feet wide apart. Her perfume wafted over him. He sneezed again.

'I got it,' Immke yelled at the top of his voice, pushing Sweet and Low aside. 'It's fucking Butler. That's who it is. My very own fucking pilot, allergic to perfume. Has to be. Same stupid cocky attitude. It's him.' He looked over at Roxie. Her hand was up to her mouth, eyes wide. 'That's right, honey, he's the same guy that was going to let you die.' She turned and walked out the door.

'I will take care of him – *morirá lentamente, cabron*.' El Hombre was standing over Mitch looking down, his gun loose in his hand like he wanted to put a round in Mitch's temple.

Immke yelled at him, 'Forget it, pal. Too many witnesses, with all these broads in the next room and the hotel staff. And we have work to do. We're finished here after tomorrow. Siegal, you do it. Take him out to the ocean. We don't want no body found in the hotel. You get rid of him. Meet us later.'

'I want this *cabron*.' The Colombian was staring menacingly at Immke.

'Who has a bigger score to settle with this prick,

me or you?' Immke shouted. Then he thought better of it and answered his own question. 'Both of us, but business is business. Siegal, leave now.'

'Maybe we should question him. Maybe he's a Fed,' Siegal said.

'Siegal, do as I say. Who cares who he's with. Tomorrow we'll be out of here.'

'The girl, what about the girl?' Siegal blurted.

'Forget the fucking girl. She was only useful in bringing Butler here. Now she's served her purpose and she's soaking up a lot of my good coke.' Immke smiled.

'If I do Butler, you leave the girl for me. I have something to settle with her. It's just between me and her,' Siegal said.

'She's just another cokehead,' Immke yelled, kicking a chair out of his way, 'and I don't like being threatened. You just do like you're supposed to.'

Siegal started to squirm as if he had to go to the bathroom. 'Look, I only meant—'

'I know what you fucking meant. Maybe we'll keep her alive, maybe we won't.' Immke was over it now. He looked at his Rolex and went out into the next room. Mitch could hear him chase Roxie's girls out and clear the room of the hotel staff.

It took all of the Colombian's will to leave. He turned at the door to face Siegal. 'Don't fuck this up, you understand?' Siegal nodded.

They grabbed Mitch under the armpits and

hustled him out the bedroom door into the corridor. Siegal yelled from the bathroom that he would stay behind for a minute to call the *White Lady* for the Cigarette boat. They took Mitch down in the elevator and out the service door. A long-body limousine was waiting.

Mitch saw the front wheel of his motorcycle barely hidden behind the trash bin just before they tossed him onto the floor of the limo.

One guard sat in the back seat, the other in the opposite jump seat. They rested their feet on him, making themselves comfortable. Both had been hand picked by El Hombre and Immke. They had pure Colombian Indian blood running in their veins. Siegal was still whining when he entered the car. He almost stumbled over Mitch's feet, telling the two bodyguards they were assholes. They looked at each other, smiled, and looked away. They had their orders. If Siegal got in the way they would leave him ashore. When they arrived at the pier and parked, both guards got out to wait for the tender. Siegal talked to Mitch. 'You know, Butler, I remember that night in Colombia. It's the only time I've ever seen Immke shitting his pants. That was some night.' He laughed his weasely laugh, squirming. 'What's with you? You just keep lying there looking at me, not blinking, like if you could get out of those cuffs you would kill me. You should be happy you're here with me and not that crazy, fucking Colombian. He had some great plans for you. You would have wound up begging him to kill you. All this trouble you're causing, I can't believe it's just for that broad. It's got to be something else.'

'Go fuck yourself,' Mitch answered, wondering what really was driving him on.

'I think it's you that just got fucked.' Siegal was laughing harder. He had worked himself up, but the laugh was hollow and flat, drifting out over the wharf.

One of the guards yelled that the boat was pulling up.

The two guards held Mitch up almost off the ground. The boat was four feet below them, pulsating with the waves bouncing softly against the pilings. Two crew men had come with it from the yacht. They moved to help load, but the guards motioned them away and then dropped Mitch hard over the side of the pier into the stern of the boat. He tried to break the fall with his legs but got tangled in the engine covers; at least they were padded.

Mitch blacked out for a second. Nothing was broken, there was just shooting pain from his side. The guards jumped down behind him and practically had to pull Siegal after them to get him into the boat. Siegal hated the water. The boat pulled slowly away from the pier. The low, throaty rumble of the exhaust sounded deep and powerful.

One of the crew came to the stern with some thin

rope and handed it to a guard, who undid Mitch's handcuffs and slipped them into his pocket, then tied Mitch's hands together with the quarter-inch nylon line, cutting the end off with his knife and singeing the ends with his lighter. He did the same thing with Mitch's ankles and then called for the other guard. Together they lifted Mitch up squarely onto the engine covers. They bound Mitch's ankles and wrists together so he was locked in a fetal position, trussed up like a hog ready for market. When they were finished they gave each of the knots a test tug that almost drew blood. Satisfied, they nodded to the captain to pick up speed.

Mitch's head was almost touching his knees. The pain in his side, where El Hombre had kicked him, was a constant throb, but the fetal position he'd been forced into helped to ease it.

Siegal walked back to Mitch, a smug look on his face. The boat suddenly broached a little on the cross-chop from the brisk wind and Siegal nearly fell. He clutched the gunnel and used it as a handrail, moving hand over hand all the way to the stern until he was finally face to face with Mitch. Mitch was lying on his side, unable to move. Siegal gave the rope between Mitch's wrists and ankles another hefty tug for good measure, saw Mitch wince, and smiled.

Mitch watched the last red channel marker fly by. In a few minutes they would be out in the ocean.

The guard who had been sitting next to him left when Siegal sat down. Siegal was green, about to be sick any minute. The two Colombian guards looked back at the two of them, then faced forward. They were enjoying the ride. A balmy, breezy night, moonless, with whitecaps in the channel.

Mitch knew he was a dead man unless he did something soon. Siegal was staring at him, about to say something, when he began to retch. At first it was a dry heave; then his hand flew to his mouth and he bent over the gunnel, leaning over from the waist. The wind was whistling by at fifty knots. No one heard or noticed him. Mitch summoned up everything he had, then somersaulted off the stern into the white wake, using the last of his strength to execute a little roll to avoid the props. He took a final deep breath and went under.

The only way to survive was to keep absolutely still. Seconds later he bobbed to the surface with his back up, his face in the water. He could hear the boat still running on full bore, the engines now somewhere in the distance. Mitch was floating like a cork. He would have to take breaths whenever he could out of the side of his mouth like a swimmer. His life would depend on his remaining calm and not rotating his body – otherwise he would sink.

The tide was running in at about two knots, with the wind steady from the south. Mitch heard the Cigarette's engines shut down in the distance. He ventured a look but couldn't see over the waves. He would have to push Siegal and friends out of his mind and concentrate on staying alive. They would think Mitch jumped or fell. In any case, Mitch knew they would figure he was a dead man, the way he was tied up.

A recon ranger in Saigon had told him that once he had been captured by the Viet Cong and taken upriver by boat, tied up like Mitch was now. They were going to torture him for information, so he threw himself overboard. He had to block everything from his mind except breathing. Mitch had to do the same now.

He was drifting back in toward Panama, but he would never survive in the channel. The waves were steadily breaking over him; every second breath wound up being a mouthful of water. If he started to choke he was dead. If he could make it past the channel over into the flats he would have a better chance. There it was calmer, breathing would be easier, and he would be hard to see in his dark waiter's jacket.

The low, throbbing sound of the Cigarette's engines returned. Mitch tried to slip the ropes, but they were too well tied. The engines were getting closer all the time. It took all Mitch's concentration to think of nothing except staying calm, and breathing.

He began to count between each breath to try and

make them last longer. He had to become one with the water, to flow with it, use it; any resistance to it and he was finished.

He was up to thirty, counting slowly and evenly, when he felt a thud against his side that sent him spinning in a 360-degree circle. He had hit the red can buoy, the channel marker. He was lucky it was his good side that hit. It meant he was on the righthand side of the channel. He estimated he had drifted a quarter of a mile to reach it. A two-knot current meant that he had been floating for about ten minutes.

Mitch tried to lift his head and find the marker again and managed to catch a glimpse of it. Good. He was blowing north, toward the flats. If he kept on this course, he would drift into calmer waters. The water was fairly warm. He figured he didn't have to worry about hypothermia for at least two hours.

He was counting and thinking of the symptoms of hypothermia when he heard their voices. They couldn't have been more than thirty feet from him. He tried to keep his count slow and even so he wouldn't cough or sputter. Siegal was muttering and every once in a while retching over the side. They were moving at about five knots in a serpentine search pattern, the engines fading in and out of earshot, along with Siegal's shrill voice. They would have to stay in the channel; the Cigarette hull drew too much water for the flats.

Mitch still had no idea if he was in the channel or had passed onto the flats. The sound of the engines was coming into and out of earshot less often. Finally the sound of both engines hitting the high revs filled the night. He could feel the vibrations through the water as they sped off into the darkness, giving him up for dead. He missed the noise; it had given him something to hate, an adversary to fight. Now the full weight of his situation hit him.

Mitch knew that panic would creep up slowly to permeate his being. It would take over his mind one step at a time, easing into his being and then hit him all at once.

It was starting now in his ankles, where the ropes were burning into his flesh, and crawling up his calves into his knees. If he let it, it would have both his legs soon; then his stomach would fall victim and he would have the impossible job of trying to stop it. He knew that pure fear would soon be as real as taking a breath. He had promised himself never again, yet here he was. He had to find something to occupy his mind to replace the panic. A wave broke right over him and drove him down into blackness. He counted to sixty before he came back up to a floating position where he could take a breath. He couldn't last this way much longer.

So he went deep-sea fishing with his father and his brother. Mitch lingered over every detail. It was

the last time they were together before Mitch left
for Vietnam. His dad had paid for all of them to go to
Islamorada in the Keys, just below Key Largo.
They stayed three days, two days fly-fishing on the
flats and one day trolling over the reef out at the
Hump, where the hundred-fathom canyon came up
almost to the surface, bringing the deep-swimming
marlin and tuna with it.

The first day Mitch's brother and he were up at
dawn, too nervous to eat breakfast. They stood on
the end of the deck waiting for their father and the
captain to show up. The mate was earning his pay,
setting up the rods and the fighting chairs, as the
sun came up red behind Mitch's brother's back. It
was then, at that moment, that his brother put his
arm round Mitch, smiled, and asked him not to go to
Vietnam – 'For Dad's sake.' Mitch could still get out
of going, his brother said, or at least stay out of the
action; no one would think the worse of him for it.
Mitch started to answer when their father showed
up and hugged them both. Mitch believed he must
have known what they were talking about, but his
father never said a word. The captain followed, and
minutes later they were out of the channel and on
their way to the reef line. They had a great day
fishing; the subject of Nam was never brought up
again.

Next day Mitch switched to the flats with them,
stalking bonefish on the pure white sand. It was

Mitch's turn to stand on the platform at the back of the little flats boat, all of them silent, his father's arm slowly rising to point out a lazy-finning bonefish skimming along in about six inches of water, looking for crabs and shrimp. The sun was shining directly in Mitch's face. He arched back to make his cast; his father and brother smiling up at him . . .

Mitch was lifted on a small wave and carried less than two feet. All of a sudden his face was into wet sand, he was sputtering and coughing, confused. At first he didn't understand, he was so deep in his reverie.

He was on a beach. He swung both legs over, out of the surf, and used a crablike motion to carry him up from the water toward the shore. His body started to heave and shake. It seemed to know that it could relax now and breathe normally. He decided to lie still awhile at the water's edge. He stayed there for at least half an hour; then he slowly started to squirm up the beach. He wasn't sure where he was going, but he had formed a vague plan – maybe if he got to the scrub line he could find something to cut his bonds.

There was no scrub line. Mitch felt the sand get soggy and soft; then he choked on a current of water that hit him full in the face. It swept the upper part of his body. He was fully immersed again, bobbing up and down with the swell. He looked back as he rose on the crest of a wave. He had washed up on a small sandbar. He had a real fight ahead of him now.

Mitch had been trying not to think about her, but his mind insisted on going back to that hotel room. The picture of her huddled in the corner like a scared animal whirled in his brain. The ropes were burning deeply into his wrists and ankles now, as the inexorable movement of the water ground out a constant hot pain. He had to concentrate on the pain, use it, but thoughts of Mai Linh pushed it aside.

He tried to think about her logically, not fight it. She had obviously tried to kill them, or at least Siegal, but she had been captured. Her face was as clear as if she was in the water under him, looking up, talking to him . . .

'I was the one, Mitch. It wasn't my sister, it was me. I am the bad twin.'

How could he be so wrong? Harry had been right, she was trouble from the start. It was Mai Linh that Siegal had recognized in the marine store. Mitch didn't have a chance after that.

There was a body, Mitch had seen the picture, so they must have killed her sister instead of her, but why would Siegal want to kill her at all? Oh God, he was losing it.

He felt a dull thud, a bump against his thigh. Then he felt it again on his back, like something was prodding him, testing. He spun round in a circle. The third time it caught him between his shoulder and his neck and drove him under. Running along his back, abrasive, coarse, rough. Shark? Mitch popped back to the surface, straining to lift his head. All he could see were moving shades of black and gray.

He wondered how big it was.

Then he heard voices. He was sure he was wishing them into existence, but words became audible now as he rose on a wave, fading as he sank into the swell. He felt something rough grab him and slip under his arm, then the same thing on the other side, then a mighty grunt, and he was lifted out of the water. Whoever was hauling him out rested him on the gunnel of their boat for a second and then gave a healthy heave to carry Mitch over and into a small skiff.

It was two Panamanian fishermen. The thud Mitch had felt was from their boat. They both had huge grins, as if he was the catch of the month.

Mitch felt the rusty fish knife sawing away at the ropes. He could feel the fish scales springing off the knife as it bit deeper into his ropes. Finally the ropes gave.

The smaller of the two men opened a paper bag — their first-aid kit. He pulled out a single leaf of an aloe plant, wiped the knife on his pant leg, and cut off an inch slice of the aloe leaf. He started rubbing

259

it on Mitch's wrists and ankles in slow, gentle circles. He gave orders to the other man to start rowing toward shore. They looked like brothers. They couldn't seem to stop smiling, as if this good deed they were doing was earning them points somewhere else. In a while they even had Mitch smiling.

The larger man put his back into it, and they headed for shore. Mitch could see the shoreline and that the current was moving parallel to it. He would have been in the water a long time before he ever drifted up on shore if the fishermen hadn't come along.

The man in the bow opened an old Thermos, wiped off the spout, and poured some coffee into a slightly used Styrofoam cup for Mitch. It was strong, pure Colombian, and it tasted wonderful. The man patted Mitch's shoulder and started to arrange their rusty hooks in some kind of order. Then he checked the live bait in the wooden bucket that hung over the side. The people who lived in this region were used to strange sights. There was only one rule in this part of the world – no questions.

Mitch lurched forward slightly as the surf caught and curled under them, the bow grinding up on the sandy beach. They helped him onto the shore. When they were on solid ground Mitch slipped his leather belt off his waist, opened the plastic zipper, and dug out three wet one-hundred-dollar bills and offered them to the smaller man. He stood there, serious for the first time, and then shook his head. Mitch looked at the other man; he looked away. They stood in silence for a minute. Mitch finally said, '*Para sus hijos* – for your children.' The smaller man looked Mitch in the eye for a second and finally smiled. He slowly reached out to take the bills. They were both smiling now, talking away a mile a minute to each other as they rowed off back through the small surf into the blackness. It was a year's wages to them. God had been very good to them that night. And to Mitch.

He walked up the beach and pushed his way through the brush to a small side trail. He followed the rough trail out to a sleepy fishing village. His watch said 2 a.m. when he knocked on the door of the first house that had a car parked in front. The car was an old Ford pickup truck with no windshield or bumpers and one front fender missing, but it looked as if it ran. Mitch waved an American fifty at the owner, and ten minutes later they were on their way into Panama City.

The warm, tropic night air coming in over the hood felt good to Mitch, and it dried out his clothes. His driver was silent for the whole journey, and except when he accepted Mitch's money he refused to look at Mitch again. He did exactly as he said he would and dropped Mitch near the hotel.

Mitch slipped into the alley next to it and was

relieved to find his bike still tucked behind the dumpster. He walked it down the alley to the street, hit the starter, and was gone.

The problem was he had no place to go. He found an open cafe and ordered an espresso and a sandwich. He had parked his bike in front, and while the waiter went to get his order Mitch checked the saddlebags. Everything was as he had left it. He strapped up the bags again. His real problem was the clock. Time was running out on him. He still had to learn where the stash was located. If he found it he might find Mai Linh. He decided to call Harry, collect. Harry was Mitch's last hope.

'Harry—'

'Mitchell, I told you the next time we talked I wanted you three hundred miles from Panama. I heard you've been a busy boy again.'

'I have to know where the stash is.'

'You and me both.'

'You know by now, Harry. I saw Roxie in their suite.' There was a long silence on the phone. Mitch could almost hear Harry thinking.

'Harry!' Mitch tried desperately to think of something he could trade, but he had nothing. 'Please.'

'You already know too much. Take that boat of yours and clear out while you still have a chance. And do me a favor, don't call me anymore. For sure, don't call me collect. You've already cost me too much.'

He hung up. Mitch banged his fist against the side of the phone booth so hard he split the wood; the cracking sound only made him feel worse.

There was something strange in Harry's voice, something that bothered Mitch. He had expected Harry to be angrier than he was. He stood in the phone booth for a minute trying to relax, to let his intuition take over and tell him what was not adding up. Then it hit him. It was the 'You already know too much'.

Maybe they hadn't found Mitch. Maybe Mitch had found them. Maybe he had stumbled on the right compound and Harry had had it under surveillance. And now they wanted Mitch out of the area. Jose had been in the car in front of him. How could he have got in front of Mitch without being seen? Impossible!

Mitch hit the starter button of the bike and headed for his Whaler.

15
Balancing on the Catwalk –
The Compound, Panama

In fifteen minutes Mitch was in the Whaler, carefully unloading the saddlebags into his duffel bag in the bow. He climbed up onto the wharf and slipped ten more US dollars to the sleepy old Panamanian dockmaster, asking him to look after the bike.

The Whaler battery was sluggish, but the engine finally kicked over. Mitch made his way up the canal slowly, trying to remember where he was in relation to the land side. As he did, he was rocked gently on the wake of a passing Panamanian-registered freighter, its propeller visible slicing the water as it thumped its way toward the Pacific.

The *White Lady*'s berth was empty; she had slipped her moorings and there was no sign that she had ever rested there. Mitch's last clue was gone. He trolled slowly down the center of the canal,

265

aimlessly checking the shoreline, when all of a sudden there she was.

The *White Lady* now sat proudly inside a marina compound, bathed in the glow of her own flood-lights, a defiant statement confirming to the world that Leonard Immke and his Cowboys were beyond the law.

The compound would have been impossible to miss, fully lit as it was, like a stadium on Saturday night. High-intensity arc lights had been installed on telephone poles every forty feet; there wasn't one square foot in shadow.

There were at least thirty buildings inside the compound, so the chances of finding the one that housed the stash, and maybe Mai Linh, were slim to none.

Mitch spotted the six-door Lincoln limo parked in the alley next to the largest building, a hundred feet square. The building was positioned in the center of the compound, with easy access to the water and the service road, a road that would lead to a hidden air strip. A figure scuttled its way from the *White Lady* into the building; it looked like Siegal. Mitch decided to target that building, but the question was how to gain entry. The entire compound was supported by pilings and stood raised off the water.

Mitch maneuvered his Whaler under the com-pound, between the pilings. It was risky because there might not be access up into the compound from underneath the wharf, and finding the right building would be tough. But it was his only chance. He had to try it.

The tide was low and coming in fast. On the full high tide there would be less than two feet of clearance between the Whaler and the wooden beams of the wharf. Mitch decided to come up from the guarded seawall, then make his way back to the compound. As the sentries made their turn to head back, Mitch slid under the wharf about a hundred yards south of the compound.

He had to kneel in the bottom of the Whaler and pull the boat underneath the wharf, grabbing at the wooden pilings and beams with his hands, centering himself in the boat so he could guide it straight ahead, making sure the gunnels didn't hit the piling. Any noise would be heard above.

It was dark and dank beneath the wharf. All the pilings and beams had been heavily coated with creosote, which filled the air with that light coal-tar aroma found only down by the docks. Mitch pulled himself under about fifteen feet and headed north toward the compound area. There were places where he could look up between the cracks and get a quarter of an inch of visibility.

They could also look down.

Mitch was happy there was no moon, but once he got into the compound he would have to contend with the high-intensity arc light. Beams of light were shining through the cracks ahead like long silver knives in the blackness. They illuminated his way; he could figure out the placement of the buildings above by studying the patterns of the light rays coming through the planks.

The guards mut have been wearing boots. Mitch could hear their hobnailed cadence as they walked in tandem precision, like the beating of a tattoo on a drum. He stopped and waited for them to pass.

He was well under the compound now, about a hundred yards, moving slowly and deliberately, keeping as silent as possible. He was reaching for a tarred piling when he heard Siegal's whining voice. There was no question about it, Siegal was standing right above him. When Mitch looked up he could see the soles of Siegal's shoes shuffling uneasily. Seconds later he heard El Hombre's voice as he walked up to Siegal, yelling at him to go into the main building. They were going to start loading. The Colombian's heavy steps echoed as he walked away. Siegal paused for a second more, then took off after him, his footsteps chattering as he tried to catch up.

There was a dark square ahead of Mitch with only a few patches of light showing through. Mitch hoped it was the shadow cast by the main building. He slid into the blackness under the building, moving very slowly, using the pilings to grasp his way along blindly. The two pilings ahead of him had rotted away completely so he had to reach up to the overhead beam.

Instantly they were on him, soft and furry. Rats. Tiny claws digging into his face and arms as they cascaded off the beam. Down his back and chest, scurrying in every direction. Mitch pushed backward off the beam, pulling them off himself, hurling them into the water. Two more jumped into the boat. Panicked and confused, they went round in circles at first. One of them got up on the seat ahead of Mitch, crouched and jumped toward him, teeth bared. Mitch caught the rat on the tip of his survival knife, squeaking and squealing as its soft body slid up to the hilt. Mitch flipped him into the water. The second had burrowed its way into Mitch's gear. Mitch took a chance and grabbed the duffel bag handle, slamming the bag against the rotting piling next to him. The rat flew off like a furry brown projectile, right into the water. It sank, then surfaced and swam off, head visible, tail snaking in an S motion as it joined the others and disappeared into the gray water.

It had all happened so fast, Mitch had just reacted. He had no idea how loud a noise he'd made slamming the duffel against the piling, so he stopped dead and sat still, listening. He could tell by the pattern of light that he was squarely under the building.

He sat tensely in the boat for almost five minutes.

Just for something to do he let his eyes track along the beam the rats had used. It led to a hole that showed half light, half shadow. It was a ragged opening about a foot square, which the rats had been using to get into the warehouse above.

Mitch tapped round the hole with the butt of the Ingram as quietly as he could. The wood was soft and corky and broke away easily, the result of dry rot and the rats eating away at it over the years.

Slowly he raised his head through the hole. It was solid cocaine everywhere he looked, neatly stacked kilos with red-embossed seals, piled at least eight feet high on pallets and covering almost every square inch of the warehouse floor. Those must have been very happy rats, Mitch thought. No wonder they were so aggressive.

It wasn't the main warehouse; there wasn't enough activity, just row after row of white powder. None had been put into duffel bags yet, and there was no forklift truck operating to move the pallets. 'Shit,' he mumbled; he was in the wrong warehouse. But at least he was topside.

The corpses of a couple of rats were in the corner of the warehouse. Several of the plastic bags on the pallets had been bitten into, causing the pure cocaine to drain out into little mounds on the floor. Once the rats start eating cocaine, it's all they want, Mitch thought, remembering how the Colombians in the mountains would put rats in cages and watch them consume the stuff insatiably until they OD'd. The Indians bet on how long it would take the rats to die.

Mitch dropped back into the Whaler to tie off both the bow and stern so the boat wouldn't hit against the pilings. Quietly he tossed his bag through the hole and followed. He used an empty wooden pallet to cover up his point of entry. The warehouse was fairly well lit. The problem was that the pallets were stacked together in solid walls with only narrow pathways in between. Once committed there was no turning back.

Mitch sat in the shadow of the stacks and put his gear together. He clipped four grenades to his belt; adjusted the Magnum in the shoulder holster; dropped two speedloaders into the zippered pocket of his jumpsuit; checked the Ingram and slipped in a double clip that he had taped together – each clip was good for thirty-two rounds and then stuffed a hundred rounds into the pouch of his web belt. He dug into the bottom of the duffel and found the little pearl-handled, snub-nosed .32, his Saturday-night special, the one he had used on Immke in the hot tub.

Mitch's father had handed it to him when he was home on leave on his second Nam tour, after he had found out what Mitch was doing in the war. It was a gift from his father's close friend, chief of detectives of the New York Police Department, who had told

Mitch's dad to give it to his son to shoot a few of those 'little Chinks' for the NYPD. Mitch fingered it for a second, rubbing the handle; it was cool and smooth. He wondered whether he was going to see Immke tonight. If he did, he hoped he would have more firepower in his hand than this. He slipped the little gun into its worn leather holster and tied it to his ankle.

Mitch was using the 'quiet' rounds Harry had given him, so he didn't need silencers. The Ingram was a Model 10 and carried .45-caliber slugs; they had plenty of impact and were deadly in tight quarters. Mitch pushed the extended tubular stock back in tight and tied the leather thong onto the magazine, then slipped it over his head so it lay flat and loose on his chest; it would have plenty of slack when he needed it. It took him only a few seconds to blacken his face so it matched his jumpsuit. He squared the black watch cap on his head and did a final check of everything, including any loose ends like untied shoelaces. He was set to go. But first he performed his usual ritual for times like these.

He squatted silently for two minutes, sitting on his calves. Hidden away in the black shadows created by those mountains of white powder, he tried to sweep his mind clear, to be single-purposed, remove his fear, heighten his powers, forget his pain, and depend solely on his reactions. Mitch willed himself to rise above his mind and go back centuries in time, to when the human tribe was living in the wild, with survival as the only objective. Gradually Mitch felt it working, raising all his instincts and at the same time calming him, so his mind would work in perfect harmony with whatever situation he found.

When he came out of this trancelike state the first thing he decided to do was find the main electrical box. The building must have been built in the middle thirties, judging from the light fixtures and wiring. Old-time green-hooded factory fixtures that housed 200-watt floodlights hung motionless over the pallets, casting a soft, dreamlike glow on the white glassine bags.

The wiring on the ceiling all came together about two rows over from Mitch and ran down the wall like thin black snakes – a primitive system, but it did the job. Mitch was betting that all thirty buildings in the compound were hooked together in series.

He started down the row of pallets. At the end of the aisle he spotted two guards near the main door, tooting coke. They must have scooped it up from the floor where the rats had done their work and figured, why should it go to waste? The two guards had it laid out on an old, spindly-legged, tilted card table with one short leg. The pure cocaine was arranged in long, fat lines that looked like cigarettes; they lay on a jagged piece of glass that

273

had been taken from one of the barred windows. These boys were deep into the powder. Mitch got the feeling they had been at it for some time. If the Colombian found them with their noses full, it would be their last toot on this planet.

There were no dogs inside. Mitch guessed that was because the rats would make them crazy, send them barking all over the warehouse.

About twenty feet off to the left of the card table was the main electrical box. It was a big one, almost three feet square, with about a dozen lines going in. Mitch dropped back behind the last stack and took out the Magnum, slipped off the safety, and crawled out round the corner prone, on his forearms.

He got off three silent shots. The box on the wall shattered and three metallic bells went off as the bullets tore in one after the other, until the box exploded in a bright yellow flash. He saw the guards look toward the wall just before all the lights went dead. The box was alive for almost a minute with yellow and red crackling sparks. A couple of wires snapped and jumped up the wall toward the ceiling, hot, nervous with wild electricity, hissing and shorting out every time they touched the wall. Finally there was a loud hum when the box started to melt. The guards, high on coke, were totally confused and bewildered. They stood staring as though this was a light show put on especially for them.

The crackling suddenly stopped, leaving the warehouse in total darkness. Mitch could see by looking through the barred windows that the whole compound was also black. His hunch had been right. But he figured it would be only minutes before the backup generators went on. The two guards ran out of the warehouse. Mitch followed. The compound was in chaos.

Mitch counted on the two guards being too frightened and coked out to figure out what had really happened. He made it at a full run to the back of what he hoped was the main warehouse and tried the door. It was locked. Mitch looked in through one of the windows, but it was black inside.

Flattening himself against the wall, he pounded on the back door as if he wanted to get in, then waited. In seconds the door flew open; a Colombian stuck his head out. Mitch came down hard with the barrel of the Magnum. The guard fell in a heap at Mitch's feet.

Grabbing him under the armpits, Mitch maneuvered the Colombian under a derelict jeep that was up on concrete blocks, headed back to the warehouse door and closed it behind him.

There was still no light inside, so he climbed up the nearest cocaine stack, using the wall for leverage. Once at the top he could see ribbons of light from hand-held flashlights, crisscrossing white rays breaking the darkness. There was no question that this was the main warehouse.

Minutes later it was lit up again.

Mitch was at the back of the warehouse, but he could hear voices and the steady groan and grunt of a forklift truck as the squeaking pallets of cocaine were hauled to the front of the building.

Mitch inched along until he could see a fifteen-foot wooden table where about a dozen men were working, steadily stuffing US Army-issue duffel bags with kilos of cocaine. The two men at the end of the table were giving the bags a final check and entering codes in ledgers that would identify each plane or boat and its destination. They slapped each kilo bag with a strip of duct tape marked with its destination point, and then neatly placed each into a duffel bag. A waiting pickup truck stood at the entrance to take the bags to a landing strip or down to the waiting flotilla of small boats.

The bulk of the powder would be flown out from a small, clandestine landing strip nearby. The planes would be touching down every five minutes tonight: duffel bags would be hurled into fuselages, as much as five hundred kilos in each plane; then the planes would be refueled by high-powered pumps – if the American pilots would accept Panamanian fuel – and flung back into the night.

They were always American mercenary pilots, with an armed, dark-eyed Colombian passenger in the co-pilot's seat to make sure the pilots stayed on the flight plan and dropped the goods at the right co-ordinates: spots in southern California, Florida, Arizona, Georgia, Tennessee, Alabama, Louisiana, and the Carolinas. The pilots made two to three thousand dollars a key, a big payday for a night's work.

Beyond the packers was a slim, gray steel table, US Navy issue, framed by six white wicker peacock chairs that made the scene surrealistic, a touch of weird elegance provided by Immke. There were five thick attaché cases on the table, all open and full of cash. It was what Immke called his 'good faith money', a small part of the value of the load, but Immke, the smart banker, always demanded to see a little 'fresh' from anyone he dealt with; it usually amounted to five or ten per cent of the loan value. Whoever dealt with Immke's Bank of Death had to put up a little of his own to get in the game.

There had to be over twenty million in hundred-dollar bills on the table. All the Cowboys loved the ritual, the drama, the exercise of their power, and Immke knew it.

Mitch was almost at the end of the row of stacked cocaine bags now, creeping along an inch at a time.

The bodyguards stood flat against the wall behind the Cowboys. No one was allowed more than two men in the room except Immke and El Hombre, and they controlled the security forces. The possibility of a rip-off was always present, but there was no one Mitch knew stupid enough to give it a shot. Immke would later leave with the cash, traveling in the Bell jet Ranger helicopter that was waiting on the rear deck of the *White Lady*.

Once the cargo was safely loaded, it was the property of the Cowboys; any losses were theirs to absorb. But there was plenty of profit – if five or ten per cent of the load was lost it was no major problem; the mark-up was at least ten times the cost.

Mitch checked out the bodyguards. The Bear had been replaced by two grisly-looking Colombians. Lynx had two big, broad-shouldered blacks standing behind him looking slightly comical, one holding Ike, the other with Tina curled up in his arms. Chico had two wiry, coked-out Cubans behind him. Both had desperate vacant stares. Sweet and Low had a mean-looking gay guy who stood six four, wore black Ray Ban sunglasses, and was packing an old Thompson submachine gun that had left some grease stains on his pale pink Giorgio Armani suit. Behind Siegal stood two blond surfer types wearing Hawaiian shirts, their tattoos showing they were both Vietnam vets. It looked like a police line-up, especially with the light from the green-hooded factory fixtures shining down. All stood silent and alert, ominous against the gray wall.

There was a fleet of small craft lying off nearby, waiting for the signal to come into the basin for the cargo. The fleet would be silently tied against seawalls somewhere in the darkness or moored in the public marinas. They would be called in ten at a time, loaded, and sent on their way. Sailboats, fishing boats, tramp steamers, and trawlers, they would all come through tonight, high-tech little beasts of burden carrying pleasurable poison. Most of their masters would have made this run before, each vowing it was his last run and meaning it, until the money ran out or he got bored or just plain missed the rush.

Mitch had never seen so much cocaine in one place. His estimate of a hundred long tons had been low.

He slithered further along the top of the row. The smell of cocaine was everywhere, a medicinal, pungent fragrance all its own. Slick plastic bags slid under Mitch's stomach as he moved forward. He looked for Mai Linh, but there was no sign of her.

The warehouse was huge; finding her was going to take time. What was it? Obsession? Pride? Love? Mitch wasn't sure he wanted to know.

Hanging high above the steel table were glass boxes holding high-pressure hoses, each folded like an accordion, positioned about every fifty feet around the entire warehouse. Mitch decided they were meant to pump salt water up from beneath the building in case of fire.

A shudder rolled down the stack. The forklift had

begun to remove the pallets from Mitch's row. He watched the stack on the end rise and then disappear toward the wooden table. The lift waddled off like a yellow insect scurrying away with a treasure.

Mitch started back down the row before he got carried away on the next load.

One pallet away from the wall he looked up and saw the catwalks near the ceiling. They were twenty feet above him and crisscrossed the entire building. He guessed they were used to maintain the roof and the lights. If he could get up to them it would give him a view of the entire warehouse. The ladder leading to them was in plain sight and too far away. But there were skylights that were open for ventilation. He slipped down from the last stack and out the back door. He would try to come in through the skylights.

Outside there was a fire escape going up the corner of the building. Mitch used it to get up to the roof and then crept along to the first open skylight. The catwalk system was arranged in a series of straight rows that bisected each other about every thirty feet. He slipped through the skylight to the front of the warehouse, where he could again look down on the conference table and the Cowboys.

A couple of bursts from the Ingram would have taken them all out, bodyguards too. But he continued past them and started to work slowly and carefully back in a search pattern. He noticed a small, windowless office in the far corner of the warehouse, its door shut. Two shining lights were suspended where there should have been a ceiling. He continued on the catwalks until he was standing directly over the office.

She was inside.

16
Fire and Water – The Warehouse, Panama

Tied in a bundle. Thrown in a corner. Discarded. Mitch couldn't tell whether she was alive or dead. There was no movement.

He remained still, watching her. Thoughts of their life together flashed through his mind: Key West, the Dry Tortugas, dinner on the bridge, watching her fish, the way the wind caught her hair, the time she'd told him about her sister . . . He took a deep breath and prayed she was still alive.

He waited a few more seconds, motionless. Then he unzipped his jumpsuit pocket and pulled out a fifty-foot coil of quarter-inch nylon rope with a bronze clip at one end. The clip snapped easily onto his web belt. He looped the coil twice round the base of the catwalk handrail. The office was located in the farthest corner of the warehouse, with only one sentry patrolling every three minutes. Mitch waited until the sentry passed on his round before he dropped off the edge of the catwalk. The rope grabbed and yanked Mitch's web belt toward the ceiling. He had to use all his strength; his forearms bulged with the strain. Suspended now like a side of beef, Mitch hung six feet below the catwalk, the soles of his shoes brushing the bottom of the steel walkway.

Slowly he let the rope out a foot at a time, lowering himself toward the office.

The guard came round the corner just as Mitch was even with the lights. There was no choice. He released the rope, free-falling the last eight feet. The rope wriggled and snaked its way up to the catwalk and stuck there, hanging like an arrow, pointing down at them.

Her hands were tied behind her back, her face against the floor. Mitch remembered Immke's last words in the hotel.

What use was she to them now? Was she alive or dead?

Mitch unsheathed his survival knife and cut away her bonds; still no movement. He slowly turned her toward him. She had a large bruise just above her temple. He shook her gently. She let out a little sigh, almost a whimper, and her eyes began to focus on him.

Over her shoulder Mitch could see the dark silhouette of a man running toward them, then an outline against the glass of the door. As the guard's hand hit the doorknob Mitch pulled on the doorknob from the inside. The force of the door opening swept the guard into the room. He had a wide-eyed, startled look on his face as Mitch kicked his feet out from under him and zapped him with the Magnum.

The forward force of the guard's momentum landed him face-to-face with Mai Linh. Her eyes popped open.

It would be minutes before they noticed that the guard was off his rounds. Mitch gave the dangling end of the caught rope two hard tugs, but it wasn't budging. Then he motioned to her to come to him. Neither of them had spoken a word.

She was on her knees. Her eyes were starting to clear, and her back was straight.

Mitch slipped the Magnum into his shoulder holster and checked the Ingram. She rose to her feet, a little shaky but determined to come with him. They met at the door. She had a cold, fierce look; her eyes were pale jade.

As she opened her mouth to speak he put his finger on her lips, indicating she was to remain silent. She nodded. Then they were out the door and running down the long aisle of pallets.

It led directly to where Immke and the Cowboys were sitting. Mitch stopped. Looked around. They had only one good choice: climb the inside ladder behind the office. They had to get up on the catwalk and try to make it out through one of the skylights.

At the base of the ladder he unclipped one incendiary grenade; the fuse was set for five seconds. He lobbed the grenade over a stack of coke and heard the metallic ring as it bounced on the floor. He heaved a second grenade in the opposite direction.

There was a soft 'phoo', then a 'whoosh' as flames suddenly shot skyward, licking the wooden walls and stacks of coke. Mitch and Mai Linh broke at the same time and climbed single file up the ladder to the maze of catwalks. It would be a long, zigzagging run to the opposite side and the open skylights.

The area that was burning was directly in front of them. The flames were leaping twenty and thirty feet in the air. Below them pallets of plastic bags were burning, the coke bubbling black and melting onto the floor. There was pandemonium in the warehouse: fires were raging at opposite ends of the building.

The grenades had been a mistake. Billowing, dirty black clouds of toxic smoke streamed out through the skylights, and the flames had swallowed the catwalk ahead of them.

They couldn't make it to the skylights, and the flames made it easy for the others to see them. They had to get off the catwalk. Mitch pointed to a ladder less than twenty feet from them that dropped down into a dark corner of the warehouse.

With the fires holding the attention of Immke's people for the moment, Mitch and Mai Linh slipped down the ladder, stopped about ten feet from the ground, and jumped onto one of the pallets stacked with coke. They lay flat next to each other.

Mitch could see the guards closing off the entrance, stopping all entry and exit.

'Mitch, I'm sorry . . .' she whispered.

'Later. We have to make it to the back door. It's six or seven rows over, against the wall. We'll jump from stack to stack and out the back door. Got it?'

'*Oui.*'

'I'll go first and stay at least two rows ahead of you. If one of us gets into trouble, the other can help out.'

There was about five feet between the rows, just enough to make it tough. Mitch bounded across two rows. Then he motioned her forward. She leaped off the stack he was on, spilling thirty kilos as she jumped. They made a loud, thumping sound as they hit the ground.

He heard the muffled sound of El Hombre's voice somewhere below. Like a hunter on the scent, he was near.

Immke stood alone in the middle of the warehouse, shouting at the guards. 'Leave those fucking fire hoses alone. Use something else, they'll destroy the cocaine.' He turned, looking down the row of pallets Mitch was on. 'Have you got the fucker that's doin' this?' Immke screamed at the top of his lungs. 'Siegal, where the fuck are you? You sure you killed Butler?'

'He's in the ocean, like I said,' Siegal whined back.

Mitch and Mai Linh slithered along the top of the pallets for about twenty feet until they were positioned against the wall. The Cowboys were assembling at the end of their row.

Siegal ran to join them, slipping into the core of bodyguards and Cowboys, disappearing into the safety of the group.

They were blocking the only exit. El Hombre was silently motioning the guards to climb the cat-walks. They would spot the fleeing couple any minute. Mitch had to do something.

The fire hoses.

The hoses were positioned within reach. Mitch slipped the coiled line of one off the runway that held it secure against the wall. It was a three-inch hose, maybe forty feet long. The on-off valve was made of stainless steel, five inches round. Slowly Mitch tried to turn it; his hands slipped. It wouldn't budge. He got under it and used his feet as leverage against the wall. He had to use both hands. It began to give, straining and squeaking at first until it finally popped free. He spun it for three revolutions until it was full open.

Nothing happened.

Suddenly the water started to fill the base of the hose, ballooning along like a wild snake, twisting and turning in its rush to the nozzle.

Mitch crawled forward ten feet until he was directly behind El Hombre. He held onto the brass nozzle with both hands, waiting for the shock, but even so the force of the water drove him back almost two feet. It shot out like a laser beam, tearing into everything in its path.

The blast caught El Hombre square between the shoulder blades, spinning him in two full circles, then bouncing him hard against the piled-up bags of cocaine and pummeling him toward the end of the row.

Mitch aimed the high-powered water cannon at the startled Immke, the Cowboys and bodyguards. The piercing needle of water blew them off their feet, splaying them into the center of the warehouse.

Mitch located El Hombre again as he tried to get his footing; he centered the jet stream of water at him, tumbling him forward until he was finally blasted into the center with the others.

Mitch and Mai Linh had to use their advantage to get out. Mitch tossed the nozzle down between the stacks. The hose danced a wild jig, shooting water in every direction and blowing bags of cocaine high into the air where they exploded into white, powdery firecrackers each time a needle of water ripped into one. Fifty-thousand-dollar firecrackers.

Mitch leaped two more rows with Mai Linh ahead of him. Then he turned on a second hose, spinning the valve three fast turns and tossing the nozzle as far as he could into the center of the rows, creating more havoc.

Mitch saw Mai Linh trying the same thing with another hose. She was struggling with the valve. He motioned to her to go forward; then he stopped to spin the valve as he went by and tossed the nozzle into the aisle.

In a matter of minutes they had six hoses snaking, spitting and hissing water at the neatly stacked rows of cocaine, blowing the glassine bags apart and shooting them high into the air, flooding the floor.

There was no sign of Immke or the Cowboys. The back door looked clear. Mitch pointed, indicating Mai Linh was to jump and wait for him near the door.

He heard her scream as she landed, then silence.

Mitch leaped the final two rows after her, landing flat on his stomach, just able to peer over into the aisle below.

El Hombre, dripping wet, had Mai Linh. His hand was clamped over her mouth; he was waiting for Mitch. The guards were up on the catwalks now. Mitch was a sitting duck. Immke was below him. He stood in the shadows directly under Mitch. They had both anticipated his move.

Mitch sprang down from the stack, landing on top of Immke. They both fell to the ground. Mitch stood up quickly with his back against the stacked coke, using Immke as a shield, the Magnum digging into his temple.

'Butler, you son of a bitch. I can't believe this. Siegal, you said . . .' Immke sputtered out, but Siegal was nowhere to be seen.

El Hombre had swung Mai Linh round in front of him. He had his gun pressed against her head. They stood staring at each other. There was a cacophony of sound in the background: fires raging, water splashing, guards screaming as they tried to saddle the runaway fire hoses that were washing away precious cargo.

Immke spoke again: 'No heroes. Nobody shoot. Butler, what the fuck do you want this time?'

'The girl.'

'The girl! I can't believe all this is for that fucking girlfriend of yours.' Mitch pushed his arm higher up behind his back. Immke let out a scream.

'Believe it, asshole,' Mitch whispered. 'We've been through this before. Remember?'

'I remember. Give him the fucking broad, if that's what he wants,' Immke yelled over at the Colombian.

El Hombre stood motionless, his gold-plated forty-five glistening at Mai Linh's temple. His eyes were black as death, not blinking, as he thought his way through this.

He finally spoke. 'Hey, you. Siegal. Where are you? I know you're out there.'

Siegal slowly peeked his head round the stack of cocaine at the end of the aisle, then darted between the broad shoulders of Lynx's two bodyguards, who had positioned themselves at the end of the row. Mitch could see Lynx running, filling in behind them.

'It's not my fault. He has to be dead,' Siegal moaned over a black shoulder.

'You do the negotiating here, Siegal,' Immke said, trying to divert the Colombian's hatred. 'You caused this fucking mess. Step forward or you never do any more business here again.'

Mitch could feel Siegal thinking, stalling, his brain whirling, weighing all his options.

Siegal smiled a thin-lipped nervous grin and stepped forward, pushing the two blacks aside, his two surfer bodyguards closing ranks behind him. He took five short, choppy little steps forward.

At the same time El Hombre suddenly brought his gun round in a wide arc, firing twice at Siegal.

The shots resounded through the warehouse over the crackle of the flames and the hiss of the fire extinguishers the men were using.

But Siegal had survived too long in the streets to be taken out this way. He had guessed what the

Colombian was going to do. He was waiting for it. He danced back into the assembled pack of bodyguards and Cowboys.

El Hombre's bullets followed him. The first shot took out one of Lynx's men. It caught him square in the chest, dropping him to his knees. Lynx lurched forward, screaming, 'Tina!' as he pulled the frightened dog out of the falling man's arms. The second shot caught one of Siegal's surfers, smashing the back of his head so it looked like an exploding watermelon.

Mitch saw Siegal running as fast as his short legs would carry him, disappearing into the blazing warehouse. The bodyguards stood motionless, bewildered, glancing from one to the other – looking for a leader.

Immke broke the silence, yelling, 'Give him the fucking broad if that's what he wants. Who cares? Get rid of the fucker. Are you all crazy?'

'He killed the Bear,' El Hombre screamed. 'He must die. *Pudrirá en el infierno, cabron.*' He spat at Mitch.

'Not tonight. Not tonight,' Immke implored, staring at El Hombre. He knew he had to take action – fast. 'How we goin' to do it, Butler? You can have the girl.'

Immke was ignoring the Colombian now.

Mitch spoke. 'Get El Hombre out of here. Let Lynx hold the girl. Then we walk to the helicopter pad and make the exchange there.'

Silence followed. The Cowboys glanced at each other, unsure of what to do.

'Okay. Lynx, you replace El Hombre.' Immke knew there was no time left. 'Hold the broad. I'll make it worth your while.'

Lynx stood for a second staring at El Hombre as he soothed Tina, stroking her little head, smoothing the fine white hair from her face while she panted and nipped playfully at his thick fingers. He looked down at his dead bodyguard, nodded, and handed Tina over to the other black bodyguard, shrugging his shoulders from side to side in a fast, dramatic motion that caused his lynx cape to slip down his back. Sweet and Low lurched forward and caught it before it hit the floor. She petted the fur gently and folded it over her arm.

Lynx strode down the aisle, unhitching a long-barreled .357 Magnum from his shoulder holster. He walked steadily until he was face-to-face with El Hombre.

Lynx hated all 'Spics'. The Ricans in Spanish Harlem had been his enemies since he could remember. He stared coldly at El Hombre, daring him now, his gun hanging idly at his side. El Hombre knew how fast Lynx was with his weapon.

With a sideways jerk of his head and a thin smile of his lips, Lynx motioned the Colombian to take off. There was too much money at stake, and El Hombre knew it. The fires were still out of control, and every minute was costing at least five million dollars in destruction.

The re t of the Cowboys had calmed down and started to put the situation in perspective. Gradually their guns shifted in the direction of El Hombre. He shrugged and walked down the row toward the group.

'He has to be out of here, out the door,' Mitch said.

El Hombre stopped dead when he heard Mitch's voice. The Colombian turned. Death was alive in those ice-blue eyes. He stared at the group for a moment, then kept on walking. Mitch watched the Colombian's shadow disappear as he walked past the fires and through the streams of water that were still shooting in every direction.

'Okay, Butler, let's get this over with,' Immke said.

'Lynx, you go first,' Mitch said. Lynx nodded and started to walk. The group formed behind him and headed for the open front doors. The forklift driver was trying to contain the fire by bulldozing the burning stacks of plastic bags and cocaine into one area. They marched along in front of Mitch with Mai Linh and Lynx in their center and Immke and Mitch bringing up the rear.

Outside on the wharf was mass confusion. At least thirty boats were backed up and rafted together waiting for their cargo. It looked like a boat show, with every possible type of pleasure craft. The guards were running in all directions, in and out of the main warehouse, carrying fire extinguishers, even pails of sand, while billows of heavy black smoke rolled out of the two massive open doors, violating the night with ugly manmade clouds.

The *White Lady* sat a few hundred feet up from the flotilla, floodlit and stark white. Rafted against the bulkhead, the blue Bell jet Ranger sat on the stern pad. The group emerged farther into the courtyard; as they appeared, a silence fell like an unfolding wave over the compound.

It was eerie. All action suddenly stopped.

Lynx took the lead with Mai Linh. Mitch was ten steps behind with Immke pressed close to him. The crews of each boat stood motionless on the decks of their boats as they passed on their way to the *Lady*. They approached the stern cautiously as Immke ordered all the crew off the boat.

'Okay, only Lynx and Mai Linh board the boat,' Mitch said. 'I'll follow. Then Immke and I will get on the aircraft. After it's started we make the exchange.' Mitch slipped a grenade out of his web belt and set the fuse for the shortest time. 'If anyone takes a shot after I take off, I'll drop this grenade on the *White Lady*. Lynx, you and Immke will be history.'

The helicopter sat squarely on the pad of the upper deck. Its tail rotor protruded at least ten feet beyond the stern flag, and its black plastic bubble gleamed in the boat's floodlights like the eye of a giant insect.

Mitch saw a movement inside the bubble, just a blink, but it registered in his subconscious. The door popped open. Standing above them was El Hombre, a beast from high in the Andes, eyes dilated. He was consumed with rage and wild on coke. His gold-plated forty-five glowed in the lights.

Immke saw him too. He pushed Mitch backward with his body as he cleared the gangplank railing in one giant hurdle. But Immke's back foot caught on the top bar and he spun, end over end, into the black water below, sinking into the darkness.

Lynx pushed Mai Linh back toward Mitch and followed Immke into the water. The splash reached up to the gangplank.

El Hombre's gun exploded in Mitch's face.

The bullet whizzed past his ear. He pulled Mai Linh by the arm and lobbed the grenade in a quick underhand motion, arching it into the cockpit of the helicopter. It sailed over El Hombre's shoulder.

He never got off a second shot.

The bubble exploded in a fiery flash of red. Mitch and Mai Linh were twenty yards farther away when the second explosion lit up the night. The fuel

297

tanks of the helicopter blew up in a huge orange and crimson blast, flames dancing up toward the heavens.

Most of the stern of the *White Lady* went with it, debris flying everywhere. As pieces of burning wreckage showered down on the flotilla, the boat people leapt in every direction, screaming and yelling at each other. Boats started to explode in a chain reaction when the flaming wreckage hit.

Mai Linh and Mitch ran across the courtyard into the second warehouse. He kicked the door open. It was empty.

Mitch stopped for a second to get his bearing and try to remember where he had left the Whaler. Mai Linh fell on the floor in a tired heap and rested her back against a stack of cocaine.

The first bullet landed with a thud only inches above Mitch's shoulder. A small puff of white powder erupted as it entered the kilo bag directly in front of his face.

Mai Linh came alive with the shot, staring open-mouthed at Mitch, eyes wide. The shot had come from the top of one of the stacks. Mitch spun round, squeezed off three fast bursts, grabbed her hand, and headed down an aisle. He slipped the leather thong attached to the Ingram from round his neck, reversed the clip, and handed it to her, pulling the Magnum for himself.

They separated and headed in opposite directions.

Two shots rang off the bricks over their heads. Mitch hugged the wall for two rows and slowly started to climb to the top of one of the stacks to look around. He was just pulling his knee up to lever his body over the top when he heard short, wheezy breaths and a small whiny voice from right below him.

Siegal.

He had stayed with Mitch all along, waiting for him to start his climb, waiting to jump down to trap him. Siegal had been hiding on top of one of the stacked pallets, waiting for the smoke to clear.

'Butler, just drop the piece real easy so it don't make no noise when it hits. Then lower yourself down.'

Mitch did as he was told and slowly dropped to the floor, turning to face Siegal. He was holding his gun with both hands, the barrel trembling. It was from adrenaline, not weakness. His face was sweating, the perspiration forming tiny drops that ran down his face.

'You're one tough son of a bitch to kill, Butler,' he whispered, 'but this time you go. Your girlfriend too. Call her. Tell her ya got me, and to come quick.'

Mitch just stood there staring at him. Siegal pulled the hammer back, cocking it.

'Mai Linh, come over here. I've got him. It's Siegal. Let's go, baby.'

Siegal backed up against the far stack so he could see both the wall and the opening at the far end of the aisle. They waited in silence. Several long seconds passed.

'Call her again,' he hissed.

Mitch was about to yell for her when there was a noise at the far end of the stack, a thud, like a sock filled with sand. Siegal turned to fire. Mitch fell to the ground, reaching for the .32 strapped to his ankle. He fumbled for the holster release, but the pearl handle stuck in his trouser cuff. Mitch looked up to see Mai Linh appear from behind the stack, her back flat against the brick wall and the Ingram blazing, jumping in her hand, silently spitting out bullets.

She must have tossed a kilo bag and then run to the wall at the other end and squirmed through. Her first burst was short, but on target. Siegal was bleeding, stitched with bullets across his chest and shoulders, his coke spoon spread flat; it had been driven deep into his chest.

He turned toward her almost in slow motion, bringing his pistol round with him. But his arms suddenly stopped working and the gun slipped from his shaking hand. It landed on the floor. His face was contorted and confused. She squeezed off a burst into his stomach. The bullets passed through him, splattering the cocaine and splitting open the bags behind him. His blood turned the white powder red as he slumped down, legs splayed, his hands opening and closing, grasping, squeezing, kneading his stomach to stop the bleeding, to keep himself from leaking out.

She walked over to Siegal and emptied the clip into the side of his head.

17
Fishing for Answers – The Cove, Panama

Mitch walked up behind her, gently took the Ingram out of her hands, and slipped the leather thong over her head. As he did, she turned to face him. Her shoulders were trembling. She started to cry. Mitch shook her back to reality, a hand on each shoulder.

'No tears now, Mai Linh,' he said softly.

He took her hand and they headed for the pallet that covered the rat hole, their way back to the Whaler.

Mitch pushed the pallet aside with his foot. Mai Linh gasped when she saw a few of the dead rats, their little legs sticking straight up in the air. She shuddered but disappeared through the hole into the Whaler below. He followed.

'Mai Linh, get the bow lines and guide us out of here. I'm going to start the engine.'

The tide was going out, but they still had less

than two feet of clearance between the boat and the deck above.

Mai Linh knelt facing forward and pulled them hand over hand between the pilings while Mitch crouched down to start the engine. He hit the starter button and got nothing at all, not even a click. The battery was dead.

She looked back toward him nervously. Mitch motioned for her to carry on with what she was doing. He took the cowling off the engine and checked the flywheel. There was a cutout for the rope hand start.

Mitch checked all the lines in the boat and finally found that the stern line was thin enough to fit over the flywheel, but they were too cramped against the floor of the warehouse for him to get any leverage to pull it.

Mitch decided to help Mai Linh instead, and together they threaded their way through the maze of pilings until they were away from the compound. They exited at almost the same spot where Mitch had entered earlier that night.

With the stern clear of the last piling, Mitch gave the engine hand start a pull. It took a lot of strength, strength he didn't have. The first try hardly moved the wheel. He rewound the rope, put both feet on the transom, and pulled for all he was worth. Still nothing. Mai Linh came back to join him on the stern seat. She grabbed the end of the rope, her hand over his, and they pulled together, their feet planted on the transom. They pulled so hard they both fell over backwards as the engine roared to life. She smiled; so did he.

She crawled up into the bow seat and faced forward.

As Mitch eased the Whaler out into the main stream of the canal, he looked back over his shoulder. It was an incredible sight. The *White Lady* was burning. The warehouse was still vomiting billows of dark smoke through the two giant front doors. The little fleet was ablaze, with an occasional red flash as another boat blew up. Immke and the Cowboys had left the floodlights on full, and the scene was lit as if they were making a movie. There was no one in charge anymore. Mitch noticed the six-door Lincoln was gone, and so was the Cigarette boat. He was mesmerized by the sight; people were like ants running around trying to cope.

Mitch called to Mai Linh to look, but she wouldn't turn round.

He kept the Whaler on trolling speed, about four knots. Two passing freighters and a tanker had stopped dead center in the canal, their crews gathered in the wheelhouses with binoculars to watch the wild scenario being played out.

Sirens screamed off in the distance. Mitch pushed the throttle up into high speed. As he did, six armed

Uniflyte patrol boats passed him going full bore, headed up toward the compound. He could see at least ten heavily armed men in each boat, and they didn't look like Panamanians to him.

Twenty minutes later the Whaler was on the high seas.

Dawn was just breaking, that first light before the sun pops up, almost an orange haze. No wind at all; the ocean was like a lake, with the Whaler up on a plane cutting a white wake that was quickly swallowed.

The air was cool and clean. It felt good to them, blowing the smoke and death out of their lungs. Mitch saw Mai Linh suddenly cradle her head in her hands. Her shoulders heaved up and down, her sobs disappearing into the whine of the engine.

He shook his head as hard as he could, as if he could shake the thoughts of death out and into the dawn. He had to get to his boat and out of Panama, back out into the ocean, for his own salvation.

A flock of seven cruising pelicans were flying in a perfect, lazy V right above them, no more than twenty feet in the air. The leader, at the apex of the V, kept looking down as if to ask for food. After a few minutes and no food he seemed to shake his head at Mitch as if he were disgusted. Then the squadron slowly peeled off toward shore to dive for some breaking bait near the beach.

The sandbar was dead ahead and just beginning

to show white water; the tide was still going out. Mitch took a deep breath and hoped the Hatteras would still be there, and not stripped.

In a few seconds Mai Linh spotted the breakers. She turned to him wiping her eyes, trying to flash a smile. Finally it came, with that lip turned down just a little. Mitch could see that some of the fire had crept back into those green eyes.

Mitch found the spot he had marked and passed full speed over the bar, right up the little river into the mangroves. In a few minutes he spotted the white of the hull through some branches.

He eased up slowly and silently tied off on the diving platform.

He slipped over into the cockpit. It took only seconds to check out. It was clean and untouched.

Mai Linh came aboard and headed straight for the couch in the salon. She curled up in the corner; it was all starting to hit her. Mitch sat down beside her. She sighed and looked sadly out the window, eyes red from crying. She turned suddenly and threw her arms round his neck. Then she crawled into his lap and buried her head in his chest.

Her quiet breathing matched his. When he put his arms round her she tightened her grip, clinging to him as though she was afraid someone was going to carry her off. Mitch thought she might be going into shock, but after a few minutes she relaxed her grip on his neck.

He broke the silence. 'Why did you come out from the wall side and start shooting? Did you know Siegal had me?'

'No. Mental telepathetic, you know what I mean? I told you never to call me baby and you say okay, so why you call me baby?' She smiled a real smile this time. Mitch laughed.

'Just don't come out shooting if I ever do it again, by accident.'

'You don't make accident, I don't come out shooting.'

'I'll try to remember that.'

He let a few minutes pass before he spoke again.

'No question, this tide is still going out. We'll have to wait for about seven hours until it's high enough for the boat to pass over the bar. You want to sleep?' he asked.

'No. I am bursting with energy.' She rubbed the needle marks on her arm, wincing slightly. Some of them were puffed up and red. Her other arm was still wrapped round his neck. She looked up at him. He squirmed and looked away.

'Mitch, you want to talk?'

He couldn't deal with it. 'Not now,' he said, dodging the problem.

She got up and kneeled in front of him. 'Why don't we go for a swim in the lagoon? My body is sore; maybe if I could swim a little it will help. Will you come?'

'Sure. How about we just float down the river into the lagoon?'

She stepped out of her clothes and stood, putting her arms round him and running her finger down the side of his face. She kissed him gently on the lips.

'You must have wanted me very bad, Mitch.' She rested her head in the crease of his shoulder for a second, then slipped away, looking back to make sure he followed as she stepped over the transom onto the diving platform and slowly eased herself into the water.

He stood watching her let the lazy current carry her down to the mouth of the river and the white sand. Her black hair was spread out, floating on the surface behind her. Her naked body was dark brown in the water. She stopped in the mangroves near a wild red hibiscus tree and pulled a flower off, turning to see if he was watching. She held it up like a trophy, smiled, and slipped it into her hair.

She had a way about her that Mitch had never known in anyone else, a way of blending in with nature, becoming part of it with no effort at all, as if it had always been there and she had always been there, through eternity.

He followed her into the water, using a smooth, easy stroke. By the time he was in the lagoon, she had made it out almost to the sandbar. Mitch headed for the beach and sat on the sand just watching her splash in the white water; then slowly she made her way back and sat next to him.

'Like a dream, Mitch, the whole thing is like a dream to me.'

'A nightmare.'

'No. Not for me. It was karma for all, even meeting you in Key West. It happened as it should. We are the same, Mitch, me and you.'

'Maybe. Maybe so.'

Mitch lay back, letting the sun soak into his body. She laid her head on his chest, and minutes later she was asleep. He drifted, waiting for the tide to rise, thinking about what she had said.

18
The Final Truth
– The Caribbean Sea

Mai Linh was half awake, sputtering and spitting out salt water as she raised her head from Mitch's chest. He felt the cool surf recede from his stomach and legs. The tide had turned and was on the rise. They had fallen asleep for several hours.

She was laughing and coughing at the same time. He gave her a firm slap on the back, grabbed her hand, and pulled her to her feet. Swimming slowly, they drifted back to the boat on the last of the incoming tide.

They dried each other off in the salon, standing there looking into each other's eyes, feeling a little strange. It was the start of sunset, and the light had a special pink quality. She shrugged her shoulders a little, almost imperceptibly, and ventured a weak smile. Mitch held out both his arms and she eased in between them, those light green eyes looking at

311

him with a trust he hadn't seen before. They kissed long and gently; then he held her for a few seconds.

He smiled at her and reached over her shoulder to grab the machete from the table behind her. She noticed what he was doing and gave him a final squeeze and a hug, then spun round and headed for the galley.

'I'm starved. How come you don't feed your guests?' she said over her shoulder, tossing her hair back and slipping on her black bikini bottom.

'You're not a guest, you're the cook. I'm starved too.'

'Before I was first mate, now I'm the cook. I think I'm going in the wrong direction. Maybe soon I be the deckhand. *Oui?*'

'Just get cooking. *Oui?*'

Mitch took the machete with him up to the bridge and started to cut away the jungle cover he had used to camouflage the boat, beginning on the bridge. The little red marine phone light was silently blinking on the console. He had noticed it downstairs and figured it had to be Harry. Mitch wasn't in the mood for Harry and didn't want him to get a fix on their position. Once Mitch answered, Harry could have them locked in on the satellite Intertel had access to.

Mitch's friend the pelican sat perched on the bow pulpit watching him, his head tilted to one side,

curious. Mitch wished he had a fish to toss to the
bird.

As soon as he cleared the mangroves from the
bridge, he moved forward to the bow. Before long
Mai Linh appeared on the bridge with an omelet on
a giant glass fish platter. It could easily have served
six. Mitch noticed her glance at the blinking red
light before she set the platter down on the console.
She called to Mitch to come. They ate in silence,
both ravenous.

The tide was about six inches from full, judging
from the waterline markings on the mangroves.
They needed the full high tide to slip over the bar.
Mitch completed clearing the boat while the tide
rose the last few inches.

The Whaler was the last chore. Mitch brought it
alongside and swung the arm of the davit over,
clipped the steel cable to the bow and stern, and
then slowly winched it up until it was level with the
bridge, swinging just above its cradle. He lowered it
into the cradle and secured it. He would change the
battery and cover it later.

It was a normal ritual for him. It was one his
father always drummed into the boys when they
were sailing: they had to make everything ship-
shape before they could leave the boat; the fun
would start after the work was done. Mitch
wondered what his father would think of all this. It

seemed odd that he should recall those racing days on Long Island Sound at a moment like this. He went below and checked out the engine room, then back up to the bridge to start both engines.

Two little clouds of diesel fumes rose as the engines cleared their throats and then drifted off down the little river like silky black cobwebs. Mai Linh was on the pulpit waiting for his signal to release the bow lines. She stood there holding her nose against the smell of diesel fuel. Mitch gave the signal to slip the line through the mangrove branches. He eased one engine forward, the other into reverse, until the stern was dead center in the little river, then slowly backed them down.

It was full high tide, no current. Mai Linh had been moody since she noticed the red light blinking on the console. She knew it was Harry. She stood next to Mitch on the bridge, silently watching what he was doing. When they got to the lagoon, he did a one-eighty so that the bow came full round, then eased her over to the far end of the lagoon until they were lined up with the markings and started slowly seaward, making about two knots. When he got to the sandbar he slipped both engines into neutral so the props would be still as they coasted over.

Mitch felt two small thuds as the boat bottom glanced off the sand. When they were clear, safe over, he put both engines into forward and ran them up to three thousand revolutions to see if there was any shudder from bent props. They were fine, so he dropped back to eighteen hundred and settled into the captain's chair on the bridge. Mai Linh had gone.

They headed due east, into open water. The sun slowly set directly behind them. He kept the heading constant. He had no idea where he was going, just away from Panama. A private jet flashed silver on the horizon. Mitch wondered if Immke was inside.

Ten minutes later he went below to the salon and the lower steering station. Mai Linh sat curled in the corner of the couch, her knees tucked under her chin, staring at the blinking red light of the marine phone. Withdrawn, distant, she didn't look at Mitch as he flipped the speaker on then picked up the receiver. She might as well hear it all.

The marine high seas operator took about five minutes to put the call through. The reception was poor. They could hear Harry yelling at his end, trying to make himself heard. Mitch could hear him but he couldn't hear Mitch. Finally Harry gave up and said he would call back off a high-priority satellite. The phone rang seconds later. Mitch picked it up.

''Bout time, Mitchell. I been calling for fucking hours.'

'Well, Harry, I needed a little time to—'

'Yeah, sure, I understand. What a mess you left.'

'I'm not in the mood for a lot of shit from you, Harry.'

'Don't get touchy, Mitchell. Besides, that's not why I'm calling. Look, I'm not pissed. You just caused us to change our basic plan, not our objective.'

'What do you mean?'

'You and me, we've both heard the band play, so I'll give it to you straight. I figured when they grabbed your girlfriend you would jump in.'

'You mean you—'

'No. I had nothing to do with them grabbing your girlfriend, but once they did, I kind of figured what you would do. At first I wanted to stop you. I even gave Jose orders to try and nab you, take you off the streets. But once you were in the hotel I figured, what the fuck, let him have at it. After you eyeballed the crop I got real specific orders from the people I work for. With their worst fears confirmed they wanted only one thing – to stop the shipment. They felt all that cheap white powder would for sure fuck up the country. So they changed all their orders to only one: don't let that shipment into the USA.'

'I thought the Panamanians were in on it.'

'Yeah. But one thing they fear is Uncle Sam. He gave them the canal, but he can sure as shit take it back if they endanger the health and safety of the USA. Get my drift?'

'Yeah.'

'You caused so much chaos and commotion it had to be recognized. Shit, Mitchell, they tell me the compound is still burning. We sent some of our own boys in, some CIA guys. If the Panamanians tried to stop us or ignore what was going on, they knew what the consequences from Washington would be. So you did good.'

'What about Immke and the Cowboys?'

'Immke got away.' Harry let the silence hang there for a moment. 'Disappeared into the water, went under the pier. He'll show up again and we will nail his ass. Crime pays, you know.'

'And the rest?'

'We picked up Lynx at La Guardia. He still had a bunch of cash, so we'll probably nail him on tax evasion, but no luck with the others. So, Mitchell, go somewhere and lie low for a year or two and don't worry about it.'

'That's all I ever wanted to do.'

'Well, go do it and stop your bellyaching.'

'Harry, you know there will be other crops as big as this one, with Nicaragua and Peru producing.'

'More contracts for me. But it won't be for a few years now that they have this manmade designer cocaine to deal with. But I hear you – it ain't the supplier, it's the demand.'

317

There was a long silence, as if they were both thinking about the ramifications of what they were doing. Harry broke the silence.

'Mitchell, about your girlfriend – I'm sorry. Did you ever find out about the hands?' Mitch could feel Mai Linh stiffen on the couch.

'No,' he said. 'Was there much press coverage of the mess at the warehouse?' he asked, changing the subject.

'Yeah. Plenty. Tomorrow's front page, the lead story on all the networks, and they're flying in all the top reporters.'

'And the White House?'

'Happy as clams. Big show like this before election time couldn't hurt.'

'Well, Harry, it's been real.'

'Like always. See ya.'

The line went dead, letting out a steady buzz. Harry always had to have the last word. Mitch flipped the speaker switch off.

Mai Linh had disappeared into the master stateroom. Mitch heard the door click closed before he hung up. He decided against going to her; instead he climbed up to the bridge, put on the automatic pilot, took out the chart of the entire Caribbean, and studied it for about half an hour. He set the sat nav for Aruba. They would hug the Colombian coast till they got to Venezuela, refuel in Aruba, and then on to Martinique. They would lick their wounds there for a while.

After he punched in the data and changed course, he settled back in the captain's chair. There was a steady west wind with gusts of up to twenty knots, six-foot waves, and a following sea. It was going to be a rough ride all night if this wind kept blowing. He fiddled with the electronics and checked the gauges, doing anything he could to keep himself from thinking.

Most of what he had done the last week had been reaction, following his training and instincts. Now he had to deal with the truth.

It was midnight when she came up to the bridge. The wind had let off a little and the boat had settled into a steady rhythm, riding along in the canyons nice and smooth. The night lights on the gauges glowed with a pale green iridescence; it gave her almost a surreal look in its reflection. She sat down next to him. He could feel her pain. She sat silently for a while, looking out to sea. Finally she spoke.

'You know, don't you?'

'Maybe. But why don't you tell me about it?'

'How long you know?'

'It doesn't matter.' Mitch felt he had to make her tell him in her own words; maybe it would release the devil inside her.

'Mitch, it's so horrible. I have been below trying to work up the courage to tell you, to come up here. Oh, God, Mitch.' She started to cry.

'Mai Linh, stop crying and tell me the truth. It has to be the truth if we have any chance at all. You can't hold back on me.'

She took some deep breaths and blew her nose.

'It was close to what I told you. I came home late, maybe midnight. The apartment was a big mess; my sister had put up a fight – tables were turned over, lamps broken. She was lying on the sofa . . . it was white canvas and they had ripped it open, and the whole end she was on . . . Oh, God, Mitch, please.' He waited in silence, watching the ocean's groundswell.

'The end she was on was dark red – brown, you know – from the blood. They had shot her in the chest and then shot her again behind her ear to make sure she was dead. It was their signature. She had been dead for maybe two hours when I arrived home. I went complete ly crazy after I saw her. I was to be her protector when our mother died. It was my only desire to see that she would get ahead, she would be the one to succeed.

'She was so gentle, Mitch, so sweet. She never saw any of it, the ugliness. Even in Saigon when it was worst of all, she was like a holy person. She should never have been put in all that death and destruction. I always kept her under my wing; the thought of anything bad happening to her would make me crazy. Me, I was on the other side. I knew what life was like from the day I was born and I knew the streets, Mitch. I liked the action and I hated myself for it. Oh, God, Mitch, you're going to hate me too. This will kill us.'

'Go on.'

'I lived with the American colonel. He arranged for the helicopter and the carrier. When we came to the carrier I brought the heroin. He gave it to me to carry for him, but then he was killed. They said he was killed in action, but it was really the Saigon underworld that killed him. I traded Siegal the heroin for coke after I moved to Los Angeles. That's when I started to sell it for him and I began to use it myself.

'Mitch, I go home and she is dead. I know it is Siegal who has done it. I sat at her side holding her hand. Then maybe an hour goes by and I start to think what trouble I am in, so I pack everything I have and take our passport. There is only one passport. That's when I got the idea, Mitch. It seemed like the only thing I could do. Oh, God. I will never be forgiven for it, but I had to, I wanted to live . . . Afterward, every time I think of it I want to die. I should have let myself die.' She had slipped out of the chair and was sitting slumped on the deck of the bridge looking up at him. She started to cry again, but she rubbed her tears away with the back of her hand.

'I don't know where the idea came from, but I was the only one who knew we were twins. I knew Siegal would not figure it out unless the ... her fingerprints were identified by the police. I packed and put my suitcase by the door, then I went into the kitchen for a tool ... Please, Mitch, no more.'

She looked up at Mitch, begging with her eyes. He stared down at her. 'Go on and tell me the rest.'

'You know. Why must I say everything?' Another minute passed before she continued. 'I went into the living room and I ... I – oh, God, Mitch – I took off the hands. I put them in a green garbage bag and threw them down the incinerator in the building. My own sister ... It was me, my awful life, that caused her death, my badness that led to her being killed. She never hurt a single person in her whole life. Oh, God, I never forgive you for making me tell you. You are a bastard, Mitch.'

She stood up in front of him. At first he thought she was going to hit him. Slowly he rose and took her in his arms. She started to sob, those uncontrollable, deep sobs of grief. He held her for a few minutes; then she pushed him away and stumbled down into the salon. He heard the door slam behind her. He was left alone with the ocean, the wind, and his thoughts.

She said she had told him everything. But why? Why did they want to kill her?

Mitch sat there for a while drifting with the motion of the boat and the roll of the waves. Then he started to do the worst thing a man can do. He started to make a mental movie, to imagine her former life. His imagination soared. He thought of her with the colonel, the things she must have done to please him. Her life in the streets of Saigon. Her words rang in his mind.

'I was the one, Mitch. It wasn't my sister. It was me. I am the bad twin.'

And then with Siegal, that slimy little bastard. Mitch thought of all the things she hadn't told him.

He had worked for these men for a year. He knew how they operated, what they extracted for cash and drugs. It made him sick to think about it; he had a hollow feeling in the pit of his stomach like there was no stomach there at all, like it had been sucked out. He had asked for the truth; now he had to deal with it.

He wondered how he had wound up here, out on the high seas with a woman who had been and might still be an addict. A woman who had run wild in the streets, testing life, paying for the consequences with the death of her sister. It was easy to see why she had taken the Uzi that night and gone after Siegal. Maybe it was herself she wanted to kill.

Mitch stood up and took a series of deep breaths, filling his lungs with pure ocean air, hoping maybe it would clean out all the blackness inside him. He stretched and went below for some coffee. Mai Linh was nowhere to be seen, but Mitch noticed the stateroom door was shut. He went up and put his ear to the door. He could hear her even breathing inside. He made the coffee and went topside.

Mitch wondered what his father would have done in this situation. He knew his father would never have been here in the first place, but what if he had? He would probably have applied his life rule; it was the best thing about his father, the reason for his success with people: if you demand the truth, especially if you know in advance it isn't going to be anything you want to hear, but if you insist on it, then you had better be able to handle it with no recriminations. Humans are frail, vulnerable creatures; if you get the truth from another person, your only way forward is simply to accept it and go on from there with no judgments. Reality is absolute.

Mitch wondered why his father hadn't applied that rule to him after he found out. Maybe Mitch was the exception to the rule.

Mitch questioned his feelings about Mai Linh: when had he first known that she had cut off her sister's hands? He believed it was when Harry called and told him the hands were gone, but why did Mitch wait so long to get the story from her? Was he afraid of losing her? And now what? Reject her and go back to a life alone, with those bad dreams and dull, empty days?

He closed his eyes and tried to remember the life

they had before Panama. Had it been just a tryst in the tropics with no meaning? Had it even been real? And the past: could they ever be free of their ghosts?

The dawn came, light in the darkness. But it had come too soon. He had settled nothing. The big question still loomed in his mind. Was she hooked, a junkie? But she had been clean from the day he met her until they got her; she had even refused the morphine for her pain. He had been around enough cokeheads to know. He had a sense for it. Mitch believed he knew if someone was using, or psychologically addicted.

They were seventy miles out in the Atlantic. Mitch checked the sat nav with the radar for his morning fix. They were off the coast of Colombia. He matched up the co-ordinates; they were within two miles of each other. He checked the sat nav twice a day; sometimes it would foul up and he would find himself off course by fifty miles. He knew all this activity was only a diversion.

He knew it wasn't what he thought. It was what he felt for her.

He loved her. There was no doubt. And they were the same person. But could he live with this love?

The wind had died down to less than ten knots; there was only a small, rolling ground swell, no whitecaps. They were on course, doing a steady fourteen knots.

Mitch yawned twice in a row and started to think

about the watches. He checked the time. It was almost seven. Except for the nap on the beach, he hadn't slept in at least a day. Maybe if he slept, his mind would clear. He was thinking of waking her when she appeared, climbing the ladder. She tried a weak smile and handed him a mug of coffee. Her eyes were red and puffy, her face pale. She plopped down in the seat next to him.

'You all right?' he asked.

'Yes. I take the watch now, if you want.'

'All right. The sat nav is hooked into the automatic pilot, and the course is plotted on this chart.' He handed it to her. 'Can you stand eight hours?' he asked.

'Yes. If not, I will come and get you.' He stood up, and she slipped into the captain's chair and busied herself studying the chart. He knew she didn't want to look at him. He turned and went below. After a long, hot shower he slipped off into a deep, troubled sleep.

Mitch was sitting in his father's den, the familiar light fragrance of leather and tobacco filling the air. His father was silent, sitting behind the solid oak partners' desk, reading the report slowly, occasionally looking up at his son with no expression on his face, his pale blue eyes revealing nothing. Mitch slipped off the arm of the couch he had straddled and slid into the thick leather cushions, making a tent with his fingers.

Finally his father finished and lightly tossed the report in front of him so it faced Mitch; it had a red cover with big, black boldface type that said 'Top Secret – Priority 5'. He leaned back with his hands locked behind his head, bobbing slightly in the big chair. Mitch knew him; he would want Mitch to speak first. But Mitch remained silent. Several minutes passed until finally his father broke the silence.

'I can handle it all but the last part. I knew what you were doing over there, and maybe all that time alone in the jungle, when you were shot down, did things to your psyche, like it says, but why did you try a stunt like that?'

'I don't know.'

'There's only one hope here. I've already contacted my friend Harry Ormsby. He's a private contractor who knows all the people you know. Maybe he has something for you, something we can trade off to get the charges dropped or buried. The government has so much invested in you, I'm sure they don't want to see it wasted. But I want to know why, son. Why would you do it?'

'We were flying it in to high officials, North Vietnamese and Cambodian. The highest people, colonels, generals, all the major politicians. We took the shit up in a Red Cross helicopter and traded it for information. It was all nuts, Dad. I'm flying in cash, coke, and heroin to the enemy in return for crucial information that most of the time we never used. I finally decided to take some cash for myself. I mean, there were millions.'

'If you wanted money, why didn't you come to me?'

'The same reason I never came to you for . . .' Mitch never finished the sentence, deciding his father wouldn't have understood.

'Well, you're looking at twenty years in the brig.' His father walked over and closed the door to the den, then checked his watch and sat down again. As he did, the phone rang. Mitch could hear only his father's side of the conversation.

'Harry, thanks for calling.' (A long silence).

'How dangerous?' (Silence).

'Can you fly a 707?' His father asked him, cupping the phone. Mitch nodded.

'Don't you have anything else?' (Silence).

'I don't like it.' (Silence).

'Yeah, good to talk to you too.' He hung up.

His father went over and opened the highly polished walnut bar, poured himself a Scotch, and plopped in two big ice cubes with the little silver tongs, one at a time. He held the glass up and pointed at it; then he made one for his son. He walked over and sat down next to Mitch at the far end of the couch. He took a long sip of the Scotch.

'There may be one chance,' his father said. 'There's an upstart, a dangerous upstart, Leonard Immke, whom we're all worried about. He just acquired the biggest mutual fund in the world. He's a bad apple; he may hurt all of us. He needs a pilot and we need to keep an eye on him.'

Mitch's father spent the rest of the afternoon on the phone, and at six that night he called Mitch back into the den. His father motioned for him to sit on the couch.

'It looks like we have a deal.' His father suddenly spun his chair round so his profile was all Mitch could see. The heels of his hands went up to his face and he rubbed his eyes. He let out a long, deep sigh and slowly spun round again to face his son. Mitch could see the mist of tears in his father's eyes.

Mitch wished he could think of something to say.

His father slowly rose and walked his son to the door of the den, then returned to his desk, picked up the report, came back to Mitch, and slipped it under his arm like it was something he never wanted to see again. Together they walked to the big carved wooden door at the front of the house. His father opened the door. There was a dark blue unmarked four-door Chevy parked in the circular drive. The car started up when the driver saw the door open; the man on the passenger side slid out to hold the back door open for Mitch. As he passed, the man slipped cuffs on Mitch's wrists.

His father shook his head slowly, bit his bottom lip, and turned. Mitch heard the heavy thud as the door closed.

Mitch woke up shaking; small beads of sweat covered his body. It was hotter, with less breeze coming in through the porthole. The engine revs had dropped. He looked out and could see landfall less than a mile away.

It had to be the coast of Colombia, near Cartagena. He slipped his shorts and shirt on, almost tripping on two large aluminum suitcases lying flat and shiny in the cockpit. He climbed the ladder to the bridge.

'Don't worry, Mitch. I know what I'm doing.'

'That's Colombia,' he said, pointing at the shore.

'*Oui*. I will be getting off today.'

'No, you won't. We're hot in Colombia, you wouldn't have a chance.'

He reached over and took the helm. He switched off the sat nav and set a new course, back out to sea, as she went down to the cockpit. The thought of her really leaving overwhelmed him. He couldn't bear it.

Mai Linh was inside him. They were reflections of each other. They could talk without speaking, hear without listening, and feel the same thing at the same time no matter where they were. Maybe, he thought, maybe he was just dreaming the whole thing, trying to romanticize some ugly business that they had both lived through. But it was still better than not being together.

She called up from the cockpit below. While he slept she had changed her clothes. She was dressed in her jeans and a pale pink T-shirt that stuck to her body as the wind blew against it and then fell away in ripples. She was looking up at him. She had a black scarf tied round her forehead, her dark hair billowing out behind her in the breeze. The aluminum suitcases, one on either side of her, flashed in the sun.

'Mitch, you please come down here. There is more.' She gave him a little wave with her arm.

'No. We'll talk tonight.'

'No, Mitch. I want you to come down here now.' Her eyes had filled with tears.

He switched on the automatic pilot and took the glasses to survey a few miles ahead of them, making sure there was no floating debris; then he slipped down the ladder into the cockpit. The smooth, rolling motion of the boat gave a peculiar feeling to the whole scene.

'I will show you why Siegal wanted to kill me, why he killed my sister, why he ransacked your boat, why they took me.'

Mitch sat down in the deck chair between the two shiny suitcases.

She knelt down beside one of the suitcases, popped both clasps with her hands, and tried to open it. It was tight, locked shut because of the vacuum created by the rubber O-ring that made it water-tight and weatherproof. He leaned forward to help her, but she held out her hand, signaling him to stop.

Finally the seal broke, giving out a long, evil hiss as she unscrewed it. She pulled at the top of the suitcase, prying it open a little with her hands until it finally came free. She flipped it open.

The lid of the suitcase hit the deck with a metallic 'ping'. It was packed solid with kilo bags of cocaine. Mitch exhaled slowly. He could actually feel his heart beat increase.

She did the same thing to the second suitcase. The bags glistened white in the late afternoon sun, the steady motion of the boat causing the lids to rise and fall on the deck, each time giving off their little metallic ring.

Neither of them spoke for a long time. There was at least two million dollars' worth of pure cocaine at wholesale lying on the deck.

There was no question of the magic in the white powder; it was almost primeval, it had a power, the power to temporarily transport a person to a higher place, to alleviate the constant human pain, to replace it with energy, momentary euphoria. It looked so innocent, white and pure, harmless, like a faithful, clean friend.

Deception in its highest form but fascinating,

captivating, providing both the riches of Croesus to those who dealt in it and death. It went back in time thousands of years, to the Incas and Mayans; it had given them the same – pleasure and pain.

The knife blade flashed in the sun, suspended at the top of an arc for a second. Mitch grabbed the arms of his deck chair and shot it out behind him. With a sudden sweep of her arm she stuck the blade dead center into a kilo bag.

She lifted the impaled kilo of cocaine out of the suitcase and placed it on the gunnel. Then she slit the bag wide open and held the corner, dumping the contents into the white, churning wake. She then offered the knife to Mitch. He reached down and took another bag, slitting it down the center and holding it over the transom. Together they watched the gust of wind sweep it away; almost like snow it drifted off behind them.

Mitch went forward to the lower steering station and turned the engines off, letting the boat drift along pushed by the prevailing southerly trades.

They each took a suitcase and slowly, as if performing a ritual, they cut and emptied the bags overboard. The wake snaked out, leaving a white trail behind them. He wondered how many lives this cocaine could have touched and what effect it would have had.

The wake of white powder started to break up, forming small, thin branches that spread out from the thick central trunk. It created a strange pattern that reminded Mitch of the many-headed Hydra – slice one head off with Herculean effort and a new one would grow back in its place, with no way to kill the central core from which the head had sprung. As long as people wanted what cocaine gave them, there would be people to provide it. Immke's Bank of Cocaine had started the cocaine kings in business – there would always be someone to finance this deadly business. But that wasn't Mitch's problem any longer. He just wanted some peace.

Mai Linh was staring at the wake. She reached out her hand for him to take. They just looked at each other; there was nothing left to say. He squeezed her hand and went forward to the V bunks.

The kite he had rescued in the Marquesas was hanging from the ceiling. He took it down and carried it to the stern cockpit. Mai Linh looked at him curiously.

He went into the galley and got the can of fire starter. He held the kite overboard and doused it in the fluid, then reached over to wash his hands clean in the ocean. He struck a match and held it to one corner of the kite.

The flame instantly started to swallow up the cloth. He dropped the burning kite into the white wake and watched it drift off, flaming bright, yellow and red for a brief moment, until the light cloth turned to ashes. It floated off smoldering, turning black and crisp.

Mitch turned to Mai Linh, who was sitting on the stern watching the remains of the kite float away, caught up in her own thoughts.

'Our bad karma is floating off, gone now,' he said.

'You think so, Mitch? You think maybe we have a chance?'

'No maybe about it, baby.'

She reached out and put her finger on his lips. 'I told you, don't call me baby.' She smiled that smile, with her lip curled down.

Mitch went forward to the lower station and started the engines, then climbed to the bridge. She was already up there. She put both engines into forward.

Neither of them looked back.

19
Postscript

Leonard Immke stayed with the cocaine trade for a few more years, partnering with a famous drug lord. Together they took over an island in the Bahamian chain just off the coast of southern Florida. Immke and the drug lord ruled this island as if it was their own fiefdom for several years, until it was finally taken back by the Bahamian government after a para-military raid. Immke and the drug lord escaped unscathed. It wasn't long before the Colombians had formed deadly cartels to administer their own marketing, financing and distribution.

In the mid-eighties, Immke left the cocaine trade and went into the next best business, a business that he knew would drain the drug lords of most of their profits: gunrunning. Immke is still at large and rumored to be under house arrest in Castro's Cuba. It is alleged that he tried to swindle Castro – and got caught – proving, perhaps, that it takes an evil monster to catch an evil monster.

Harry Ormsby's business prospered in the years to come and his company still offers the same services. Harry died in a bordello in Haiti in 1989, they say with a smile on his face and a clean uniform waiting. His son now runs the business.

Sweet and Low quit the drug business and married a Senator, whom she is now grooming to become President.

Lynx was tried in New York City on unrelated murder charges and given twenty-five years in federal prison.

Mitch and Mai Linh have disappeared; their whereabouts are unknown.

More Thrilling Fiction from Headline:

EDWARD STEWART

A DANGEROUS COCKTAIL OF WEALTH, SEX AND MURDER

DEADLY
RICH

In the fashionable night spots of Manhattan the
beautiful people indulge in their games of sin and
sex. On the crack-infested streets a serial killer
stalks. His victims: those whose names adorn the
society columns.

With the politicians yelling for action and the press
screaming for a suspect, Lieutenant Vince Cardozo
of the NYPD is appointed to find 'Society Sam', the
name the killer uses in his first gloating letter to
New York's biggest tabloid.

The forensic evidence presents a puzzling set of
contradictions, but Cardozo discovers a twisted
logic in Sam's crimes, which leads to a connection
between the sensational murder years before of
movie star Leigh Baker's daughter, a smart dinner
party and a deadly mix of sin, cocaine and lies...

'A tasty, gossipy, suspenseful read' (*Publishers
Weekly*) from the international bestselling author
of *Privileged Lives* – 'Money, sex, clothes, greed,
revenge, drugs and murder – all in one glossy
package...glamorous, glitzy fare' (*Kirkus Reviews*).

FICTION/THRILLER   0 7472 3813 8

More Thrilling Fiction from Headline:

SUZY WETLAUFER
JUDGEMENT CALL

Ambition... Obsession... Retribution

She is the pampered rich girl determined to make a name for herself as a newspaper reporter.

He is the mysterious sixteen year old with a chilling secret. As hired assassin for a Miami gang, he has already killed eighteen victims.

In a different place, a different time, Sherry Estabrook and Manuel Velo would never have found each other. But now their dreams of fame and revenge collide and explode with deadly consequences.

For as Sherry's eagerness to scoop this story lures her ever deeper into the mind of a killer, she is blind to his sinister obsession which is rapidly spinning out of control.

'A whirlwind of threats, betrayals, counterplots... goes for the jugular' – *Kirkus Reviews*

'Wetlaufer's evocation of steamy Miami, her unusual villain and clever plotting create a gripping, often horrifying thriller'
– *Publishers Weekly*

'Intelligent and suspenseful... passion, obsession, insanity, ambition, dread, and violence' – *Booklist*

FICTION/THRILLER   0 7472 3931 2

A selection of bestsellers from Headline

SEE JANE RUN	Joy Fielding	£4.99 □
STUD POKER	John Francome	£4.99 □
REASONABLE DOUBT	Philip Friedman	£5.99 □
QUILLER BAMBOO	Adam Hall	£4.99 □
SIRO	David Ignatius	£4.99 □
DAY OF ATONEMENT	Faye Kellerman	£4.99 □
THE EYE OF DARKNESS	Dean Koontz	£4.99 □
LIE TO ME	David Martin	£4.99 □
THE LEAGUE OF NIGHT AND FOG	David Morrell	£4.99 □
GAMES OF THE HANGMAN	Victor O'Reilly	£5.99 □
HEARTS OF STONE	Mark Timlin	£4.50 □
JUDGEMENT CALL	Suzy Wetlaufer	£5.99 □

All Headline books are available at your local bookshop or newsagent, or can be ordered direct from the publisher. Just tick the titles you want and fill in the form below. Prices and availability subject to change without notice.

Headline Book Publishing PLC, Cash Sales Department, Bookpoint, 39 Milton Park, Abingdon, OXON, OX14 4TD, UK. If you have a credit card you may order by telephone — 0235 831700.

Please enclose a cheque or postal order made payable to Bookpoint Ltd to the value of the cover price and allow the following for postage and packing:
UK & BFPO: £1.00 for the first book, 50p for the second book and 30p for each additional book ordered up to a maximum charge of £3.00.
OVERSEAS & EIRE: £2.00 for the first book, £1.00 for the second book and 50p for each additional book.

Name ....

Address ....

....

....

If you would prefer to pay by credit card, please complete:
Please debit my Visa/Access/Diner's Card/American Express (delete as applicable) card no:

Signature ....Expiry Date ....